With a Mind to Kill

ALSO BY ANTHONY HOROWITZ

The House of Silk

Moriarty

Trigger Mortis

Magpie Murders

The Word Is Murder

Forever and a Day

The Sentence Is Death

Moonflower Murders

A Line to Kill

With a Mind to Kill

A James Bond Novel

Anthony Horowitz

HARPER LARGE PRINT

An Imprint of HarperCollinsPublishers

First published in the United Kingdom in 2022 by Jonathan Cape, an imprint of Penguin Random House UK.

FIRST HARPER LARGE PRINT EDITION

ISBN: 978-0-06-324220-3

Library of Congress Cataloging-in-Publication Data is available upon request.

22 23 24 25 26 LSC 10 9 8 7 6 5 4 3 2 1

Contents

In *You Only Live Twice*, James Bond was sent to Japan, where he tracked down Ernst Stavro Blofeld on the island of Kyushu. Following a pitched battle in Blofeld's 'Garden of Death', Bond received a traumatic head injury which resulted in amnesia. He spent the next year in a Japanese fishing village. He was reported as missing in action. His obituary was published in *The Times*.

In *The Man with the Golden Gun*, the twelfth and final James Bond novel written by Ian Fleming, Bond returned to London after having fallen into the hands of the KGB. He had been brainwashed and ordered to assassinate M with a cyanide pistol. The attempt failed. Bond was deprogrammed and sent to Jamaica to kill the freelance assassin, 'Pistols' Scaramanga.

With a Mind to Kill begins two weeks after that mission ends.

PART ONE

London Calling

1
Dead Man's Mile

In death, as in life, the navy leaves nothing to chance. The *Royal Navy Ceremonial and Drill*, a drab-looking publication first printed in 1834, devotes no fewer than eleven pages to funerals, with everything from the transport of the body to the firing party to the playing of the last post set down in carefully measured words. So, for example, 'the coffin will always be carried feet end foremost'. The Union Jack 'is to be placed over the coffin as though the upper left quadrant is over the left shoulder of the deceased'. Funeral honours can be given to any officer or rating in active service at the time of his death although special dispensations may be made 'provided that the burial ground is within reasonable distance and that no public expense is incurred beyond the value of the blank ammunition required'.

At exactly eleven o'clock on a perfectly English spring day, three cars emerged from the central arch of the sprawling Royal Hospital Haslar in Gosport and cruised gently forward towards the cemetery with its long lines of white gravestones standing to attention, the silent testimony of two world wars. The hospital, built in the eighteenth century, had once been the largest brick building in Europe. At the time of the Normandy landings, it had operated the country's first blood bank. Over the years, it had seen more than its fair share of death with so many funeral processions that the road in front of the hospital was known as Dead Man's Mile.

The cars were black and brightly polished, glinting in the sun: a Daimler hearse flanked by two limousines. They pulled in at the edge of the cemetery and the pall-bearers – two warrant officers and two senior non-commissioned officers (as set out in paragraph J/9513 of *Ceremonial and Drill*) – busied themselves with the coffin, which was draped with its correctly placed Union flag.

The death of Admiral Sir Miles Messervy, known to some as 'M', had been announced to a largely uninterested world a few days before. The lack of attention was far from unexpected. Only forty or fifty people – most of whom were present in the cemetery – would have been able to identify the head of the British secret service, and not even they, or very few of them, had ever known his real name or the exact nature of his work. His career had been sketched out in the short obituary which had appeared in the press. Educated at the Nautical College, Pangbourne, and then at HMS *Britannia*, Dartmouth. Service in the Dardanelles, commander of the battlecruiser HMS *Renown*, director of Naval Intelligence and then the inexorable rise . . . rear admiral, vice admiral, admiral. Companion of the Order of Bath and, for good measure, chevalier of the Légion d'honneur. He had turned down the post of Fourth Sea Lord explaining, as *The Times* put it, that 'there were other arenas in which he felt he could be of greater use to his country'. The secret service was not mentioned in the obituary. Nor was the fact that he had been murdered. It was stated only that he had died suddenly and unexpectedly whilst at the height of his powers. Both the prime minister and the First Sea Lord had paid tribute to his long and exemplary career.

Neither man had made the journey to Gosport although they had both sent representatives. A funeral, particularly a military one, has a way of making every participant look much the same and the crowd of mourners that had gathered in the cemetery were unremarkable, most of them with grey, thinning hair, dark suits, white shirts and black ties, standing in silence, spread out across the green baize.

There were just two women. One was Sir Miles Messervy's widow, Lady Frances Messervy. She was standing quite still, supported by a young man who was not her son. The two of them had lost their only son in the war. Her face was hidden behind a veil. The other, who had possibly known him better than anyone and who had certainly spent more time in his company, was his secretary, Miss Moneypenny. She was wearing a sleeveless dress with a short-waisted jacket, not black but midnight blue. She did not need a veil. Her face gave nothing away.

Had any journalists been allowed anywhere near the cemetery, they might have been interested in the man with the look and the deportment of a professional butler, standing next to the grave with a single black rose in his gloved hands. His name was Porterfield and he was in fact the head waiter at Blades, the gentlemen's club to which Sir Miles had belonged. The club, in Park Street just off Pall Mall, has only 200 members and it is a tradition there that should one of them die, a black rose will be sent to the funeral. There is only one place in the world where true specimens are cultivated: the village of Halfeti on the banks of the Euphrates in Turkey. This specimen had been flown in specially and Porterfield had taken it upon himself to bring it to the grave. He'd always had a fondness for the admiral. He had wanted to show his personal respects.

As the hearse had begun its journey from the hospital, two late arrivals had reached the entrance to the cemetery and had fallen into step. The two men, similarly aged and identically dressed, would have been indistinguishable to anyone who did not know them although they came from very different worlds. One was an eminent neurologist, the recipient of a Nobel Prize for his work on psychosomatic disorders. The other was permanent secretary at the Ministry of Defence.

It was this man, Sir Charles Massinger, who spoke first as they made their way towards the open grave. 'So what exactly happened?' he demanded. There had been no greeting, no expression of condolence.

The other man seemed surprised by the question. His name was Sir James Molony and he was something of a rarity in that he'd actually had a close personal relationship with the deceased. He had also been the first person to arrive at the scene of the crime and it had fallen on him to pronounce his old friend dead. 'It seems that the Russians managed to turn one of his own men against him,' he said. 'I'm sure you've heard all the hoo-ha about new brainwashing techniques coming out of Korea. I'm afraid I'd always taken it with a pinch of salt, the idea that you can get into someone's head. It's the stuff of John Buchan and George du Maurier . . . at least, that's what I thought. Clearly I was wrong.'

'I know what happened,' the permanent secretary snapped. 'I have read the file. What I was asking was, how was he able to get away with it? You were there, I understand.'

'I arrived soon afterwards.'

'And? This is the second time the department has lost its top man in that very same room. You'd have thought they'd have learned from their previous mistakes.'

Sir James couldn't argue. M had only been appointed head of the secret service when his predecessor had been shot with a single bullet between the eyes. 'There's not very much I can tell you,' he said. 'The weapon used was a bulb-shaped pistol loaded with cyanide. Only the Russians could come up with a contraption like that. M had taken precautions – bulletproof screens and that sort of thing – but clearly they didn't work.'

'And the man who killed him. He was one of our

own!' It wasn't a question. It was an expression of contempt. 'James Bond.'

The name joined all the others in the cemetery, carved in stone.

'Yes, sir. You'll recall that Bond went missing in action a year ago. God knows how long the Russians had him or what they did to him. But in the end, they gave him the gun and sent him home and he was programmed to kill.'

'M should never have allowed him to come anywhere near him.'

'I agree. But that was M's decision.'

Sir Charles Massinger scowled. 'Well, it's a damned nuisance. And it doesn't say very much about our overall competence, does it. Let's hope we can keep it out of the press.'

'We're doing our best.' Sir James Molony struggled to keep the smile from his face. He had only met the permanent secretary on a couple of occasions but he recognised him for what he was. Almost certainly an Old Etonian with a father and possibly a grandfather in the Civil Service. Disgorged into the adult world with an iron determination to succeed built on the foundations of low self-esteem, a fear of women and the emotional range of an adolescent. He remembered that Sir Charles had never liked M. He had considered the head of the Secret Intelligence Service to be a loose cannon, headstrong and unpredictable, and had resented the fierce loyalty shown by those around him. As for M, he had of course kept his opinions to himself.

They reached the crowd and went their separate ways, facing each other across the grave. Sir James crossed over to a younger man who was standing on his own, looking tired and a little wary. The two of them shook hands. 'How are you holding up?' Sir James muttered, taking his place beside him.

Bill Tanner, M's chief of staff, raised an eyebrow. 'I'll be glad when this is over, Sir James.'

'We all will.' He lowered his voice. 'Are they going to bite?'

By way of an answer, Tanner turned his head, his eyes settling on a car parked on the edge of Dead Man's Mile, beside a public telephone box. The car was a two-tone Hillman Imp, grey on beige, the colours trapped in a loveless marriage. He could just make out the shape of the two men inside it, both of them watching the funeral. It was what he had been expecting. By the time he got back to the office, there would be photographs of both the driver and the passenger on his desk and the registration number would have been traced, probably to the Russian embassy. Only the Soviets could have chosen a car that was so poorly designed and engineered and then made even worse with such a dismal colour scheme.

Sir James had seen it too. 'Do they have to be so bloody obvious?' he asked.

Tanner smiled. 'Well, that's Redland for you. They've never been strong on finesse.'

Inside the car, the driver was unaware that he was being observed. He watched the coffin being carried into the cemetery, then turned to his companion and nodded. '*Pozvony im.*' Make the call. His lips were bulbous, the words spat out like grape pips.

The passenger got out and walked over to the telephone box. He inserted the money into the slot and dialled a number. He was connected immediately.

'The funeral is taking place now,' he said, still speaking in Russian.

'So the old devil is dead. And Bond?'

'He has disappeared. We have people who can make enquiries. Do you want us to make contact?'

'Do nothing yet. We are to wait for further instructions.'

The phone went dead. The man walked back to the car. He wondered what would happen to the spy who had killed his master. Bond's name had not appeared in the newspapers and there had been no mention of him over the official airwaves. It was almost as if he had become, like so many members of the Russian intelligentsia during the Stalin years, a non-person.

Would he be put through the British justice system? It would be easier to deal with him quietly in some anonymous basement. A bullet in the head or perhaps an injection. That was certainly how it would be done at home. On the other hand, this was a country that prided itself on its legal system going back centuries with its bizarre rituals and its barristers and judges, still in wigs. They would almost certainly insist upon the full procedure: a magistrate's court, remand, a trial, the inevitable death sentence for treason and murder, prison followed by a hanging at dawn.

Ridiculous, really. The end result would be the same.

All in all it had been a good day in the struggle against Western imperialism. The man reached the car just as a series of shots echoed in the air somewhere behind him. He did not look round. He got in and a moment later the two of them drove away.

2

Urgent Repeat Urgent

A week before the funeral, with M very much alive, James Bond had been sitting in the front row of the BOAC Boeing 707-436 carrying him from Kingston International to London Airport, with a one-hour stopover in Bermuda. It felt strange to be surrounded by people, to be trapped inside a metal tube, even to be fully clothed. Jamaica had let him leave reluctantly. Bond had all too quickly grown used to the little villa close to the Mona dam with its views of the harbour and the sea, the heavy scent of passion flowers in the air, the dazzling colours of the warblers and the streamertails as they hovered over the branches of the poinciana trees and the sound of steel drums echoing up the hillside.

As he picked at the 'Médaillons de foie gras de

Strasbourg' which had been served to him, along with an overbearing Margaux Casque du Roi 1950, as part of the airline's Monarch Service, he reflected on the events that had brought him here. It was strange to think that just a few months ago, he had been considered a basket case, unemployable, a danger to himself and everyone around him.

He had been captured by the Russians, brainwashed and sent back to England to kill M. Mercifully, he remembered very little of that episode; the interview in M's office, the insane dogma he must have spouted, the moment when he had produced the poison gun with its deadly cyanide spray. Fortunately, M had been prepared. At the touch of a button, a glass screen had come hurtling down, protecting the head of the Secret Intelligence Service. It was Bond who had collapsed. He had been carried, unconscious, out of the office and taken to a secure hospital in the countryside.

That should have been the end of it. Anyone else would have had Bond thrown out of the service, perhaps given a small pension, but ultimately forgotten. Not M. If the KGB had the nerve to throw one of his best men at him, he would simply throw them back. Bond had been treated, reprogrammed, healed – and then sent to Jamaica on a mission that even his chief of staff had considered suicide. But as M had argued, Bond had to prove himself. This was his chance.

His target was a Cuban-based assassin by the name of Francisco 'Pistols' Scaramanga; a man who had killed several British agents with his famous golden gun. Bond had tracked him down and, working under the name of Mark Hazard, had managed to talk his way into becoming Scaramanga's personal assistant. This had led him to the Thunderbird hotel resort and a scheme to undermine Western interests in the Caribbean headed by Scaramanga with a group of American gangsters and operatives from the KGB. It had all ended with pain and bloodshed, as these things always did. Bond had almost been killed. He had spent the last few days recuperating, with the close and personal attention of his former secretary, the always captivating Mary Goodnight.

The only trouble was that he had become exactly that.

A captive.

Goodnight was a wonderful girl with her golden hair and deep sunburn, the perfect bosom and hips. She had been a first-rate nurse, secretary and lover. He would never have been able to take on Scaramanga without her. But Bond had felt her arms too tightly around him and had known almost from the start that he would have to find an excuse to get away.

That excuse had come earlier than expected in the shape of an 'Eyes Only' cable which had been signed PRISM – meaning that it had been personally approved by M. Mary had patiently set to work with the Triple-X deciphering machine, but even as she worked out the settings and began to crank the handle her face had been filled with foreboding as if she had somehow guessed what was to come.

PERSONAL FOR 007 EYES ONLY STOP REGRET MUST CURTAIL REST AND CONVA-LESCENCE WITH IMMEDIATE EFFECT STOP RETURN TO LONDON FOR URGENT REPEAT URGENT BRIEFING ON ARRIVAL STOP PASS-PORT, TICKET AND ALL PAPERWORK FOR TRAVEL TO BE UNDER COVER OF MIAMI HOTEL ENDIT PRISM

Bond still had no idea what it was all about. It was interesting that he had been ordered to travel as Mark Hazard, working for Transworld Consortium, the same alias he had been using throughout his time in Jamaica. The cypherines had adroitly coded it into 'Miami Hotel'. Bond sipped his wine. Perhaps he was being too self-critical but it occurred to him that neither of his last two missions had been entirely successful. He had allowed Blofeld to capture him in his 'Garden of Death' on the island of Kyushu and had suffered the head injury that had put him out of action for a year. He had wandered into the hands of the KGB in Russia. And even Scaramanga had almost killed him. The bullet fired by his concealed Derringer pistol had miraculously missed all Bond's vital organs but it had been steeped in enough poison to kill a horse, and but for the quick thinking of the policeman who had found him, Bond and Scaramanga might now be lying side by side.

So why had he been the one to survive? Bond had been careful not to read his own obituary – it had been published after he had disappeared in Japan. But the very fact that it had been written had given him pause for thought. How much longer could he go on before he was signed off for real? Le Chiffre, Mr Big, Hugo Drax, Rosa Klebb, Dr No . . . there was a very long line of people who had tried to kill him, now all of them queuing up at the gates of hell. Bond had been superbly trained. He had excelled at Close-Quarters Battle Combat while he was at Naval Intelligence and he was proficient at boxing and judo. He was the best shot in the service. But he could not deny that at the moment he most needed it, luck had always been on his side, and he understood that luck has a way of moving on when it decides it's had enough.

He was also getting older. Would a wounded and dying Scaramanga have been able to pull that trick with a second gun hidden behind his neck twelve years ago when Bond had been sent on his first mission? Bond had managed to twist round and fire five shots from the ground but had he moved quickly enough? He remembered not just the hurt but the exhaustion he had felt when he had recovered consciousness in the Kingston hospital. He was still painfully aware of the entry wound rubbing against his shirt. Did he really want to keep putting his body through that?

Bond had lost his appetite. He called for the stewardess, who took away his dinner tray. Then he settled back and allowed himself to be lulled into sleep by the hum of the four Rolls-Royce Turbofan engines which propelled the plane at 600 miles per hour across the edge of the world, passing through the shimmering mauve and silver haze of the lower stratosphere, leaving Jamaica with its secrets and its guilty pleasures far behind.

'Mr Hazard?'

The official was young, dressed smartly in a suit,

standing at the bottom of the steps that led down from the plane. He had recognised Bond on sight. 'Your luggage will be sent on to your home, sir,' he continued. 'I have instructions to take you directly to your briefing. Will you be all right in the back?'

'Yes. That will be fine.'

Bond was impressed. Not for him the white and yellow buses lining up to transfer the passengers to the Oceanic Building. A black saloon had been parked on the tarmac with a uniformed driver sitting behind the wheel. The sun was shining but the air was cool and smelled of aviation fuel, a poor exchange for the Jamaican climate. Carrying his briefcase and with a lightweight raincoat over his arm, Bond got into the car and sat back as the young man closed the door and climbed into the front. He would have liked to have gone home and taken a long shower, as hot as he could bear, then icy cold. Then a plate of his housekeeper May's scrambled eggs and perhaps a Bloody Mary. That would have cleared away the detritus of international travel. Sadly, it was not to be.

The car left the airport and turned immediately away from London. Bond was not being taken to the office building near Regent's Park where, he had assumed, M would be waiting for him on the ninth floor. They made their way across the sprawl of south

London and suddenly they were in the countryside passing through first Sevenoaks and then Tonbridge on their way into Kent. It was only when they reached the village of Matfield that Bond began to feel uneasy. He recognised the little church of St Luke's, the village green, the pubs. He had been here all too recently and had hoped never to come back.

They continued towards Brenchley and by now there could be no doubt of their destination. Sure enough, the car slowed down in a narrow lane hemmed in by poplars and then turned into the gateway of a huge mansion carefully tucked away in 200 acres of its own land. This was The Park. It was the convalescent home where Bond had been sent three months ago, immediately after he had tried to kill M.

Despite the coolness of the air inside the saloon, Bond felt the sweat break out on his forehead and the back of his neck. Once again he saw M sitting opposite him, the Armourplate glass falling. He still wasn't sure what sickened him more: the knowledge of what had been done to him during his long imprisonment in Russia, or the fact that he had come so close to killing the man he most admired in the world.

Bond put the thoughts out of his head. A moment later the car pulled in and stopped. The young driver was immediately there, opening the door. 'I hope you enjoyed the journey, sir.'

'Yes. Thank you.' Bond wished he had never got into the saloon. Were they seriously going to strap him down and connect him to the black box that, day after day, had fried his brain? But looking towards the front door, he saw a man emerge and recognised Bill Tanner, his closest friend in the service. Tanner was smiling, pleased to see him. Bond relaxed slightly. Perhaps he had nothing to worry about after all.

The two men shook hands.

'Good flight, James?'

'Not too bad. What's this all about? I wasn't expecting to find myself back here.'

'Yes. I'm sorry. But M wanted to meet you somewhere out of the way and this seemed the best place.'

'M's here?'

'And Sir James Molony. They're waiting for you now.' Bond hesitated and the chief of staff smiled. 'You did a good job with Scaramanga. M was very pleased. It's a bore having to cut into your holiday but something rather odd has come up. It's not like anything we've dealt with before and . . . well, you'll see. I'm afraid you're the only man for the job.'

'Tell me, Bill . . . how is he?'

They both knew what he meant. Bond had not seen M since the assassination attempt. It had been Tanner who had given him his signed orders once he had returned to duty, sending him to Jamaica. At the time, Bond had been grateful. He wasn't sure how he could face M after what had happened and he felt the same now.

'You don't need to worry, James,' the chief of staff assured him. 'There are no hard feelings as far as he's concerned. None at all. He knows you weren't responsible for your actions and, as things have turned out, it may be that the Russians have handed us an opportunity.'

'Why here?'

'The Park? Yes, I can imagine it's not one of your favourite places. But it'll make sense once you've spoken to M.'

Bond fell silent. He knew that it wasn't Tanner's job to comment or to expand on any assignment he might have been given, and already his old friend had probably said too much. Bond kept his eyes down, focusing on the ornately patterned carpet in front of him and wondering in the back of his mind why the furnishings in government institutions always have to be so unspeakably ugly. In this way he was able to avoid any sighting of the corridor that led to the room where he had been locked up or, worse, the door that opened onto the 'treatment centre'. They came to a corridor and went upstairs. A nurse in a starched white uniform walked past and Bond turned away. But even if she had recognised him, she did not slow down or break her pace.

They reached a heavy oak door set in a solid frame. Tanner glanced at Bond, who nodded. Tanner knocked and they went in.

The room was large and airy, with three windows looking out onto the grounds. There was a heavy, antique desk but M had ignored it in favour of an armchair where he was sitting, talking to another man whom Bond recognised at once. During his treatment at The Park, he'd had many conversations with Sir James Molony and had been grateful to him for his cold professionalism. The neurologist had never made any judgements. He had made it clear that Bond was his patient and that he was there only to help. Both men got up as Bond came in. They were pleased to see him.

'Welcome back, 007,' M began and despite everything, Bond felt glad to be hearing, once again, the metallic voice that he knew so well. 'A good journey?'

'Yes, sir. Thank you.'

'I'm sorry to have to drag you back here. I'm sure

you had enough of the place on your last visit. But we had good reason to keep you out of London and the people who you need to meet happen to be here. You remember Sir James, of course.'

Sir James Molony smiled. 'How are you feeling, Mr Bond? No more of those memory issues, I hope.'

'No, sir.'

'How's it been going with the programme I set out for you?'

In fact, Bond had given up the so-called reconstructive memory and confabulation exercises he'd been given almost the moment he'd set foot in Jamaica. He'd also jettisoned his various medications. Now, he smiled thinly. 'It's been very helpful, sir.'

'Please sit down, 007. Chief of Staff, you can stay too.'

M and Sir James returned to their seats. Bond took his place on an unyielding leather armchair. Bill Tanner hovered by the door. The room was somehow too large, too empty for a conversation such as this. Bond rather missed the intimacy of M's office in Regent's Park with its wood panelling and pipe smoke. He would have liked to have seen Moneypenny too.

But M had got straight down to business. 'I want to say straight away that what happened between us three months ago is gone and forgotten,' he began.

'You weren't responsible for your actions. You were injured in Japan and fell into the hands of the KGB. They brainwashed you and turned you against me but we've put paid to all that. I'll tell you now that the main reason I sent you to Jamaica was to demonstrate – to you and to myself – that you were still a first-class operative and, with the death of Scaramanga, you've once again proved to my complete satisfaction that I can rely on you.

'Now, I won't beat around the bush, 007. What I'm about to suggest to you is very dangerous, even by the standards of your remarkable career. There are plenty of people, including my chief of staff, who think I'm crazy even to be considering it. You've been to Moscow, haven't you?'

'Yes, sir.' It was true. Bond had been attached to the British embassy for a few months although that had been a long time ago, at least twelve years, just before he had joined the Double-O Section.

'Well, something is happening there,' M went on. 'It is my belief that it could have serious repercussions for the safety and the security of the West. Last week I received a piece of intelligence that suggests to me that you, and only you, are uniquely suited to finding out what's going on.

'The Russians sent you to kill me and if it hadn't

been for the Office of Works and that gadget of theirs, they might have had their way. But very few people know what actually happened that day and let's imagine for a moment that things worked out differently. Let's imagine in fact that you never went to Jamaica. You returned to London four months ago but you and I only met this week. You were still brainwashed and you tried to kill me exactly as you'd been instructed. Only in this version of events, you succeeded.

'That's what I want them to believe. I want them to think I'm dead. We'll even have a funeral if it will help persuade them.' M smiled. 'And then I want to send you back.'

3

Steel Hand

'There are people who say that the Soviet Union has changed in the eleven years since Stalin did us all a favour by dropping dead,' M continued. 'They talk about the Khrushchev Thaw. Political prisoners released. Forced labour abolished. A certain amount of liberalisation in the arts and that sort of thing. Khrushchev has been more open in his dealings with other countries, too: Yugoslavia, Estonia, Lithuania. He even made that visit to the United States – not that it achieved a great deal. He and Nixon didn't see eye to eye. I'm told that the First Secretary was quite disappointed that he wasn't allowed to visit Disneyland, which might give you some measure of the man. You can't imagine Stalin or Beria queueing up to shake hands with Mickey Mouse.

'But all of that's only half the story. I don't need to tell you that the Russian bear will never retract its claws. You had a KGB man chasing you round Jamaica. What was his name?'

'Hendriks,' Bond said.

'That's right. Operating out of the Havana centre and perfectly happy to be working hand in hand with Scaramanga, the Mafia and anyone else who might harm our interests. The KGB is fast becoming the largest security agency in the world, with a whole department dedicated to political assassination. For all his Disneyland aspirations, Khrushchev is as cruel as any of them. Look at the Berlin Wall! Families divided for eighteen months, parents and children torn apart and it may be years before they can see each other again. And then there was his ill-judged excursion into Cuba, taking the world to the brink of nuclear war.

'I talk about the Russian bear but it's more like the double eagle from the days of the tsar. They look one way and they're smiling. But at the same time they look the other and there's murder in their eyes.'

M reached into his pocket and drew out the pipe that never left his side. He cradled the bowl in his hand but, perhaps out of deference to the building in which he found himself, refrained from lighting it.

'Now, you may be wondering where this is going,'

he went on. 'So I'll get to the point. About a month ago, while you were in Jamaica, we became aware of a new state security agency that seems to be some sort of successor to Smersh even though it's shrouded in secrecy. It actually meets on the eighth floor of their old building on Sretenka Street in Moscow, which has to be a statement of some sort, and when I tell you that the man in charge is General Nicholai Grubozaboys-chikov, well, the connection could hardly be clearer.'

Bond caught his breath. General Grubozaboys-chikov, a Hero of the Soviet Union for his part in the Defence of Moscow and the Capture of Berlin, had been the head of Smersh at the time when they had put together an elaborate scheme to discredit the British intelligence service.* Their plan, involving a beautiful woman and the latest cipher machine, would have suc-ceeded if it hadn't been for Bond, and shortly after-wards General Grubozaboyschikov had gone missing, presumed executed as the price of failure. But now he was back, perhaps even in his old office, dreaming up fresh conspiracies.

'The organisation calls itself Stalnaya Ruka, which translates as Steel Hand,' M explained. 'The name may be fanciful but it allows us to construe a certain amount

---

* See *From Russia, with Love.*

of information about them. First of all, clearly, they're taking a hard-line approach. More to the point, that first word must have been chosen deliberately with its reference to Stalin. This is the murderous side of the eagle. They're going back to the old rules.'

'Nice of them to let us know,' Bond muttered.

'They can't help themselves,' Sir James remarked. 'The Russians have to behave like cartoon villains. They've been brutalising each other for hundreds of years. For them, it's an endless power game and they have to play the part.'

M gave a brief nod. 'There are four other senior officers who make up the central committee of Stalnaya Ruka,' he said. 'It's interesting that they've been drawn together from different parts of the Soviet machine. General Volkhov works in the Central Intelligence Directorate, or GRU. Lieutenant General Kirilenko is KGB. She heads up Department V of the First Chief Directorate dealing with what they call *mokrie dela.*'

Bond knew what that meant. Wet cases. Or, in plain English, murders, kidnappings and acts of terror. He noted that Kirilenko was a woman. She had presumably followed in the less than delicate footsteps of Rosa Klebb.

'And perhaps most interestingly, we have Erik

Mundt, who has no rank and isn't even Russian but is the third most senior officer in the East German Ministry for State Security – the Stasi. Nasty piece of work. He came late to communism, which only makes him all the more fanatical, as if he's making up for lost time. He deals with informers and potential defectors, which is ironic in the light of what I'm going to tell you. They call him The Hammer because that's his weapon of choice. No one has ever walked away from one of his interrogations.'

M coughed. He had been smoking for more than forty years and the pipe nestled guiltily in his hand as if it knew it was to blame.

'So you have KGB, GRU, Smersh and from East Germany, Stasi. Four major intelligence agencies who have been merged into this new outfit, Stalnaya Ruka . . . for what purpose?' M glanced at Bond. 'That's why we're here today. We need to know.'

'Are we certain this is actually a Soviet organisation, sir?' Bond asked. 'How do we know General G hasn't gone into business for himself?'

'That's a good question, 007 – and one we have, of course, considered. But we know for a fact that Stalnaya Ruka is reporting directly to the Kremlin . . . to Alexander Shelepin, the first deputy prime minister of the Soviet Union no less. He listens in to the meetings at the end of a telephone and he's the one pulling the strings. You don't get very much higher than that.'

'We have someone inside the group?'

'We had one, yes.' There was a file on the side of the desk. M reached out and took it. He extracted a black-and-white photograph which he handed to Bond. It showed a man of about Bond's age, dark-haired and handsome but for a scar that had disfigured one side of his face so badly that at first Bond had thought that the photograph was creased. 'This is Karl Brenner. Born 1927 in Berlin. For a time he was the star player for the East German junior handball team. He got that scar when the coach carrying the whole team to an engagement crashed on the autobahn. Six players were killed.

'Brenner joined the Communist Party the year after and became an unofficial collaborator for the Stasi. He was promoted to *Hauptmann* although he had no military experience and wound up as ADC to Mundt. The trouble is, he began to have his doubts about the political system in East Germany and cast his eyes to the other side of the wall. He approached us six months ago with classified information about Stasi operations. The deal was, we'd help to get him out and he'd give us more.

'It was Brenner who told us about the existence of

Stalnaya Ruka . . . much of which we've been able to verify. He also told us that they were planning something big, a single event that would completely smash the balance of power between East and West. He said it was going to happen soon. The only trouble is, he wouldn't tell us what it was or where it was taking place. He wanted to be sure that we'd go ahead with our side of the bargain and help him with his defection. Station G had made all the arrangements to get him out of Berlin – across the wall – but Brenner was adamant that he wouldn't give us the whole picture until he was safely on the other side.

'Unfortunately, a week ago, the axe fell. Or perhaps I should say, the hammer. Brenner must have made a mistake and one mistake was all it took. He was taken to the Stasi prison in Hohenschönhausen and beaten to death.

'And that's where we are now, 007. The only way we're going to find out what these people are up to is to put someone in among them and I'm afraid you're our best chance.'

M stopped. Bond was aware of Bill Tanner, standing just out of the corner of his eye, and Sir James Molony, watching him intently. He wanted to ask how this was all meant to work. Why him? But even as he turned over what he had just been told, he was aware that something was missing. What was it? Yes. That was what M had deliberately left out.

'You said there were four senior officers working under General G in Stalnaya Ruka,' he said. 'General Volkhov, Lieutenant General Kirilenko and Erik Mundt. Who is the fourth?'

M was pleased. 'That's right. You've put your finger on it, 007. The fourth member of the executive is a man who is very well known to you. We have no idea what he's doing as part of this set-up but we've come to the conclusion that he has to be our best way in.' M paused. 'His name is Colonel Boris.'

Bond should have been expecting it. Given what M had said at the start of the meeting, nothing else would have made any sense. But the two words had an extraordinary effect on him. It was as if the glass screen that had shot down to protect M had fallen again but this time it had smashed, fragmenting everything on the other side. Bond found himself staring into another world. At the same moment, all the lights seemed to go out and darkness fell on him like a wave.

He saw himself standing naked, in a cell. He had been there for a long time. He was filthy. Someone was shouting at him . . . in Russian, in English, he couldn't tell. He was punched. He was beaten. He was injected, the needle entering the cephalic vein of his left arm. He felt the surge of the hallucinogen as it entered his bloodstream and invaded his brain. Then everything broke up and once again his mind and his body were somehow disconnected until he was dragged back out of the tunnel and found himself in a leather chair in a brightly lit room with a man sitting opposite him, calmly watching him.

Colonel Boris.

He was dressed as he always had been, like a dentist with that white, collarless jacket, buttoned at the neck, smiling at him with the same kindly manner before the drill enters the tooth. He was almost too good-looking, with his perfect smile and his hair cut symmetrically, the pale gold strands framing a face which could have come out of one of those Renaissance paintings depicting a hero or a demigod who might be more than human or less than human, but who was either way missing the human element. He had extraordinary eyes. It wasn't just their intelligence, the way they dissected you. They were also different colours. The left eye was a pale grey. The right eye a brilliant blue. This disparity made it almost impossible to look at him for any length of time. It was like staring at someone who had lost an arm or a leg. It felt intrusive. How old was Colonel Boris? He had the smooth, untarnished skin of a very young man and the experience and authority of a much older one.

He seemed to notice Bond for the first time. He spoke.

'How are you, James? Are you feeling recovered?'

'I'm feeling . . .' The voice was a whimper. It wasn't his.

'There, there. You still have difficulty seeing things the way they should be.'

'I am trying, Colonel Boris.'

'I know you are. But you're not ready yet. Perhaps you need a little more time.' A pause. Then: 'I think you should go back to the magic room.'

Hearing the words, Bond felt the familiar terror rush in on him and he closed his eyes, holding back a well of tears, his heart hammering at his chest and the blood pulsing in his head. Acting on their own, his hands curled around the sides of the chair. He took a deep breath, fighting for control. He opened his eyes again and found himself back in The Park in the Kent countryside with the sun shining and the dust hanging in the air. M was watching him, concern etched into his face.

'Are you all right, 007?' he asked.

'Yes, sir. I have to say, I was rather hoping I wouldn't hear that name again.'

'I'm sorry. I'm afraid I rather threw it at you.'

Sir James poured a glass of water and offered it to Bond. 'Drink this,' he said. 'You may have had an acute stress reaction . . . exactly what we talked about. The name acted as a trigger. You need to take a moment to relax.'

Bond waved away the water. He looked M straight in the eye. 'I'd like to have a cigarette, if you don't mind, sir.'

'No. Not at all. Go ahead.'

Bond would never have smoked in front of his commanding officer. And M would never have countenanced it. But these were extraordinary circumstances and nobody in the room spoke as Bond took out his gunmetal case, withdrew a single cigarette and lit it with his black oxidised Ronson lighter. He immediately felt better. It wasn't just the jolt of nicotine. It was the familiarity of the Morland cigarette with its blend of Turkish and Balkan tobacco and of course the three gold rings. It gave Bond the sense that he was once again in control.

'You want me to pretend that I'm still brainwashed,' he said. 'You're going to persuade the Russians that I attacked you in your office not three months ago but today, now, and that I did actually manage to kill you. And then somehow you're going to arrange for me to go back . . .'

'It's our belief that the Russians would do anything in their power to get hold of you again,' M continued. 'First of all there's the propaganda value. They might put you in court, get you to confess to God knows what. That seems to be what they did with Cardinal Mindszenty and again at those bloody Moscow show trials. Or they could make a hero out of you. There have been plenty of defections from East to West. A prominent British agent heading the other way would certainly give them something to crow about.'

Bond considered. 'I'm sure Colonel Boris would be delighted to see me,' he agreed. 'If we tell him I've killed you, I'll be one of his greatest successes. And you believe that if he took me under his wing, so to speak, I might be able to find out what Stalnaya Ruka is up to.'

'That's about the long and the short of it. Losing Brenner was a disaster as far as we're concerned. General G, Kirilenko and the others are untouchable. But Colonel Boris may have further use for you and that could give us an opportunity. We'll of course make sure that you're looked after. We have people in Moscow who will keep an eye on you. But at the same time, there's no question that you'll be putting yourself in harm's way. What do you think?'

'Well, sir, I'd certainly be up for it. Stress reaction or

not, I'd welcome the chance to settle a few scores with the colonel. The only trouble is, I'm not sure it would work.' Bond exhaled smoke. 'How am I going to explain what really happened after the Russians sent me back to London? After all, that was four months ago. You said it yourself. I spent six weeks being treated here and another six weeks chasing Scaramanga all over the Caribbean before I finally caught up with him. What am I meant to have been doing in all that time?'

It was Bill Tanner who answered. Up until now, the chief of staff had been silent, watching the encounter with a wary eye. 'You could have been on sick leave,' he said. 'Recuperation. Retraining. You could have had a desk job until M was prepared to see you. As a matter of fact, that was exactly what I advised when you showed up again.'

'Except that I was in Jamaica. The Russians must know that. You mentioned Hendriks just a moment ago. When I was at the Thunderbird hotel, I overheard him talking to Scaramanga and he'd worked out exactly who I was. He'd talked to his people in Havana and they'd identified me.'

'But Hendriks died a few hours later,' Tanner reminded him – although Bond was unlikely to have forgotten. It was he who had fired the single shot between the Russian agent's eyes. 'And you know as well as I do how the KGB operate. It's all about oblique control. What happens in Havana stays in Havana and it's more than likely that they'll have done their best to close the file on Scaramanga. After all, it was a colossal failure on their behalf.'

'But the order to kill me came from Moscow.'

'That's not entirely true,' M cut in. 'It was Mark Hazard that Moscow wanted dead. That was the cover you were operating under and they had no idea it was you for the simple reason that Havana hadn't informed them.'

'We've had GCHQ at Oakley listening out for transmissions,' Tanner added. 'Your own name hasn't come up once in any of the chatter coming out of the Kremlin since Scaramanga died. Anyway, we'll know we're on safe ground the moment we get started.'

'Exactly.' M nodded. 'If they think you want to defect and agree to help take you back, then we'll know they've swallowed the bait. It won't be easy for them, getting you out of England.'

Bond considered everything that had just been said. He drew on his cigarette. 'So I kill you,' he concluded.

'That's right. We do it as soon as we can and we announce my death immediately afterwards. We have a funeral. You'll be taken into custody and somehow, you'll make contact with your handlers. I understand they gave you a telephone number to use once the job had been done.'

'Yes, sir.' Bond had provided this piece of information during his extensive debrief.

'The number belongs to an out-of-work journalist in Ruislip,' Tanner said. 'We could have arrested him but we thought it was more useful to keep him under surveillance. He'll just be a cut-out. The moment you call him, he'll pass the message on to his superiors and with a bit of luck they'll come for you.'

'I have to tell you that no one apart from the four of us will know the truth of what's happening,' M added. 'You may find yourself getting some rough treatment from some of our own people. We'll do what we can to protect you but we can't risk anyone outside this room knowing that you're still working undercover for us. Once the news of my death has been announced, you're going to have to look out for yourself.'

'Where will you send me?' Bond asked.

'We don't have very much experience of this,' Tanner admitted. 'I suppose the closest parallel is George Blake. He wasn't technically an assassin although the swine was responsible for the deaths of dozens of our people. He went through the classic route . . . magistrate's court, Old Bailey and finally Wormwood Scrubs. That sets up a pattern of behaviour that the Russians would recognise so we'd do the same for you. Except with a bit of luck they'd come for you long before you reached trial. All you have to do is contact them and let them do the rest.'

'If they do come for me, people could get hurt.'

'That's a risk we'll have to take. But they're not going to start a war. They'll want to extract you as quickly and as cleanly as possible.'

'At which point, the police and the secret service will begin a nationwide hunt to find you,' M said. 'So let's just hope the Russians know what they're doing.' He paused. 'We also need to talk about what might happen to you if you do return to Russia. We know what they did to you the last time you fell into their hands. We need to be sure that they can't continue the treatment if they get you back.'

'That would be reassuring,' Bond agreed.

M thought for a moment. He came to a decision and lit his pipe. 'Very well,' he said. 'There's someone I want you to meet.'

4

C.C.

'Chief of Staff . . . ?'

Bill Tanner had been waiting for M's instruction. He nodded and left the room.

'I'm going to introduce you to Major Colin Cunningham,' M began. 'He's a remarkable man . . . a clinical psychologist. Worked in Science 4 as a senior adviser to the Air Ministry during the war and since then he's been an integral part of A19.' A19 was the intelligence department dealing with prisoner interrogation. During the war, in its former incarnation as M19, it had advised officers on how to conduct themselves if they fell into enemy hands. 'He's produced outstanding work on German interrogation and communist indoctrination techniques,' M continued. 'Right now, he's the leading clinician here at The Park.

We're lucky to have him. You may have seen his initials on some of the reports that have landed on your desk over the years.'

So Bond was about to meet the man who was C.C. It had never occurred to him that the appellation, the double letters stamped at the end of so many secret documents, concealed a name that belonged to a man who had been quietly serving his country for more than twenty years.

M pointed at Bond with the stem of his pipe, the smoke rising gently from his fist. 'If I'm sending you back to the Russians, I want to know that you're mentally equipped – so listen to what he has to say. And don't be put off by his manner or his appearance. I don't know why it is, but a lot of these psychologists come across as a bit barmy themselves.'

Sir James Molony frowned. 'I'm not sure that's entirely fair . . .' he began.

'It's entirely unfair and that's exactly the point I'm making,' M growled, his voice more gravelly than ever. 'I'm making no judgement and I want 007 to do the same.'

The door opened and Tanner returned, followed by a man who hesitated in the doorway and seemed uncomfortable about even entering the room. Major Colin Cunningham was in his sixties, wearing a sports jacket with patches at the elbows, baggy corduroy trousers and a bow tie. He had lost most of his hair and what few curls remained sat awkwardly, thin and colourless, on his skull. His eyes blinked rapidly behind tortoiseshell glasses and Bond noticed an angry rash on one side of his neck. He understood immediately what M had been saying. Cunningham really did have the appearance of an absent-minded professor.

Tanner closed the door. Bond stubbed out his cigarette and got to his feet. He held out a hand. 'Good morning, sir. I'm James Bond.'

Cunningham gripped the hand briefly, and only with his thumb and fingers, as if he was nervous of too much contact. 'Yes,' he said. 'I know who you are. We actually met when you first came here although you've probably forgotten. You were in no state to remember anything.'

'I'm sure that's true.'

'But I understand you've made a complete recovery. That's quite remarkable – a credit to you, Mr Bond. What the Russians did to you makes the blood run cold. It really was quite disgusting.'

He searched for what he was going to say next, couldn't find it and fell silent. M had also put out his pipe and gestured at the sofa. 'Would you like to sit down, Major Cunningham?'

'Yes. Yes. Do you think we could open a window? It's quite smoky in here.'

There was a hint of petulance in his voice. Tanner did as he'd been asked and the major took his place on an empty sofa, perching on the very edge as if he might need to leap to his feet at any moment. M waited for him to speak and, when he remained silent, gently prompted him. 'You were going to talk to us about brainwashing.'

'Brainwashing?'

'We spoke on the phone.'

'Yes, sir. Of course I know that. It's just that I don't very much like the terminology. It was the Chinese who invented what they called *xi-nao*, which translates as "mind-cleanse". But then the Americans had to make it their own and came up with "brainwash", turning the whole thing into hocus pocus which is all very well if you want to sell cheap paperbacks but doesn't do justice to the sheer nastiness of it all. I prefer the term "menticide". Or menticidal hypnosis. That was very much what was done to Mr Bond. I have to say that his description of his time with the Russians was most informative and sheds completely new light on the subject. I very much hope it will have made you reconsider your own opinions, Sir James.'

'Absolutely.' Sir James Molony frowned. This wasn't what any of them wanted to hear.

'What we want to know,' M cut in, 'is whether it is possible to resist the techniques of menticide or whatever you want to call it. If we send Bond back, how do we know they won't indoctrinate him a second time?'

'To answer that, you have to understand how they succeeded the first time,' Cunningham replied indignantly, glancing at M as if he were an indolent schoolboy. 'Now, the point is – as I understand it – that Mr Bond was already suffering from a traumatic injury following his experiences in Japan. This resulted in almost total amnesia which turned him effectively into a blank canvas. When he inadvertently fell into the Russians' hands, he had no defences at all.

'Even so, this didn't stop them throwing the book at him; by which I mean extreme violence, starvation, autohypnosis, hours without rest, isolation and above all total confusion. They also used narcotics and we can only guess what filth they injected into him. Mescaline, morphine, marijuana. The Americans have been experimenting with LSD although they have no idea what they're playing with. Really!' He tut-tutted. 'One-millionth of one gram will drive an artillery tractor through a man's mental capabilities. It's one of the most destructive ingredients on the planet and if they decide to use it on Mr Bond when they get him back, there's no saying what the result will be. I have to say that I doubt very much that he will be able to withstand it – no matter how much faith you have in his capabilities.'

Despite M's defence of Major Cunningham, Bond found himself becoming annoyed. The psychologist was talking about him as if he wasn't in the room. In fact, for all the emotion in the man's voice, he could have been a footnote in an oversized textbook. He decided to answer back. 'I very much doubt that they'll drug me,' he said. 'After all, if they believe I've killed M and managed to make my way back to them, they'll have to assume that I'm still brainwashed.' He enjoyed using the forbidden word and the tic of irritation it drew from Cunningham. 'Why would they need to start again?'

'You have a point.' To Bond's surprise, Cunningham agreed with him. 'But whatever happens, the important thing – and this will make a huge difference – is that this time you'll be prepared. Back in the fifties, President Eisenhower made his soldiers sign a declaration that they would never yield to brainwashing techniques if they were captured by the Russians. Now, you might think that it was a fool's errand. "I will never forget that I am an American fighting man, responsible for my actions." What would that even mean? Well, actually it was cleverer than it seemed. It prepared the soldiers for what they might expect and so became a shield against it. It reminded them that they *were* soldiers, that they had to obey orders and to conform.

'The Dutch psychoanalyst, Dr Joost Meerloo, put it very well in his book, *The Rape of the Mind.* "The soldier has to know not only his rifle but his sense of mission and the nonsense of his enemy." That is precisely where Mr Bond will begin this time round. He will also know the enemy's aims and techniques.'

Major Cunningham turned to Bond and fixed him with his small, bright eyes.

'When you first fell into their hands, they will have deliberately set out to cause you the greatest anxiety. What will the day bring? When *is* the day even and when is it night? Will you be starved or given food? Will there be another physical assault or will you be allowed to rest? For long periods of time you will have been left completely isolated, feeding on your own fears. This will have had the effect of causing your own psyche to turn against you. It will have created a form of menticidal hypnosis which will have done much of their work for them.

'But this time there will be none of the terror or the paralysis that comes with deliberate bewilderment. On the contrary, the fact that you have an understanding of the enemy's tactics and a knowledge of what to expect will make you stronger than they will ever suspect. More than that, you know something they don't. You have not obeyed their orders and killed your commanding officer. You have returned in full possession of your senses. That places you in a position of superiority which they will find very difficult to undermine.

'You know what to expect so you are already armed,' he concluded. 'You will remember this meeting and that will help you too. It will remind you that you have friends who want you to come home to them. I'm sure you'll think this is all very trite but I assure you it is your psychological armour. Why do you think the BBC with their "London Calling" broadcasts and – on the other side of the Atlantic – the Voice of America were so effective in the Second World War? Why did our enemies do so much to silence them? It was because they reminded the occupied countries that they had not been abandoned. At the end of the day it was not the athletes or the blowhards who necessarily survived the POW camp experience. Physical strength and courage were admirable but not always effective. The survivors were the ones who never felt they were alone.'

Major Cunningham fell silent. He seemed to notice a speck of dust on the sleeve of his jacket and picked at it with a look of dismay.

'Well, thank you very much, Major,' M muttered. He glanced at Bond. 'Is there anything further you want to ask, 007?'

'No, sir. I think that was very helpful.'

Cunningham realised that he was being dismissed. He got to his feet. 'I would add just one thing, if I may be so bold,' he said. 'I think that sending Mr Bond back is a very bad idea. I wouldn't recommend it at all. They're bound to be deeply suspicious of him. They'll be watching him every minute of the day. This man, Colonel Boris, knows what he's doing and clearly sees people as nothing more than commodities. If he thinks he's been tricked, he'll kill Mr Bond without a second thought. Personally, I think it very unlikely that he'll be able to pull this off.'

'Thank you,' Bond muttered.

There was silence in the room after the man from A19 had left. There was no need to discuss what he had said. The four men were agreed.

A week later, with full military honours, Sir Miles Messervy was quietly laid to rest.

5

'Do as you're told . . .'

13, Sretenka Street is a very ugly building even by the high standards of Stalinist architecture. The street itself, in the Meshchansky district of Moscow, is wide and empty, with four lanes for traffic which are quite surplus to requirements as there are seldom enough vehicles to fill one of them. The eight-storey construction stretches for an entire block, crowding out its neighbours, and seems to have been thrown together by committee. It's a mishmash of concrete, wet stucco walls, pointless balconies and narrow windows that allow in almost no light. A wide staircase with a marble facia, dirty and cracked, rises to a pair of solid iron doors that give the impression more of a prison than an office. When Smersh was in residence, this was even more the case with two sentries, armed with sub-machine guns, standing outside, twenty-four hours a day, menacing anyone who had the misfortune to pass by. It is now home to a number of less prominent government organisations including the Council of Artistic Culture, the Central Economic Mathematics Institute and the headquarters of the Machine Tractor Station, responsible for the rental of agricultural machinery to collective farms.

The day after M's funeral, four men and a woman met around an oval-shaped table on the top floor. All of them had brought with them an ADC: a general assistant and, if necessary, a witness to what might be said. These people, young and smartly dressed, were standing in respectful silence a few paces behind their superiors, their faces blank, their hands clasped behind their backs.

The room was bare, without even so much as an official portrait on the walls. A pair of windows looked out over the courtyard at the back of the building, a square of concrete some distance below. There was a fifth man listening to the conversation although he was not present. A fat Bakelite telephone, shaped like a pyramid, squatted in the middle of the table. The very latest in Soviet technology, it was completely transistorised with four built-in amplifiers and electronic voice control. Only forty or fifty such models could be found in the country, all of them connected to the high-frequency network whose beating heart was located in the Kremlin. The man at the other end of the line was silent but occasionally the phone hissed and squawked as if to remind the company that he was still there.

'So news has come in from the south of England,' General Grubozaboyschikov was saying. 'It would seem, comrades, that we have reason for celebration.'

In fact, Grubozaboyschikov was no longer a general in anything but name. Gone was the uniform that he had once relished: the tunic with its crowd of medals, the cavalry trousers, the highly polished black leather riding boots. He was dressed in a dark suit, a white shirt and a maroon silk tie. The fabrics were expensive and doubtless imported but the style and colours had been deliberately chosen so as not to appear flashy or, worse still, degenerate. The clothes did not fit him very well. Sitting in a high-backed chair at the head of the table, he appeared to be shrinking into them. His whole body had a crumpled appearance. Even the shaven skull appeared to have suffered a slow puncture, and the bright eyes that had both inspired and terrified those around him had lost some of their fire, smouldering dully, deep in their caves.

He had paid a heavy price for the failure of the *kon-spiratsia* that he had organised in this very building, several floors below. He was nine years older and he had spent five of them on the penal island of Sakhalin in Eastern Siberia. His health was shattered. He walked with a limp – very little of his left foot remained – and his lungs had been burned by the freezing air, making it difficult to sleep, to eat and, of course, to smoke.

'The head of the British Secret Intelligence Service is dead,' he continued. 'And it is a matter of consid-erable satisfaction that he was killed by the notorious *Angliski spion*, James Bond.' He pronounced 'James' as 'Shems' and the soft sibilant carried with it a whis-per of the hatred that had been building up inside him over the years. 'Bond had been a thorn in our flesh for a very long time and was personally responsible for the elimination of several of our most significant as-sociates across the globe. Le Chiffre, Buonapart Ignace Gallia who called himself Mr Big, Hugo Drax . . . each one of them defeated through no fault of their own. This man had the luck of the devil and you are to be congratulated, Colonel Boris, not just for recognising the opportunity that had fallen into your hands but for exploiting it to such an appropriate end. The English have long had a liking for irony and here we have the chief spymaster, M, killed in his own office by the man he most trusted. Bond is still alive?'

This question was addressed to Colonel Boris, who was sitting at the other end of the table with his hands crossed in front of him, his long, elegant fingers with their perfectly manicured nails on display. An L-shaped, metal inhaler such as might be used by an asthmatic lay within close reach. He was wearing a collarless jacket that was black rather than white but otherwise he was exactly as Bond had remembered him; poised and elegant, the high priest of an evil religion, listening to what was being said but making no comment, his oddly coloured eyes staring into the mid-distance as if examining a world that only he could see.

'Yes, General.' His voice was barely more than a whisper, the words framed by perfect, slightly feminine lips. 'Mr Bond did not attempt to escape from the building in Regent's Park after he had killed M. He would have been perfectly happy to die for the cause and, for what it's worth, if I'd had more time, I would have suggested he should do just that. Certainly, I did not feel I had any further use for him. As it is, he was taken prisoner and is still, as far as we know, in custody.'

'In that event, since he is alive, might it not be

possible to extract him?' It was Erik Mundt who had asked the question, speaking in perfect Russian but with a heavy German accent. There was something of the college professor about the man from the Stasi. Aged in his early fifties, with thinning grey hair and intelligent eyes, he weighed his words carefully before he allowed himself to express them. Like General G, he was wearing a suit with a gold tiepin. The symbol of proletarian solidarity was stamped into the metal . . . or at least half of it. The tiepin had a hammer but no sickle.

'To what purpose?' Grubozaboyschikov asked.

Again, there was a brief pause before Mundt spoke. 'I was thinking that he could be useful to us.'

The four other heads swivelled towards him. The pyramid-shaped telephone sat implacably between them.

'Comrades, there is a proverb: "*Einem geschenkten Gaul schaut man nicht ins Maul*" or, as you say, "Do not count the teeth of a horse you have been given". We have here an opportunity. If Bond is under the control of Colonel Boris, could we not use him for the action that we have planned? Could he not replace the agent – Ivan Aranov – whom we have chosen? He has, after all, the requisite skills. And think of the message it would send to the Russian people – and indeed to the world – if they believed that British intelligence was involved.'

'Bond is a traitor.'

General Grigory Volkhov of the GRU was ginger-haired, with the stolid features and the thickset physique of Georgian peasant stock which was, indeed, where he had originated. Born in a village fifty miles south of Gori (the birthplace of Stalin), he had travelled to Moscow as a teenager and joined the Young Communist League before becoming a junior officer with the OGPU, the secret police force charged with the eradication of saboteurs and counter-revolutionaries. As an assistant to Vasily Blokhin, the world's most prolific executioner, he had witnessed more than a hundred deaths and had personally shot nine of the sixteen defendants following the Moscow Trials.

'He has been disowned by his own country,' Volkhov continued. 'He is in custody, presumably awaiting trial. Even if he were to be involved in our planned action, why would anyone believe that he was acting under the instructions of the British secret service?'

'His name has not been mentioned in connection with M's death,' Mundt replied. 'The British press did not report what actually took place, and even to the intelligence community it remains a closely guarded secret. We can understand why. It was a humiliation! The secret service opened its door to an armed assassin and invited him into his superior's office, perhaps to take tea. Would such a man have been allowed anywhere near any of us? I don't think so. It's hardly surprising that they have remained silent.

'And yet, as a consequence, Bond's reputation is intact. To many people around the world, in the CIA and the Deuxième Bureau for example, Bond is still one of his country's most trusted agents. This can be useful to us. After the event, they may try to deny his involvement. By then, it will be too late.'

'You make an interesting point.' General G took out a packet of Moskwa-Volga cigarettes, extracted one and squeezed the cardboard tube flat before sliding it between his lips. His ADC stepped forward with a match and lit it for him. General G knew he should not smoke but he could not stop himself. These days, there were few enough pleasures in his life. He drew in the acrid smoke, then turned to Lieutenant General Kirilenko. 'Your thoughts?' he asked.

'I do not agree.'

The only woman at the table spoke with a voice that sucked the life out of everything she said. General G still found it difficult to imagine Irma Kirilenko running a department of the KGB, particularly one that occupied itself with murder on a daily basis. She was, like General Volkhov, in full uniform but even so she seemed too prim, too orderly with her hair tied back, the schoolteacher's spectacles, the studied blankness of her face. She was at least thirty years his junior, younger than his youngest daughter, and represented the new breed of Soviet apparatchik: business-like, efficient, utterly lacking in imagination. He wondered if she had ever allowed a man to touch her body, if she had ever had sex. He doubted it. Comrade Kirilenko was in a full-time relationship with her work.

'We have been discussing this operation for months,' she continued. 'We have spent many hours poring over every last detail. The timing. The location. The choice of weapon. We had examined many candidates for the final action before we selected Ivan Aranov, a loyalist and a professional killer on whom we were all agreed. Are we now going to replace him? Are we seriously going to consider making such a major adjustment at this late stage?'

'Both men are weapons,' Mundt said. 'Why should we not discard one if the other is superior?'

'How can you be certain that is the case? Bond seems to have been effective with regard to this business in London, but how can we be sure that he could be trusted a second time, particularly when the stakes are so much higher? It is well known that Colonel Boris has done exemplary work in the field of mind control but, comrades, it has always been my practice not to believe anything until I have seen it with my own eyes. We only have his word for it that he can control this man, Bond. What if he is wrong?'

Colonel Boris spoke for the first time. 'You would like a demonstration?' he asked with a half-smile, as if he found the challenge amusing. 'Unfortunately, Mr Bond is not with us presently but even so, it would be my pleasure to educate you as to the extent of my capabilities. Mind control, as you call it, is an exact science and I would like to think that, working at my institute in Leningrad, I have developed it further than any person in the world. Any one of you could be in my complete power even now, without realising it. In fact, one of you is.'

He paused. The other four committee members were looking at him uneasily. He allowed the silence to insinuate itself into their darkest thoughts. Then his long fingers tapped gently on the table. 'Ilya Platonov?'

These last words were addressed to his ADC, who had been listening to all of this with interest. Now he stepped forward, his face politely enquiring. He was slim and attractive, with the looks of perhaps an actor or a dancer, dressed in a suit and tie.

'Have you been paying attention?' Colonel Boris asked.

'Certainly, Comrade Colonel.'

'Can you tell us how long you have been with me?'

'Two years, Comrade Colonel.'

'And how old are you, Ilya Platonov?'

'I'm twenty-seven, Comrade Colonel.'

'Do you enjoy working for me?'

'Very much so, Comrade Colonel.'

'I am grateful to you, Ilya. I have enjoyed your company. But now I'm afraid I must ask you to leave the room.'

The young man looked puzzled. 'I'm sorry, Comrade Colonel?'

'I want you to leave.'

The ADC opened his mouth as if to argue. He thought better of it, nodded and took a step towards the door.

'Not by the door. The window.'

Suddenly, the room was very still.

'I don't understand, Comrade Colonel?'

'It's perfectly simple.' Colonel Boris raised a single finger and touched his own face, just below the blue eye. It was not an affectation. It was a signal and the young man jerked back as if a switch had been thrown. 'I am ending our association. Leave by the window.'

'But—' The word caught in his throat.

'Do as you're told, Ilya. You always do as you're told.'

Ilya Platonov stared as he attempted to make sense of what he had just heard. He had broken into a sweat. His whole body was gripped in some sort of paroxysm as if he had lost control of his own limbs. He tried to speak but no words came. The veins on the side of his neck were pulsating as blood rushed into his face. At the same time, he had begun to cry. His head twisted to one side as he tried to fight whatever it was that had overtaken him. His jaw was clenched so tight that his entire mouth seemed to have dislocated.

And then he came to the decision that had never actually been his to make. Moving jerkily, he walked to one of the windows and opened it. For a moment he stood there, the breeze tugging at his dark hair. He didn't look back. He was unaware of the nine faces watching him in silent horror. He threw himself forward and disappeared from sight.

'*Ty che – blyad!*' General Volkhov was the first to recover. He spat out the obscenity and hurried over to the window. He looked down eight floors. Ilya Platonov was not dead yet. He was lying in the courtyard in a spreading pool of blood, his body mangled, one leg still twitching. Volkhov closed the window.

'How?' he muttered. He thought for a moment. Then: 'Why?'

'Comrade Kirilenko left me with no choice but to provide you with a demonstration of my capabilities,' Colonel Boris remarked. 'Let us not mourn the loss of Ilya Platonov. He was sent to me by his father for retraining. He was, I regret to tell you, a sexual deviant. His family will not miss him and I kept him with me only until such a time as it amused me to be rid of him. He is easily replaced.'

General Volkhov returned to his chair and sat down heavily. Colonel Boris reached for the atomiser and pressed the button with his thumb, spraying vapour into his mouth. The smell of peppermint hung briefly in the air. He turned, once again, to Lieutenant General Kirilenko. 'I hope I have dispelled any doubts you may have had, Comrade,' he continued, smoothly. 'But whether it is the decision of this committee to use Bond or not, let me give you some further assurance.

'Return him to me and I will examine him with great care. I will look into every corner of his mind. James Bond may have had a certain success as a secret agent and there are those among you who may respect or even fear him, but to me he is nothing more than a microorganism on a slide. He can hide nothing from me. And when the moment comes for him to make the kill, he will not hesitate. It will be my finger on the trigger. The trigger is deep inside him. He is not aware of it but I know because I placed it there.'

General G finished his cigarette and pinched it out between his index finger and thumb. When he spoke, he chose his words carefully. He had to appear neutral. He did not want anyone else around the table to see how much he was motivated by the simple, primal desire for revenge. It was not enough that Bond had been humiliated and destroyed. General G wanted to see him killed.

'There are many advantages to be gained by this change of plan,' he said. 'It will certainly add emphasis to the message that we wish to send the world. But such a course of action will not be easy. First, we have to help him with his defection and bring him back to us here in Moscow. That in itself will not be without challenges. Then we require Colonel Boris to examine him extremely carefully – as he has just described. But were these two stipulations to be met, the reward would be considerable. It is, as Comrade Mundt said, an opportunity that we cannot ignore. So let me ask you, comrades . . .' He turned the remains of the cigarette between his fingers, reflecting that once there

would have been no need to ask. 'How are we to proceed? Are we to adopt the proposal?'

Kirilenko was the first to reply. 'It was a remarkable
demonstration,' she exclaimed. 'I must apologise to
you, Comrade Colonel, for having any doubts in your
abilities. However, even so, it is my opinion that we
should stick with what we have decided. We already
have a candidate. I think it would be dangerous to
make changes at this late stage.'

General Volkhov spread his hands. 'I'm afraid I
concur with Lieutenant General Kirilenko,' he said. 'I
can see advantages to using this man, Bond. But even
if he is under our complete control, there will be risks.
And in this affair, we already have enough risks. I pro-
pose we stick with Ivan Aranov and continue with the
plan that we agreed.'

'I can see that General Grubozaboyschikov and I are
in agreement,' Mundt remarked. General G nodded.
'We both support the proposition. It is two against
two. Therefore it would seem that Colonel Boris has
the casting vote.'

Colonel Boris did not speak for a long moment. His
eyes gave nothing away. He raised his fingers and in-
terlaced them like a pianist about to perform. 'I would
very much like to make use of James Bond,' he said,
eventually. 'It would amuse me to have him back in

my hands and I agree with General G. Just think of the message it would send when it was discovered that British intelligence was involved!

'But at the same time,' he continued quickly, 'and with the greatest respect, I do wonder if the decision is mine – or any of ours – to make.'

Everyone in the room knew what he meant. Their eyes turned to the telephone. There was a pause and then the voice came, clear and distant.

'We will use Bond.'

There was a click and the line disconnected.

The decision had been made.

6

A Room with No View

It was an Edwardian, double-fronted residence, a short distance from the river on the wrong side of Richmond Bridge. It looked unloved. The windows had a sheen of dust that was too ingrained to be cleaned, the roof was missing tiles, the garden was overgrown, with a stagnant ornamental pond and a stone Cupid blunted by the rain and wind and disfigured by pigeons. People came and people went but nobody knew who actually lived there. A gate and a short gravel drive separated it from the main road. The house was called River View although it didn't have one.

Bond had been kept here for a week, interrogated continuously by a succession of men and women who arrived with their briefcases and their compact cassette recorders and sat at one end of the table in the basement with the single window behind and above them so that Bond, sitting opposite, saw a narrow rectangle of grey sky and wild grass just over their shoulders. Each of them had their own style. Clipped and efficient. Vaguely sympathetic. Or threatening with a hangman's smile.

It made no difference. He gave them all the same answers, trying to explain that he was fighting for peace and that killing M had been the only reasonable thing to do, given what he had learned during his time in Moscow. He was without remorse, speaking with endless patience, as if they would see things his way if only they tried a little harder. Bond knew that – if all went according to plan – this was just a rehearsal for what was to come. It was a chance to get it right. At the same time, he hated what he was doing. None of these people knew the truth. He was pretending to be everything he had spent his whole life fighting against.

He felt this most keenly when he was alone with the young agent who was looking after him. He remembered the driver who had met him at the airport and reflected that a great many of the people he encountered in the intelligence service these days were ten or fifteen years younger than him. Despite everything, Bond had developed a liking for Sam King, a fair-haired ex-grammar school boy from the Ribble Valley who represented the new intake. In the long hours they had spent together, they had talked about tennis and the pleasures of cross-country versus Alpine skiing (Sam enjoyed both); anything that wasn't related to politics or current affairs. Sam was puzzled by Bond. He spoke with a soft Lancashire accent and there was always an element of disappointment in his voice.

They were not going to be together much longer. During his last interview (a prim civil servant who looked bored and regarded him with distaste) Bond had been told that he was being taken to Bow Street Magistrates' Court to be charged and remanded in custody. The intelligence services wanted nothing more to do with him. As he sat on the single, wooden chair in the basement room with its barred window and bed, Bond reflected that very little would be changing in his current circumstances. He also knew that if he wanted to make contact with the Russians, it would have to be now.

River View had its own internal clock. At exactly six o'clock, the door opened and Sam King came in carrying a tray with Bond's evening meal. The food was bad, almost deliberately so, as if to remind Bond that he wasn't actually worth feeding. He set the tray down on the table below the window.

'You'll be leaving tomorrow morning,' he said.

'So I understand,' Bond replied.

'I imagine you'll want to shave. I'll make sure your stuff is brought to you.'

'Thank you.'

Bond had wandered over to the table as if he was interested in seeing what was on his plate. Sam King had been leaning towards him with the tray and as he straightened up, Bond hit him once, an elbow strike behind the ear. The younger man pitched forward. Bond caught him and lowered him onto the bed. It occurred to him that the next time he saw Bill Tanner, he would mention that combat training within the service needed taking up a notch or two. The young agent had allowed the relationship between them to undermine his defences. Certainly, he should never have turned his back on his prisoner. In other circumstances, he might have ended up with a broken neck.

Sam had brought no keys with him. Bond quickly frisked him but his pockets were empty. It didn't matter. He had already worked out that there was no easy way out of the house, which was much more secure than it looked. The windows on the ground floor were barred. Only the front door actually opened to the outside world and it was guarded around the clock by a second man called Harrison who had positioned himself at the end of a long corridor so that it would be impossible to approach him without being seen. There were panic buttons everywhere, discreetly placed next to every doorway. If one of them was activated, it would take reinforcements minutes to arrive and Bond would be trapped inside, waiting for them.

He left the room, closing the door behind him, and made his way up the blank, concrete stairs that led to the ground floor. There were no lights on and although it was still early evening, very little sunshine made its way into the house. Gloom and shadows clung to the walls like mildew, and the very air had a grey quality as if the house was trying to keep its secrets to itself. Bond looked round the corner and saw Harrison, sitting in a chair, reading a paper. Another security lapse. How was he supposed to do his job when half his attention was on the day's news?

Bond knew what he was looking for. When he had first been brought here, he had noticed an open door and, on the other side, a study, obviously in use as it was in better repair than the rest of the house. He waited until Harrison turned a page and used the rustle of paper as the cue to slide across the corridor and into the doorway opposite. With his back against the wood and his eyes still fixed on Harrison, he reached down, found the handle and turned it. The door opened behind him. He went in.

The room was empty apart from a desk, some old armchairs, a two-bar heater and a filing cabinet. But it was what stood on the filing cabinet that Bond wanted. A telephone. He crossed the threadbare carpet and snatched up the receiver, still wondering if he would be rewarded with a dialling tone. Almost to his disbelief, the phone was connected. He wondered if Bill Tanner had deliberately made this easy for him. He dialled the number that he had memorised while he was still in Moscow, before he had been sent home to kill M. The phone rang three times. Then it was answered.

'Yes?'

'This is Diamant.'

It was the code name Bond had been given. Diamond. He almost heard the gasp at the other end of the line as the Russian collaborator in Ruislip realised who he was. He might have been waiting much of his adult life for this, his moment in the sun.

'Where are you?' he asked.

'In a house just south of Richmond Bridge.'

'Are you at liberty?'

'No. They're taking me to Bow Street tomorrow morning.'

'Where in Bow Street?'

'The Magistrates' Court. Where do you think?'

'Whose telephone is this?'

Bond felt something press against the back of his head and knew at once that it was the muzzle of a gun. A voice said: 'Put that down.'

He lowered the telephone receiver back into its cradle.

'Turn round.'

Bond did as he was ordered and saw Sam King holding a Walther PPK, the same pistol that he favoured himself. The younger man took a step sideways, keeping a careful distance between himself and Bond now that they were face to face. Bond saw a dark swelling on the side of his neck. The younger man's eyes were ice cold and when he spoke, he had to fight to control his voice. 'Who was that?' he demanded.

'My mother,' Bond said. 'She worries about me when she doesn't hear from me.'

Sam was holding the pistol in a two-handed grip with the thumbs kissing. It wasn't just to help his accuracy. Bond saw that the agent was almost shaking with fury. He was fighting with himself, forcing himself not to pull the trigger. He wanted to kill Bond.

'We'll check the number,' he said. 'We'll know who it was.'

'Then why ask me?'

There was a movement at the door. The second agent, Harrison, had arrived. He was the same age as Sam and stood there, in shock, almost afraid to come into the room. 'Are you OK?' he asked.

'Just watch my back.' Sam's eyes never left Bond. 'I want you to know something,' he said. 'You disgust me. Everything about you disgusts me. I know who you are. The great James Bond, 007. Everyone talks about you. They told me that the Russians got their hands on you and did something to your brain and it wasn't your fault and I've tried to make allowances for that. But what you tried to do just now, you had to think about that . . . didn't you. You had to plan it. So you *can* think. You know what you're doing. I don't accept that anyone can mess with your head so much that you actually turn against your country. I think there must have been a part of you that wanted to do it from the start.

'I'm going to take you back downstairs now. You're going to keep your hands clasped behind you and if you try anything, if you even look at me, I will put a bullet in your neck. From what I understand, I'll only be saving everyone a lot of time and money because they're going to hang you anyway. You know the mistake I made tonight? It was believing in you. Well,

Mr James Bond 007, whatever you were is gone. It belongs to another time. There are no heroes any more.
And you're just the lowest of the low. Now move.'

They went back down to the basement in silence.
Harrison followed King who at least knew enough
to keep carefully to one side so as not to obstruct the
other man's line of fire. Bond stepped into his room
and heard the door close behind him. A key turned in
the lock. His food was still on the table, quite cold by
now. He sat on the bed.

There are no heroes any more.

He reflected on what had just happened and on what
Sam King had said and felt the whisper of unease that
had been pursuing him ever since he had stepped off
the plane from Jamaica. It had begun with the driver
who had driven him to The Park. How old had he been?
Twenty-eight? Twenty-nine? There is a moment in
everyone's life when they discover that the waters that
were once so familiar have somehow receded and that
they have been left exposed on a solitary mound of dry
land. Bond wasn't feeling his age but he was, perhaps,
feeling the age in which he lived.

He had lost the comfort of certainty. Tanner had
mentioned the double agent, George Blake, now serving forty-two years in jail. It wasn't just Blake. The rot
had started with Guy Burgess and Donald Maclean,

who had both defected at the start of the fifties. More recently, there had been the improbable Portland spy ring, headed up by an alcoholic civil servant and his damaged, foolish wife. He had just spoken to a journalist in north-west London who had quite possibly been waiting half his life for the chance to betray his country. To look at the newspapers, you would think the whole of Great Britain was riddled with traitors. There was no trust any more. Even Macmillan, when he was prime minister, had expressed his doubts about military intelligence, referring in one of his speeches to 'the so-called security services'. The war, which had given the young Bond so much of his motivation, had ended almost two decades ago. It was accumulating the dust and the fuzziness of past history.

He was still a member of the elite Double-O Section of the secret service. He had his licence to kill. But was it possible that in this new, more questioning age, that licence might have expired? Perhaps killing had become too blunt an instrument for the new realpolitik.

For a long time, Bond sat where he was, gazing at a window which gave him no view. Not of the outside world. Not of his own future life.

7

The Killer Instinct

It was six o'clock the next morning when the convoy arrived. Apart from a solitary milk float whirring past on its three wheels, the streets were empty, the curtains in the houses still drawn. The sky had that slate-grey quality that comes when the sun has just risen but has yet to drag behind it any warmth. The river birds, flying overhead, seemed to pass slowly, with a certain hopelessness.

There were three vehicles. Two of them were Wolseleys, the 'area cars' favoured by the Metropolitan Police. A Ford Transit van had travelled between them; midnight blue with a single light set in its roof, no windows in the back but narrow, glass-covered slits along the sides. As the three of them crossed Richmond Bridge, the distance between them didn't vary by so much as an inch. They continued down the road and then, in perfect unison, pulled in outside the house called River View. The engines were left running. Nobody got out.

Inside the house, in the room that had been his home for the past week, James Bond was sitting on the edge of the bed, dressed in a suit, his arms folded in front of him. He had been handcuffed. Harrison and King stood over him, both men holding guns. Harrison was also cradling a radio in the palm of his hand. It suddenly squawked into life, a metallic voice barking out information that was close to indecipherable.

'They're here,' he said.

Sam King nodded. The bruise on the side of his neck seemed to have darkened. He turned to Bond. 'We'll be travelling with you to Bow Street,' he said. 'Once we get there, you'll be handed over to the Special Branch of the Metropolitan Police and you're no longer our responsibility. You will not speak to us during the journey. You will not move. You will keep your hands in sight the whole time. Do you understand me?'

'You make yourself very clear,' Bond said, with a thin smile.

'Good. We'll leave now. You can stand up.'

Bond did as he was told. The younger agent had

slipped up badly the night before and he was obviously doing his best to show that he was still in control. Was he about to be proved wrong? The Russians now knew where Bond was. They knew when he was being transferred and where he was going. The one thing they didn't have was the route. If they were going to arrange a snatch, it would have to be at the beginning or the end of the journey – in Richmond or in Bow Street. As far as Bond could see, the Magistrates' Court would be the more likely option. There were plenty of narrow streets with flats and offices providing opportunities for concealment and evasion. The police officers guarding him would be fully alert when they set off but they might make the mistake of relaxing once they felt they had arrived. If the Russians were going to bite, that was surely where their teeth would snap shut.

Bond was wrong.

The moment they had decided to extract him, Stalnaya Ruka had swung into action and during the past week, while Bond was being interrogated, their agents had been looking for him all over London, using every means at their disposal. The Russians had people in government ministries, in police stations, newspaper offices, embassies, even inside the intelligence service in the very same building where Bond had once worked. They had intercepted letters and listened in on telephone conversations. They had a list of ministers and civil servants who drank too much, who owed money, who had cheated on their wives with girls or with boys. Anyone who might have information had been approached, questioned, bribed, threatened. Bond. James Bond. The man who killed M. Have you heard anything about him? Do you know where he's being held?

At the same time, anyone associated with Bond – and that included Bill Tanner, his former secretary, Loelia Ponsonby, and even his housekeeper, May – had been closely monitored. The Russians had guessed that Bond was being kept somewhere in the city. His telephone call had told them they were right.

It was that brief contact that had changed everything and had, inadvertently, given Stalnaya Ruka exactly what they wanted.

The call had lasted less than a minute and the journalist in Ruislip who had answered – and who had already been arrested – was insisting that he was an innocent victim and that it had merely been a wrong number. But there could be no doubt that a major security leak had been allowed to occur. As a result, all the officers involved in Bond's transfer from Richmond to the Bow Street Magistrates' Court had been reassigned and replacements had been drafted in. They had come to the house an hour earlier than was necessary. And, most significantly, the route that the convoy would take had been changed. From Richmond, it would follow the south bank of the river, continuing past Waterloo Bridge (close to Bow Street), only crossing the river at Tower Bridge before looping back past St Paul's.

The new instructions were typed by a senior secretary at the Home Office. Selina Wilson was single-minded and superior and like so many women at the top level of the Civil Service, married to a job which had never treated her very well. Miss Wilson prided herself on her work. There were no typing errors on the two sheets of paper that she sent – FOR YOUR EYES ONLY – to the chief constable and four other senior officers at New Scotland Yard. She had carefully laid out the new route in a neat column on the second page.

She was working on a brand-new Selectric type-writer. Introduced by IBM just a few years earlier, the machine utilised an advanced technology: instead of striking keys, there was a silver golf ball that swiv-elled and then leapt up to plant the correct letter on the page. Miss Wilson was justifiably proud of the ma-chine as there were very few of them in London and when it had first arrived at the Home Office, she had insisted that it should be assigned to her. She had no way of knowing that the typewriter had been delivered for exactly that reason. It was bait.

The machine was bugged. There was a metal supporting bar underneath the keyboard mechanism which had been hollowed out and contained a series of magnetometers connected to a compact foil capacitator – also known as a 'bleeding unit' – concealed inside the power line. The bug registered the movement of the golf ball and recorded the magnetic disturbances made by the metal arms that supported it. This data was sent by radio to a listening post outside the building and although it wasn't complete, it was enough to allow the individual letters typed by the efficient Miss Wilson to be reassembled, with the result that the information had arrived at the Kremlin minutes after it had reached New Scotland Yard.

Even as the convoy waited in the street, it was being watched. The man in the milk float spoke briefly into a microphone concealed behind the steering wheel.

'They're here.' He spoke with an Irish accent. 'No sign of our man yet.'

The milk float wheezed on, stopping a few doors down. The milkman stayed in the front seat, watching events in the driver's mirror.

Meanwhile, Bond had climbed the stairs and stood

in the corridor that he had reached the night before. There were two more men waiting for him at the door, Special Branch obviously: he would have been able to tell from their short cut hair and thankless eyes. He glanced at their badly cut suits and guessed that they were wearing bulletproof vests beneath: for his sake or for the Russians, he wondered? Had they been tipped off that some sort of attack might be likely?

He walked towards them. 'Good morning,' he said.

They looked at him indifferently.

'Is everything ready?' King asked.

'The limo's outside.'

'Then let's get him on his way.'

Two men in front, two behind. They were taking no chances. One of them opened the front door and Bond stared at the grey light of morning, the first time he had seen the outside world for a week. He passed through the doorway and into the street, noting the empty pavements, the drawn curtains, the single milk van parked a short distance away. As soon as he appeared, two more officers moved towards the Black Maria – Bond supposed that was what he should call it – and threw open the back. Just five steps and he would be inside. So it didn't look as if the Russians were here. Would they be waiting at Bow Street? Perhaps nothing would happen until he was in jail.

He just hoped that M was right and they would actually decide to come for him. The intelligence service had put a lot of time and effort into creating this trap. Would the mice sneak in to steal the cheese?

Bond had reached the van.

'Mind your head,' one of the police officers escorting him said.

'Thank you . . .' Bond began, then grunted as the same man grabbed hold of his head and slammed it against the side of the van. The sound of bone hitting metal was loud, amplified by the empty drum of the interior which was lined with wooden panels. But although Bond was startled, smarting from the blow, he knew that the damage would have been minimal. They wouldn't want to leave bruises when he was about to appear in court.

'Traitor,' the police officer muttered.

Bond stumbled as if dazed, and as the man reached out to steady him, Bond lashed out with one fist, the short chain of the handcuffs forcing the other fist to follow through beside it. His three outstretched fingers knifed into the edge of the man's throat. Bond had been careful to avoid the soft tissue around the tracheal cartilage – he could have killed the Special Branch man instantly – but it had exactly the effect he wanted. Suddenly he was surrounded by guns.

Everyone was shouting. The man he had attacked fell sideways, retching. Bond felt a heavy object crash into his back, propelling him into the van. The world twisted briefly and then King and Harrison were with him and the door was slamming shut. He heard the locks turn.

The three of them were alone in a wooden box. The side of Bond's head was smarting and his back was bruised but otherwise he was unhurt. He examined his surroundings. There wasn't much to see. Two benches faced each other, running the length of the van, bolted to the floor. The glass in the narrow windows was thick enough to obscure the view but allowed enough light to bleed in to demonstrate to any prisoner the hopelessness of his situation. Bond sat down, pleased with himself. If the Russians were watching, they would have seen exactly what he wanted.

'You never stop, do you?' King said with quiet loathing.

'He hit me first,' Bond replied, reasonably.

He felt the van sway as the driver got back into the front. A moment later, the engine started. The turn of the pistons echoed through the closed interior with its wooden panels, drowning out any other sounds. Harrison was sitting in one corner, clearly unhappy to be there. King sat opposite him, next to Bond but keeping as much distance as possible between them. The van pulled out and at last they were on their way. There was no conversation.

Still sandwiched between the two police cars, the van made its way across Richmond Bridge and then along the south bank of the river, heading through Putney, Wandsworth and on into Lambeth. Had Bond been given the opportunity, he would have had a fine view of Battersea power station, then the Houses of Parliament, Big Ben and – at the bend in the river – the majestic sprawl of Somerset House. Bond had a certain fondness for London. It wasn't just that he lived and worked there. He'd always thought the city had an unchanging quality. It struck him as stolid and loyal. But in recent years it had come under attack from a new generation of architects full of ambition and fresh ideas, their towers of glass and concrete redefining the horizon. It was ironic that the Luftwaffe had paved the way for them. The new London was feeding on the empty spaces where the old had once stood.

King and Harrison were saying nothing. Bond could only work out where he was by the shifting of the van, the left and the right turns, the amount of time that had passed and the few audible clues: a helicopter landing at what might be Battersea heliport, a train passing close by, perhaps at Hungerford Bridge. There didn't seem to be much traffic around them. Their progress was smooth. And they were barely stopping at any traffic lights, suggesting to Bond that they had bypassed the centre of the city and instead were skirting round the edge.

He only became aware that something was wrong when they came to a sudden halt, all three of them jerking forward on their opposing benches. The secret service men sensed it too, their hands moving towards their guns. There could have been a traffic accident just ahead of them. A careless pedestrian or a stray dog could have walked into their path. But instinctively, Bond knew that it had to be something more.

In fact, the convoy had just turned onto Tower Bridge. That was where the attack began.

There were roadworks on the bridge; a temporary traffic signal next to a makeshift work tent with a group of labourers in hard hats and fluorescent jackets, picking at the surface. As the convoy approached, the light unexpectedly turned red and that was what had caused the immediate brake. The three police vehicles were suddenly trapped, twenty-eight feet above the water, surrounded by the other cars and buses that had been crossing at that time. For a few seconds, nobody was aware that anything was wrong.

And then the missiles were launched, sweeping

down from the two bridge towers at either end of the upper walkways. There had been men concealed behind the cathedral-like windows, looking out for the convoy which they had spotted long before it had arrived. They had passed the information to the workmen, using handheld transceivers, and the lights had been primed to turn red at exactly the right moment.

The men in the towers were equipped with modified versions of the RPG2 anti-tank missile launcher first developed by the Soviets at the end of the war. But instead of high explosive, the missiles contained white phosphorus which, at the moment of impact, burst into brilliant yellow flame, releasing pillars of white smoke which billowed out in every direction. Within seconds, the convoy had disappeared from sight. The central span of the bridge itself had vanished. The smoke seemed to cling to the surface with a life of its own, keeping everyone – innocent motorists, bus drivers and police – in its grasp.

Bond felt his eyes smarting. The smoke was creeping under the door. He could hear the panic outside. People were shouting. A car had begun to sound its horn repeatedly. God! The Soviets must have mounted an operation bigger than any of them could have imagined. Was he that important to them? And did they really think they could get away with a pitched battle in the middle of London? He saw Sam King draw his Walther PPK and knew instantly that the young agent was out of his depth, that he had no experience of this sort of action.

'Put that away, you damned fool,' he snapped.

King looked at him, astonished. 'What . . .?' he began.

'It sounds like my friends have come for me. There could be twenty of them out there.' Bond's throat was burning as the phosphorus gas filled the van. 'They're obviously armed and you're not going to stop them on your own with that. Do you really want to die for me?'

'I'll kill you before I let them take you.'

'You think you could look me in the eye and kill me in cold blood? You don't have it in you, Sam. Put that down.'

King kept Bond in his sights. On the other bench, Harrison had taken out his gun but he was even less sure of himself. He looked ill.

The van's engine had stalled. The noise of battle penetrated the wooden shell. Bond tried to make sense of what was happening, waiting for the next phase of the assault which he knew must happen soon.

The gunmen in the towers had fired off two more missiles, which had burrowed into the dense, white cloud and exploded invisibly inside. There was the scream of rubber and then the smash of metal against metal as a driver in a Ford Cortina, half-blind and panicking, tried to drive off Tower Bridge only to crash into the side of a bus. The fake workmen were running towards the convoy. They had dropped their tools. Instead, they had produced pistols and AR-10 semi-automatic rifles. They had also pulled on gas masks which hid their faces as well as allowing them to breathe. They surrounded the two police cars, shouting at the officers to stay inside. A burst of machine-gun fire shredded the tyres of the leading vehicle. More men, spectral figures in the smoke, moved towards the van.

King was still aiming at Bond but his hand was shaking. Harrison had slid further up the bench, backing into the far corner. The white smoke was rolling across the floor, bouncing off the walls. It was becoming difficult to breathe.

'He's right,' Harrison rasped. Tears were streaming down his cheeks and it was hard to be sure if they were caused by the fumes or by his fear. His pistol hung helplessly in his hand. 'There's nothing we can do.'

But Sam King had already failed once. Bond saw that nothing would make him give up a second time. He realised that the whole situation was out of control. The convoy had been ambushed earlier than he had expected. Somehow the enemy had got hold of their route. Was he going to have to sit there and watch these two beginners die?

'Listen to me . . .' he began.

It was too late. The lock at the back of the van exploded. Bond felt the compression and the rush of overheated air. He recognised the sour, almond smell of plastic explosive. The doors were flung open and he saw two figures wearing balaclavas, both with pistols, standing against a twisting curtain of white smoke.

'Bond?' one of them asked.

'That's me,' Bond said.

'What are you waiting for?' The voice was high-pitched, with an Irish accent. 'Get the hell out!'

'No!' King had half-risen to his feet. His hand was stretched out as if he wanted to keep his gun as far away from himself as possible, as if he didn't want to be connected with what he was about to do. Harrison was cowering behind him.

'Leave it!' Bond snapped.

King fired at one of the masked men in the door. The man cried out and fell back. The bullet had creased his arm, high up, close to his shoulder. At once, King brought the gun back and aimed at Bond. Bond kicked out, the tip of his shoe scything into King's wrist just as the gun was fired a second time. The shot went wild, hitting the roof, and the gun fell to the floor. Bond was still chained. He clasped his hands together and then swung the ball made of his ten fingers and knuckles, crashing it into the side of King's face. King was thrown into the corner of the van, colliding with Harrison. Bond leaned down and snatched up the gun.

It was over. Bond looked out the door and saw the skeletal outline of one of the towers and the walkway cutting through the sky. He heard machine-gun fire and, in the distance, the sirens of approaching police cars. It was time to leave but just as he made his move, a figure loomed towards him, blocking his way. It was the man who had been wounded by Sam King. He had climbed back into the doorway and now he stood there, clutching his injured arm with one hand, holding his pistol in the other. Quite deliberately, he took aim at the young agent.

Bond knew, with sickening certainty, that the Irishman – furious and in pain – had decided to take revenge. He had seen it enough times, the moment when any sense of humanity falls away and the killer instinct is all that remains. King had stumbled against Harrison so that even if the other agent had wanted to help, there was nothing he could do. Bond himself had been forgotten. In the middle of all the swirling chaos, he was about to witness a cold-blooded execution.

He couldn't allow it to happen. He had no choice. He brought the Walther PPK round, feeling the familiar weight in his hand, and fired off a single shot. At this range, he couldn't miss. The bullet struck the wounded man in the forehead, killing him instantly. His partner had appeared just behind him and saw what had happened. The shock of it froze him to the ground. So be it. Bond fired again and watched as he fell backwards with a scarlet bloom bursting from his chest.

Both Sam King and Harrison had observed all this in stunned silence. There was no time to explain. Bond fired two more shots at the ground, then turned on them with icy determination in his eyes. 'Listen to me,' he snapped. 'When anybody asks, you say you killed the two men who broke in here. In other words, you did your job. Those two shots I fired just now . . . I want the Russians to believe that I killed you and that's how I got away. Do you understand me? You stay in the van. You don't show yourselves. Play dead until the intelligence services get here. If you say anything to anyone, you will do incalculable damage.' He remembered he was still holding the gun and slid it across the floor. It came to a halt just in front of King's foot. 'Find Bill Tanner at the intelligence service,' Bond added. 'You can tell him what happened. Tell no one else.'

'But . . .' Sam King glanced down at the gun and then looked up at Bond, seeing him in a completely new light. At the same time, there was the admission that everything he had thought and said the night before had been wrong. 'Thank you,' he whispered.

Bond didn't reply. He stepped out of the van and, like a magician leaving the stage, disappeared into the smoke.

8

Over the Edge

Bond had stepped into a war zone. He was surrounded by chaos and destruction; a crashed car with its nose buried in the side of a bus, a woman and a child running between the stalled traffic, both screaming, broken glass, the pulsating yellow of another smoke grenade, thick white clouds spreading out between the two towers. The police cars that Bond had heard were getting closer. Their sirens were converging from both sides of the river, reminding him that Tower Bridge only had two exits. Even as he stood there, trying to find air that was actually breathable, Bond knew that if he didn't move quickly, he would be trapped.

The Wolseley 6/99 that had come for him in

Richmond was right in front of him, the Special Branch men trapped inside, watching helplessly as their worst fears played out around them. Somehow the route that they were taking had been revealed to the enemy. The security services were responsible for all this destruction. They could do nothing about it. Two men in balaclavas stood either side of the car, their rifles slanting down towards the windows. Bond didn't need to look to know that it would be the same for the other car. He recognised the officer who had slammed his head into the van, sitting in the passenger seat, almost writhing with frustration. Bond smiled at him. He deserved it.

A figure lumbered towards him, a thickset man dressed like all the others in a donkey jacket, fluorescent vest and dungarees, cradling an ArmaLite in his arms, the wooden stock pressed against his chest. As he drew closer, Bond saw a lock of ginger hair, watery brown eyes, a boxer's nose pushed flat against his face and thick lips. This was all the balaclava gave away. The man stopped inches away from him. He recognised Bond. He was angry.

'What happened to Brendan and Sean?' he demanded. Irish names to match the Irish accents of the two men Bond had shot.

Bond glanced behind him, at the open door of the

van, relieved that King and Harrison were obeying his instructions and hadn't appeared. 'They didn't make it,' he said.

'That's not what I asked you. What happened to my people?'

'There were two agents with me. They were armed.' Bond lifted his arms, showing the handcuffs. 'There was nothing I could do.'

'So how come they let you get away?'

Before Bond could answer, the first police car arrived, speeding onto the bridge from the north side of the river. Most of the smoke had dissipated. Bond saw the car swerve to a halt. All four doors burst open.

'You want to talk about this now?' he demanded.

The Irishman wanted to talk. He wanted to interrogate Bond. He wanted to go into the van and examine the agents. But he had no time. There were no more smoke grenades being fired and Bond saw the men emerge from the towers, still carrying their weapons as they made their escape. He heard the angry roar of motorbike engines and two 700 cc Royal Enfield Interceptors came bursting out of what, just moments before, had looked like a work tent. The twin-cylinder motorbikes were capable of speeds of up to 130 mph and even as Bond watched, the men ran towards them and climbed onto the pillion seats, to be swept away in a cloud of exhaust, heading south, away from the new arrivals.

The men guarding the police cars were waiting for their cue. The man Bond thought of as Boxer was torn between the unfinished business in the van and his own escape. He made his decision and nodded. Everyone broke at the same time.

But not off the bridge. They were running to the side, close to where Bond was standing.

'Move it!' Boxer demanded.

Puzzled, Bond went with him. What were they going to do? Jump?

There was no other way. Seconds after the two motorbikes had gone, more police cars arrived, blocking the south exit. The Special Branch officers were scrambling out of their cars. Suddenly Tower Bridge was full of policemen. They reached the edge of the bridge, looking downriver towards Bermondsey. Now Bond saw the ropes that had already been looped round the balustrade that ran the full length of the central span. Two of the gunmen were uncoiling them, dropping the ends down into the water. So it looked as if it was going to be sink or swim after all! Bond had to admire the planning that had gone into the operation even if the endgame still wasn't clear.

The Special Branch men who had picked him up at

Richmond were running towards him. Bond grabbed hold of a rope and threw himself over the parapet, his body swivelling in mid-air. Now it was just a question of lowering himself as fast as he could, using the 'break and squat' technique he'd learned as part of his training with Naval Intelligence. He saw men in balaclavas on either side of him. They were already underneath the bridge, out of the line of fire, and they slowed themselves down as the water drew near. It seemed they had no intention of getting wet.

Bond heard the sound of engines and twisted round, the rope looped between his feet. Three boats were skimming along the river, rushing past the Tower of London on their way to the bridge. They were sleek, white, low in the water: turbocraft jet speedboats powered not by propellors but by water which was being sucked in and then expelled at forty-five gallons a second. There would almost certainly be no faster vessel on the Thames. It was all part of the same efficiency he had noted just moments ago. Nothing had been left to chance.

One of the boats pulled in directly beneath him and Bond dropped the last few feet onto the back seat. The driver, also wearing a balaclava, spun the wheel. The turbocraft had no rudder but the twin flow of the jets allowed it to manoeuvre itself adroitly into place. A second man dropped down beside him. Three boats. Six men. The others had made their escape on motor-bikes and the police and Special Branch were left with the wreckage of an operation that had gone catastroph-ically wrong and the knowledge that the prisoner had been snatched out of their hands. Bond reached out for balance as the boat accelerated away. He thought he heard shots being fired from the bridge but the rush of water drowned them out and they were already too far away and moving too fast to be in any danger of getting hit.

Bond crouched down, feeling the wind and the spray in his eyes. They were heading downriver, but he knew they would have to pull in somewhere before they came to Southend and the North Sea. Even if it were possible to avoid the coastguard, the water would be too rough for a crossing to Belgium or the Nether-lands. And they weren't clear yet. Someone had been smart enough to call ahead and a fast-response vessel had been launched from the Marine Policing Unit at Wapping. It was twenty yards ahead of them, perched in the middle of the water. A voice was booming at them through a loudspeaker, the words snatched away by the breeze.

The speedboats didn't hesitate. They split in dif-ferent directions, two heading one way and one the other, leaving the fast-response vessel in their wake. The police boat spun round and gave chase. At the same time, Bond saw police cars speeding up Wapping High Street with their blue lights flashing, following the bend in the river. He got the impression that the whole of London was hunting him down, the sharks everywhere while the minnows tried to find a place to hide.

More police boats appeared ahead of them. These were duty boats, thirty-two-footers with single engines, wearing the same blue and white livery. They would be slower than the other police vessels but it would be impossible to get past them without colliding: they had turned themselves horizontally, leaving only the narrowest space between them. Bond glanced at his own driver, standing behind the wheel, seemingly relaxed. He wondered what trick he was about to pull out of the bag.

The driver spun the wheel. The three turbocraft wheeled to one side, avoiding the duty boats and cutting a graceful arc through the water, heading towards the right bank. There was a man-made canal cut into the river, leading to a long, rectangular docking area. A metal footbridge crossed over the entrance, forming a sort of gate. Bond saw a barge and an old clipper moored on the other side but the tide was low. The boats were resting at an angle with only a few inches of water shining underneath them. Ahead of them, a ramp slippery with black water and oil rose up to an abandoned yard with weeds sprouting through the gravel and broken bricks. It was being used as a make-shift car park. Bond saw a few dusty cars but no drivers. They had arrived at one of those little pieces of London that had somehow been forgotten in the rush to the future.

The speedboats passed under the bridge almost side by side and continued across the docking area with no attempt to slow down. The fast-response vessel with its crew of marine police officers followed. Bond saw it pass the bridge then heard the brittle cacophony of metal hitting concrete. The police boat slewed to a halt, spinning wildly out of control. One of the officers was thrown out and landed in the water. Bond didn't need to worry if he could swim. The water was only a few inches deep and the man was already sitting up, dripping wet, looking a little foolish. The boat had capsized, its propellor shattered. But the speedboats had no propellors. They were gliding over the surface, the glass fibre hulls barely touching the water. They continued up the ramp and into the centre of the car park. Here, finally, they came to rest.

'Out!' Boxer gave the order but his men were

already ahead of him, racing for the cars which, beneath the dust, were both newer and in better condition than they had seemed. The Irishmen stripped off their work clothes to reveal smart woollen trousers and jerseys beneath. One of them was in a suit. The balaclavas were thrown away. A few seconds later, three cars pulled out of the yard carrying what could have been young friends on their way to the office or the golf club.

At the same time, Bond was pushed towards a fourth car by Boxer, who had removed his mask to reveal an unsmiling man with a lined, tired face. He opened the boot.

'I prefer the back seat,' Bond said.

'I don't care what you prefer. This is how you're travelling. If you don't like it, you can stay behind.'

It went against every one of his instincts to put himself in a position where he would be powerless but Bond knew he had no choice. He climbed in. The boot slammed shut.

For Bond, the next three hours were spent in darkness with only his own imagination for company. Who were these people? Mercenaries or sub-agents hired by the Russians, people with an insider's knowledge of London. From their accents, he guessed an affiliation with the Irish Republican Army or one of its offshoots, the Curragh faction, for example, named after the men who had met in the military detention unit in Curragh, County Kildare. In the brief moment that Bond had seen Boxer without his balaclava, he had certainly looked like an older man with the unhealthy pallor of an ex-prisoner. Where were they taking him? The borders would be closed by now. M had warned him that he would be on his own once this operation began. The whole country would think of him as a traitor and a fugitive. It would make an interesting end to his career if he was shot on sight by one of his own people!

He shifted position and winced as the bullet wound he had received from Scaramanga reminded him once again that it was there. That was something he would have to think about. If he did make it to Russia, they might give him a full medical examination. He would have to think up a good explanation for this fresh injury.

Bond stretched out as much as he could and rested, wrapped in the darkness and the vibrations of the engine which were all around him. He lost track of the time until suddenly he was aware that they had stopped, the boot was thrown open and daylight poured in.

'Move!'

Bond swung himself out of the car and his feet landed on grass. He looked around him and saw that he was in an area surrounded by woodland. In front of him there was a small, wooden building that looked like a clubhouse, a runway and a light aircraft, one of the old three-seater Auster 5 Autocrats, waiting to take off. There were two men in overalls, one of them feeding the plane from an oil drum. A windsock hung limply behind.

'It looks like this is where I say goodbye,' Bond remarked. 'Thank you for your help. I have to say, your organisation was meticulous.'

'Wait one moment.' Boxer was holding a pistol, pointing it directly at him. 'You still have to answer for Sean and Brendan.'

'And what exactly is the question?' Bond replied. He wasn't going to let this man bully him. 'They broke into the police van but they were slow. The people guarding me were armed. They were shot.'

'Since when did the Special Branch carry guns?'

'Maybe that was the mistake you made. They weren't Special Branch. They were military intelligence.' That gave Boxer pause for thought and Bond pressed on. 'There wasn't very much I could do. I was still wearing these.' He showed them his wrists, still chained to each other by the handcuffs. 'I don't suppose you could do me a favour and take them off me? It would make for a more comfortable flight.'

Boxer wasn't giving up. 'Two of our best men are dead. How come you walk out unharmed?'

'The people who were guarding me decided to let me go.' Bond allowed the sarcasm to sink in, then shook his head. 'What do you think? The agent who shot your friends was barely out of kindergarten. I managed to grab his gun and disarmed him. I killed him and his colleague at point-blank range. You must have heard the other gunshots. Then I got out.' Boxer was still looking doubtful so Bond decided to seize the moral ground. 'Your friends died for the cause, Comrade,' he said. 'You should be proud of them.'

Boxer spat. 'I'm not your comrade.'

'Really?' Bond looked surprised. 'Would you like me to report that to my superiors? That you don't believe you're on our side?' The Irishman faltered and Bond went on quickly, pressing his advantage. 'Your men were carrying ArmaLite semi-automatic rifles.'

'What of it?'

'They're no longer manufactured but they were the weapon of choice for the Harrison network in the fifties, supplying the rebels in Cuba. We controlled the pipeline. Is that where they came from? Or from Libya? You used Soviet-made missile launchers on the bridge and that gun you're pointing at me now is a Makarov which has been used by our glorious army for the last ten years. If we're talking about loyalties, Comrade, you've got yours written all over you. We're fighting for the same cause.'

Boxer looked at Bond long and hard, the Makarov still drawing a line between them. Then he lowered it. 'You need to be on your way,' he grunted.

As if on cue, the propellors of the Autocrat spluttered and began to turn.

'Together, we have struck a blow for world peace and the destruction of the capitalist machine,' Bond commented. He wondered if he was laying it on too thick. But no. Ideology could never be too thick for these self-styled freedom fighters.

'Get on the plane,' Boxer said.

Bond crossed the grass and the mechanics watched him as he climbed into the cabin and fastened his belt. They closed the door and stood back. Meanwhile, the pilot was checking his instrumentation. He did not look round.

The man who had brought Bond here watched as the plane bumped along the runway and turned before take-off. He heard the four-cylinder engine rise in tone until it became an angry growl. The plane rolled forward, picking up speed, then left the ground.

The two men in overalls had joined him. 'What do you think, Charlie?' one of them asked.

The Irishman took out a cigarette and lit it. 'I think we should call Moscow,' he said. 'I don't trust him.'

The plane was already a speck in the air. It veered left over the treetops and began the journey east.

PART TWO

Moscow Nights

9
Truth and Lies

The office was, quite simply, enormous. If Colonel Boris was modelling himself on the spider at the centre of the web, he had at least got the proportions right although instead of filaments around him, there was only empty space.

From the double doors that were the main entrance, he could count exactly twenty-three steps to the metal desk with its swivelling metal chair and his soft leather boots had rapped out each one of them as he made his way across the polished concrete floor and sat down. The office was at ground level but the windows behind the desk, taking up almost the entire wall, continued up for four more floors, a great square of grey-tinted glass criss-crossed by metal frames. Two more chairs, a filing cabinet and a pair of surgical lamps, leaning forward as if they were trying to eavesdrop, defined the actual work area. Dressed as always in his clinician's jacket, he could have been a doctor in the world's emptiest hospital.

The room had once been used as a refectory, feeding 12,000 workers a day, 2,000 of them at a time. When it had opened, in 1922, the building had been known as the Ulyanka Factory Kitchen. It had been constructed to provide hot, nutritious meals to workers from the surrounding industrial enterprises in Ulyanka, an administrative district of Leningrad. It had closed down in the mid-fifties due to lack of demand – according to the authorities. The actual reason (as everyone knew) was that the factory kitchen had become unable to provide the number of meals required due to food shortages. The portions had become smaller and, at the same time, increasingly inedible until suddenly there were no takers any more. The building had remained empty for five years. Then it had been requisitioned by the USSR Academy of Medical Sciences, who had assigned it to a highly secret department exploring psychopolitics. It was now known as the Institute although people who lived nearby never mentioned it by name, trying to pretend that it did not exist at all.

From the outside, the Institute was a solid block of off-white concrete and glass, designed in the constructivist style and erected in private parkland just off Prospekt Marshala Zhukova, to the south-west of the city. It was surrounded by lawns which were in bad need of watering and by fountains which hadn't been switched on for so long that the ornamental basins were cracked and dry with sprouting weeds. It looked a little like a railway terminus as designed by an over-ambitious architect . . . one obviously with ideas above his station. In fact, very few people saw it from the outside. Most of the patients arrived in closed vans. Quite a few of them never left at all.

There were twenty rooms for patients, another thirty for security guards and staff. Other areas had been converted into lecture theatres, various sorts of treatment rooms, a gymnasium and a private *banya* – or steam room. Colonel Boris had a suite of rooms in a separate wing.

He had taken his place with his elbows resting on the desk, his long fingers forming a steeple in front of him. Apart from a small medical screen, there was no other furniture or decoration in his office. Even if Colonel Boris had put pictures on the walls, they would have been too far away for him to see them. For a long time, he remained silent. All his concentration was focused on the man in the chair in front of him, the oddly paired eyes examining him intently. It was the first time he had seen James Bond since he had sent him on his way to London more than four months ago.

James Bond was watching Colonel Boris with something close to disinterest. His eyes were glazed and his whole body was relaxed to the point of inertia. The sleeve on his left arm had been rolled up and there was a tiny trickle of blood where he had been injected by a male nurse shortly before being brought here. He was wearing the same uniform as all the patients at the Institute: a pale grey cotton tunic cut low at the neck, loose-fitting cotton trousers and slippers. If you wish to remove a man's identity, you begin by removing his clothes. Bond's hands were still tied together but this was more to remind him that he was a prisoner than to physically restrain him. He would barely have been able to move anyway. Two armed guards stood behind him but they weren't needed either.

'It's very good to see you, James,' Colonel Boris muttered, at last. His voice was soft and even. It sounded as if he was speaking the truth.

'It's very good to see you too, Comrade Colonel.'

The Botticelli lips stretched themselves into something faintly resembling a smile. 'And yet it's been such a long time. I was beginning to think that you were never coming back to us.'

'I came as soon as I could, Comrade Colonel.'

'But where have you been? What have you been doing? You were instructed to kill M immediately. Why did you wait?'

Sitting in the chair, Bond's face remained expressionless even as he fought for control. Almost a whole week had passed since he had left England. After a refuelling stop near Groningen in the Netherlands, he had travelled all the way to Karl-Marx-Stadt, close to the border with Czechoslovakia. Then he had been transferred to a flight run by Czech Airlines, the plane itself being a Russian-made Illyushin 11-14, an old warhorse with twin propellors and a bad reputation. It had been built to carry thirty-two passengers but seldom managed to attract more than a dozen and Bond recalled that it was notoriously unreliable with engines that might cut out at any time. Well, that would be an unfortunate end to the adventure, a cut-out 20,000 feet above Warsaw. However, the plane had made it all the way across Lithuania and Latvia, finally coming in to land at Pulkovo Airport in Leningrad. By now, two burly escorts in matching light raincoats had joined him . . . straight out of KGB central casting, Bond thought. Neither of them spoke to him throughout the journey. An unsmiling air hostess in a calf-length, turquoise uniform had given him a glass of water and a sandwich but otherwise he'd had nothing to eat.

A van had brought him to the Institute. There was a part of Bond that had dreaded returning but he had also expected it and he was prepared. He had been taken to a room which might have been the same one that he had occupied when he first came here although he knew that all the rooms were designed to be identical; it helped with the general sense of disorientation. He had been left alone for three days. That, too, was expected. And then, finally, the orderlies had come in with the trolley and the hypodermic syringe and Bond had known that the real ordeal was about to begin.

He had not struggled. He had held out his arm and smiled as if he welcomed the medication. Everything he said and did would be noted and reported back to Colonel Boris. He had to demonstrate, beyond any doubt, that he was here willingly and had no concerns about his own future. He had waited while his sleeve was rolled up and had watched with polite disinterest as the needle had entered the skin. He saw the plunger pressed and almost felt the contents gleefully mingling with his blood, rushing through his system, propelled by the beating of his own heart. What had they given him? A cocktail of psychoactive drugs which would almost certainly include scopolamine or sodium thiopental: the so-called truth serums. Lying back on the bed, left once again on his own, he recognised the moment when the barbiturates found their way into his brain, smashing his defences and leading him down the path to self-destruction. From that moment, Bond was at war with himself. He knew that he would have to weigh every word before he allowed it to leave his mouth. One mistake could kill him.

There is no such thing as a truth drug.

As he waited for the orderlies to come back for him, Bond allowed the thought to whisper itself to him over and over again. If a truth drug existed, the Secret Intelligence Service and the CIA would have used it but despite all the experiments with mescaline, scopolamine, sodium amytal and all the rest of them, no one had ever achieved a satisfactory result. He remembered what Major Cunningham had said to him. '*Whatever happens, this time you'll be prepared.*' He was right. When Bond had first come to the Institute, he'd had no defences. He hadn't even known who he was. This time it was different. Drugs could make him more loquacious. He might talk all night. But if he reached far enough into his consciousness, he could still choose what he wanted to say.

M is not dead. This is a trick. That was what they wanted to hear. That was the truth. But Bond had put the truth in a box and slammed the lid.

'Why did you wait?'

That was what Colonel Boris had asked him. He had rehearsed the story many times. Now he just had to believe it.

'They wouldn't let me anywhere near him,' Bond explained. 'I was taken out of the Double-O section and given desk duties. They didn't trust me and I obviously couldn't argue. Then, finally, M agreed to see me and I was able to carry in the weapon that you'd given me.' Bond allowed himself an edge of protest, as if he wasn't being given the credit he deserved. 'And it worked! I killed him. He was an imperialist warmonger and a liar, just like you told me. He died in front of me and I was glad.'

Colonel Boris did not look convinced. 'After you killed him, what happened?'

'I don't remember, Comrade Colonel. I think I passed out. There were cyanide fumes in the room and the next thing I knew, I was in hospital. Then they took me to a house in Richmond. They kept me there for a week and they interrogated me.'

'Did they torture you?'

'No. They treated me well.'

'You telephoned our agent from the house. How did you manage that?'

This part was easier. Bond could describe what had really happened and did so at length, speaking like a schoolboy in class, eager to please his teacher. He told Colonel Boris how he had knocked out Sam King and gone upstairs. 'The agents were young and inexperienced,' he concluded. 'I thought of killing the one who was guarding me but there was nothing to be gained by it and as far as I could see there was no way out of the house. I knew that you would come for me, Comrade Colonel. You'd promised. All I had to do was wait.'

'We lost two men on Tower Bridge.'

'That was unfortunate.' In a strange way, Bond found that the drugs he had been given were helping him. Once he had decided on what was true, he was able to relax into it. He repeated the version of events that he had told the Irishman at the airfield, adding only how grateful he was that two freedom fighters had been willing to sacrifice their lives for the cause.

Was he being too glib? Colonel Boris still looked doubtful. 'It seems strange that the British agents you describe as young and inexperienced should have got the better of Ross and O'Leary.'

Ross and O'Leary. Sean and Brendan. Bond made a mental note of the names. They might be useful if there was any future investigation into the Republican Army and its involvement with the communists. He realised Colonel Boris was waiting for him to answer.

'It all happened very quickly,' he said. 'There was smoke and it was difficult to see. The man who was guarding me fired two shots before I could get hold of his gun.'

'Why didn't he kill you first?'

'I wasn't a threat to him, Comrade Colonel.' Bond searched for the right words. 'The simple fact was that the two men – King and Harrison – had received their training from a corrupt and arrogant intelligence organisation. They could have killed me and should have killed me. It should have been their first instinct. But instead they thought only of their self-preservation and turned their guns on comrades Ross and O'Leary. They did at least forfeit their own lives as a result.'

'You shot them.'

'Yes.'

Colonel Boris considered what he had just been told. 'It seems you've done very well, James. And you must forgive me for being so remiss. Sitting there with your hands tied and two armed guards! What must you think of me? You should have been given a hero's welcome but . . .' He spread his hands. 'We have to be so careful. I'm sure you understand.'

He opened one of the drawers in his desk and took out a packet of Marlboros. 'Let me offer you a cigarette. I'm afraid we don't have your brand but this is

American tobacco which I'm sure will be acceptable to you. Some habits die hard!' He had added these last words with a twinkle, as if he were telling a joke. Bond leaned forward and took the proffered cigarette, cupping it in both hands.

Colonel Boris lit it for him with a gasoline lighter, an angry tongue of flame leaping up. 'You must be wondering why we went to such trouble and expense to bring you here,' he said.

'I'm very grateful to be here, Comrade Colonel.'

'There's no need to be.' Colonel Boris waved away the gratitude. 'The fact of the matter is that we may have further use for you. Another assignment.'

'I'll do anything,' Bond said. He blew out smoke. 'It would be an honour to serve the party – and the country – that I once thought of as my enemy but which, thanks to you, I now see as my true and only home.'

'Thank you, James. That's very good to hear.'

Colonel Boris reached into the drawer a second time and removed an inhaler, similar to the one he had used in Moscow but with a differently coloured cylinder. He placed the nozzle close to his mouth and pressed the button. As he breathed in the vapour, Bond caught the scent of eucalyptus.

'I have made a lifetime study of the human brain,

James,' Colonel Boris observed. 'I would imagine that you and I see the world in very different ways. You are a spy, a womaniser, a killer. You have no interest in books or great art or natural science. When we first met, I saw at once that you were a blunt instrument who could be used just as your masters in London had used you for much of your adult life. What you saw as loyalty, I saw only as crushing stupidity. I have to say that I found everything about you utterly disgusting.'

'I'm sorry, Comrade Colonel . . . ?' It was a question, not an apology.

Colonel Boris held up a hand, stopping him. His face showed no malice whatsoever. 'Please. Let me finish.' He waited for Bond to settle down. 'You and I have nothing in common, James. Look at me! I think most people would agree that I'm the foremost scientist in my field. I have written books that are studied by my peers all over the world. At the same time I love poetry – Pushkin and Baratynsky – and classical music, the orchestral works of Rimsky-Korsakov, Borodin and Tchaikovsky. I collect fine art. Whereas the only taste or discernment you have shown in your entire life is the way you take your martinis.

'I think it would be hard to imagine two people more different than you and me. But here's the thing.' Colonel Boris raised a single finger. 'If someone were to take out our brains and lay them side by side on a tray, they would be identical. Three pounds of water and soft tissue making up only two per cent of our total body weight and yet fundamental not just to who we are but to how we feel, how we see the world, the actions we choose, every decision that we make every second of our lives. The brain is the most wonderful machine on the planet and we need to look after it, to fine-tune it if it is going to give us the best results.'

Colonel Boris picked up the inhaler. 'You are perhaps puzzled by this,' he said.

'Not at all, Comrade Colonel . . .' Bond had been glad that he hadn't needed to speak. At the same time, he had been wondering where this was all going.

'There's no need to be embarrassed, my dear James. I could see that you wanted to ask but you were too afraid. Well, I'll tell you. Have you heard of aromatherapy?'

'I had an aunt who was a great believer.'

'It's a science that goes back to the first century. A Greek physician by the name of Pedanius Dioscorides wrote about it in a book called *De Materia Medica*. What he was interested in was the power of the olfactory process – how our sense of smell can affect our thoughts and emotions, in fact our entire rationality, in much the same way as the cigarette you are smoking.

The nicotine in your tobacco is mimicking the characteristics of dopamine, and stimulating the pleasure centre in your orbitofrontal cortex, disguising the truth, which is that it is in fact a dangerous poison. I can assure you that any pleasure you are feeling right now is completely illusory.'

'Even the pleasure of seeing you, Comrade Colonel?'

'Well, I suppose that's real enough.' Colonel Boris returned to his theme. 'Did you know that there are five million receptor cells in the human nose? If we take essential oils and introduce them to the olfactory bulb . . .' he tapped his own forehead, '. . . here, it can enhance our performance in ways that are quite remarkable. Lavender, for example, releases hormones that make us happier. Peppermint acts on the theta waves in our brain which are connected to creativity and imagination. And eucalyptus, which I inhaled a moment ago, increases awareness and is particularly useful when you need to analyse something, which is what I'm attempting.' He leaned forward. 'Because you see, James, I believe that everything you're telling me is a pack of lies.'

The words were no sooner spoken than Bond felt something crash into the side of his head and he was thrown out of the chair and onto the floor. The guards had crept up on him and one of them had hit him with the barrel or the grip of his pistol. With his hands still tied in front of him and dressed in the flimsy tunic and trousers, there was nothing he could do except to curl up and take the kicking that was now inflicted on him. The guards were wearing leather boots and they aimed at his back, the side of his head, his shoulders, his arms. Colonel Boris sat impassively, watching, as if he'd had no part in what was taking place. Bond was furious with himself. He should have been expecting it. How could he have forgotten? The polite conversation, the pleasant discussions about the weather, the news, the result of the last Zenit Leningrad football match . . . how often had they suddenly lurched into exactly this sort of violence? A beating, a whipping, on one occasion a near-drowning in an ice-cold bath.

One of the guards stamped down on him and Bond was tempted to grab hold of the man's foot, twist it and break his ankle. It would have been the work of two seconds. But there could be no resistance. If there was any chance of persuading Colonel Boris that the brainwashing had been effective and that he hadn't been deprogrammed, he had to remain completely passive. Once again, the drugs that he had been given came to his assistance. To a certain extent, they dulled the pain.

Eventually, it was over. Bond lay still as normal

feeling returned to his body, easing itself into the areas that had somehow been left untouched. He wasn't sure how badly he had been hurt but he knew that he had endured much worse in his time. For some reason he was reminded of Wint and Kidd and the Spangled Mob, who had come close to killing him in a ghost town outside Las Vegas.* That had been a carefully measured beating, a 'Brooklyn stomping' dished out with custom-made football boots. What he had just been given was amateurish by comparison and it occurred to him that, as with their tobacco, the Americans left the Russians far behind.

Colonel Boris spoke again, first in Russian and then in English for Bond's benefit.

'I think you need some time in the magic room. Perhaps it will help you see things more clearly.'

The magic room.

Bond felt the sweat break out on his forehead as tangled, half-forgotten memories rushed into his brain. He saw the two guards reach down for him and cowered away. 'No! Please, Comrade Colonel! No!' He was still shouting as they dragged him across the improbably huge floor with the desk and the two lamps

---

* See *Diamonds Are Forever*.

and the vast windows disappearing down the tunnel that the room had become. Bond had no doubt that he was putting on a good act. He looked and sounded terrified. Except – there was a small part of him that had to ask the question. Was it really just an act?

10

Behind the Screen

The doors on the far side of the room swung shut and the cries and protests of the British agent disappeared down the corridor. Colonel Boris did not move. He waited until silence had returned before he reached for his inhaler. He picked it up, then, after a moment's consideration, replaced it. His thinking was utterly clear. He had no need for artificial stimulation. What was more important to him was a second opinion.

'You can come out now,' he said.

There had been someone sitting behind the medical screen throughout the interview and the subsequent beating. The fabric rippled slightly as a figure stood up on the other side and then stepped into view. It was a young woman, holding a notebook and a pen, wearing a severe, tight-fitting dress of a nondescript colour and fabric with a matching half-length jacket. She came over to the desk.

'Comrade Leonova. You heard everything?'

'Yes, Comrade Colonel.'

'And you were able to observe?'

There had been a gap between the fabric and the metal frame. The girl had seen Bond brought in. She had watched what had happened. 'Yes, Comrade Colonel.'

'So let me have your thoughts. The *Angliski* spy. Is he still in my control or do you think he was dissimulating?'

Katya Leonova was far too beautiful for the uniform she had chosen. She had everything that is desirable in a woman in her late twenties, starting with her eyes which were the softest shade of blue with lashes that might be coquettish, modest, even childlike. Her hair was blonde but appeared almost white in the sunlight. It was cut short with a very straight fringe at the front and tied efficiently at the back as if better to show off the elegant nape of her neck. This, along with her eye colour and pale, unblemished skin, suggested Belarusian parentage, at least on one side of her family. There was something of the young Jean Seberg about her face, an indecisiveness, a sense almost of androgyny.

The very straight nose, the cheekbones and the strong chin had a certain masculinity but the mouth was unashamedly feminine, small with full lips parted slightly to provide just a suggestion of the pink tongue and perfect teeth that any man would want to explore.

This same contradiction could be found in a body that might on first appearance have seemed boyish. Katya was barely taller than Colonel Boris, who was seated while she was standing, and it was as if everything about her – her arms and legs, her breasts and her thighs – had been scaled down. In other circumstances, and dressed differently, she could have resembled one of those Russian gymnasts who have sacrificed their sexuality in their endless quest for physical perfection. But in fact many of the young orderlies who worked at the Institute were attracted to her. Late at night, after a few vodkas, they would talk about her in whispers, taking it in turns to describe what they would do to her if they were ever lucky enough to get her into their bed, their descriptions becoming ever more filthy as the vodka was consumed.

So why was it that not one of them had even tried? Part of the answer was her position in the Institute, her role as a senior clinical psychiatrist. She was close to Colonel Boris and one word from her could mean immediate dismissal . . . or worse. But she had never invited friendship. She showed no interest in men. And there was something cold about her, an authoritarianism in her eyes and in the way she moved that made her untouchable. She never laughed when she was in the building. She seldom even smiled. She was a specialist in a psychiatric hospital and she gave the impression that there was nothing else in her life that mattered to her and never had been.

Now she considered what she had been asked. 'It is hard to be sure, Comrade Colonel,' she replied after a silence that many would have found intimidating. 'His explanation about the death of his superior was certainly convincing and his general demeanour was everything I would have expected following his treatment here.'

'What about the business on Tower Bridge?'

'He was vague. But as he said, there was smoke and it happened quickly. If he had been able to provide more detail it might well be that the story had been fabricated.'

'But you still have your doubts.'

'There were two things that he said . . .'

'Go on.'

'The first was that he was grateful to be here. Of course he is thankful that you extracted him from his country and saved him from almost certain execution.

But nobody who knows what happens at the Institute or who has experienced it themselves is ever glad to return. It may be that he was attempting to ingratiate himself with you but he was certainly lying.'

'And the other thing?'

'When you gave him the cigarette, you remarked that all pleasure is illusory and he replied . . .' She glanced at her notebook. ' "Even the pleasure of seeing you, Comrade Colonel?" ' She turned the notebook down. 'I have a suspicion that he was being sarcastic,' she said. She looked ashamed. 'If so, that would suggest that he is aware of his situation and that he is play-acting.'

Colonel Boris smiled. 'Yes. I thought the same. That was when I decided to have him taken to the magic room.'

There was another long silence. Colonel Boris was still seated, the clinical psychiatrist still standing before him. He ran his eyes over her body then suddenly spoke. 'Tell me, Katya Leonova. You had plenty of opportunity to see this man, Bond, when he was with us the first time. What did you make of him?'

'I provided you with a full report, Comrade Colonel. As soon as his memory had been restored, Mr Bond was revealed to me as an archetypal product of the outdated British class system, extroverted, highly self-opinionated and borderline psychotic—'

'I know all this.' Colonel Boris cut her off with the disapproving wave of a finger. 'Your work was exemplary. But that's not what I'm asking.' He paused. 'What do you think of him . . . as a man?'

'I don't know what you mean, Comrade Colonel.'

'Don't play games with me, my dear. It's a simple enough question. Do you find him attractive?'

Katya jerked back as if she had been slapped. It was the last thing she had expected to be asked. She grasped for the right words. 'He is handsome enough,' she admitted, 'but I do not find him attractive.'

'And why is that?'

'Because he is too sure of himself. Or at least, he was. He has had many sexual conquests but all his relationships have ended quickly and with no sign of any regret on his part. There was of course the woman he married and who died very soon after their wedding. He spoke fondly of her although I do not think the marriage would have lasted long. He would have found it inconvenient and ultimately unnatural and I am quite sure he would have either cheated on her or dropped her altogether . . . although it might have been difficult to explain his actions to his father-in-law, given that Mr Draco was the extremely dangerous leader of an international crime syndicate. But still it was inevitable. For James Bond, all the women in his life have been little more than a commodity.'

'Do you think he has treated them badly?'

She shook her head. 'No.' She paused, as if she had managed to surprise herself with the certainty of her answer. 'From what he told me in our sessions – both with and without medication – I am sure that he never forced himself on a woman who did not want him and, during the time of the relationship he treated each one of them with kindness and consideration. He is even capable of love. His problem is his inability to commit. It is quite possible that he has a paranoid personality disorder. That was covered in Section 27/12 of my report.'

She had tried to find a way back to safe ground but Colonel Boris hadn't finished yet. 'Could you have a relationship with him?'

Katya clapped a hand over her mouth and for a moment her eyes widened like a schoolgirl's. 'Do you mean a physical relationship?' she asked.

'That's for you to decide. What I mean is, could you allow yourself to get close to him?'

Once again, Katya searched for the right words. 'Why?' was all she could come up with.

Colonel Boris leaned back in his chair. 'I have become involved in a very serious enterprise about which I can tell you almost nothing,' he began. 'I will say only that my orders come directly from the Presidium and that the stakes could not be higher. If all goes according to plan, we intend to change the course of history and return to the motherland the authority and the world dominance which some would say have, in recent years, been foolishly squandered.

'You do not need to concern yourself with the politics. You need to know only that it is this man, Bond, who has been chosen as the linchpin on which the entire operation turns. He is British. He is a spy. More than that, he is extremely well known and admired in certain circles. This is what makes him useful to us.

'But I need to know that he is what he seems to be, that he will do exactly as I tell him without question. When the critical moment arrives, I must know that he is reliable, that there will be no hesitation. I would like you to spend time with him, to become his friend, his lover if that is what it takes. And while you are with him, you will scrutinise him minutely. You will look deep into the workings of his mind and report back to me on anything that raises your suspicions.'

'But why me?' Katya faltered. 'Bond will remember me from our many sessions together and he has no reason to confide in me. Comrade Dr Krylov is more qualified. Or Comrade Dr Irina Blavatsky is a superb analyst . . .'

'Dr Blavatsky has a brilliant mind but the looks of a carthorse,' Colonel Boris replied. 'She would never get close to Bond. And Dr Krylov is an old man. If Bond remembers you from his past treatment, that may help you with your enquiries. You were never unkind to him.' He waited for her to speak, then added: 'I would not be asking you, Katya Leonova, unless it was of the first importance.'

'Are you *asking* me, Comrade Colonel?'

Colonel Boris looked at her sadly. 'No.'

She saw that there was no point arguing. 'Are we to stay here?' she asked.

'No. I think it would be better if Mr Bond was removed from the Institute and even taken out of Leningrad. While he is here, he will think himself under examination, while it would be much more helpful to us if he were relaxed. That way he is more likely to make mistakes.' Colonel Boris considered. 'You can take him on the Red Arrow express to Moscow. Mr Bond has always enjoyed train journeys. I will arrange for you to have adjoining suites at the Hotel National. There will be a communicating door. You shouldn't look so dismayed, my dear. It's going to be quite an adventure.'

Katya knew she was being dismissed. But before she went, she had one last thought. 'If I discover that Bond is lying to us, what will you do?' she asked.

Colonel Boris smiled and his eyes gleamed unevenly. 'I will have him killed, of course.'

Katya nodded. 'Of course.' She turned and left.

11

The Magic Room

Bond had been taken down a flight of metal stairs that led to the basement, far beneath the Institute. He knew where he was and where he was going. It was impossible to say what would happen when he got there.

A series of doors led to the magic room, each one of them set at a different angle, each one smaller than the one before. There was a cacophony of sound blasting out of hidden speakers – a mixture of military commands being barked out in Russian, the whinnying of horses, gunfire and short bursts of martial music. The volume was turned up deafeningly high and as his ears coped with the barrage, Bond was dazzled by spotlights that burst into life above his head, one after another, as he passed. The whole corridor had been constructed to give every Alice their very own rabbit hole. By the time they arrived at the end, they would already be doubting their sanity.

But it had been different when he had been brought here the first time. Then, he had been drugged and disorientated, barely aware of his own identity. This time, at least, he knew what to expect. Sure enough, the last door opened into a small, neat room which might have belonged to a cheap hotel except that it had no window and no carpet on the smooth, cement-covered floor. Ahead of him was a bed, a washbasin and, partly concealed by a small wardrobe standing at right angles to the wall, a toilet. The pictures opposite the bed showed views of Leningrad. There was a wooden table with two chairs.

Except that, with Colonel Boris, nothing was ever what it seemed.

Bond was propelled through the door and as he stumbled forward, his foot disappeared through the floor that was not solid at all but the surface of a tank filled with some sort of filthy, grey oil. So how was the furniture floating? Bond had no time to work it out as his entire body followed and he suddenly found himself floundering, up to his neck in the stuff, blind and choking. He couldn't remember when the guards had untied his hands but somehow they were free and he was able to swim to the bed which must have been bracketed to the wall because it took his weight and allowed him to pull himself out.

As he lay there panting, the lights went out. The darkness was absolute. Bond hadn't heard the door close but he knew that he was alone, the only sound in the room his own tortured breathing. He could feel his clothes sticking to his body and the oil dripping out of his hair. He realised now that solid or otherwise the bed had been deliberately constructed at an angle to ensure that he could never actually relax or fall asleep. He had to cling to the edge to prevent himself rolling over and sliding back into the ooze.

The room was refrigerated. Bond could feel his body temperature plunging as the cold air, exaggerated by the soaking he'd received, bit into him. There was to be no comfort. The bed had no mattress or pillow and the single blanket was too thin to offer any warmth. Bond curled into a foetal position, using the edges of his feet to keep himself in place. He already knew that there would be no sleep tonight or any night and that every minute would crawl past in a procession of endless misery. The worst of the punishment was that it had no foreseeable end. Colonel Boris would not let him die. But he could arrange things so that he would no longer want to live.

And yet, somehow, minutes or hours later, unconsciousness came to him and drew him into its embrace. Perhaps it was the drugs he had been given. Perhaps it was simply that his body could take no more. There was no transition. All Bond knew was that he opened his eyes to find that he was dry, lying on a mattress on a decent bed with proper bedclothes and now there was a window showing daylight and a drive with a van parked outside. How was that even possible when the room was in the basement, below ground? Bond sat up. He was wearing pyjamas although he had been in his hospital patient's uniform when they had brought him here. There was a plate on the table. Some black bread, cheese and Russian tea. Bond rolled over and cautiously placed one foot on the concrete floor. This time it supported his weight. He went over to the table, sat down and ate.

Bond knew that the respite he had been given would not last long. That was how the magic room worked. It could be your friend or your torturer. It whispered gently to you one minute, screamed in your ear the next. Always it played with you so that whatever happened would come as a shock, disorienting you, making you question your own sanity. If he was being given breakfast now, he would be starved tomorrow. The food he was eating might be poisoned. A minute from now, he could be on the floor in convulsions. It had happened before.

But this time he would be grateful for whatever time he had, using it as a respite before the next nightmare began. Bond poured the tea and watched the steam creep over the edge of his glass. He smelled cinnamon and lemon. He collected his thoughts.

Nothing he had said in the interview with Colonel Boris could have given him away. He had been careful not to describe too much of what had happened in M's office, at the Richmond house or on Tower Bridge. The fewer details he offered, the less chance he had of being tripped up. The very fact that he was being tested could be considered a good sign. Colonel Boris wanted to trust him. Could he be watching even now? Bond was staring at a fixed point on the wall, showing no interest in the view out of the window, which might not be a view at all but some sort of projection. He was tempted to search for hidden cameras but if they were actually there, Colonel Boris would be watching him and would know that he was in command of his senses. Instead, he sipped the tea, which was hot and far too sweet although he could still taste the bitterness of the oolong leaves beneath the sugar.

He was in pain and he wondered how badly he had been hurt. He casually ran a hand over his ribs. They didn't seem to be broken although he guessed he would be covered in bruises from the kicking he had been given. He couldn't see his face. There was no mirror in the room and the tea had come out of a white china teapot rather than a samovar. Nothing in the magic room had been left to chance. A samovar would have had a silver surface which would have offered him the comfort of a reflection. Bond examined what he could see of himself and noticed a damp area on the side of his pyjama jacket. He touched it with one finger and winced. The bullet wound he had received from Scaramanga had opened again and it was leaking. That was bad news. It wasn't just the fact that the wound hadn't healed. It had also made itself known. Colonel Boris's people would have seen it. He might have to explain how it had come to be there.

'Looks like you're gonna be joining me soon – right, mister?'

There was someone else in the room. Bond looked up and, somehow, he wasn't surprised to see that Scaramanga had joined him at the table. The light brown eyes were regarding him with a quiet malevolence. The oversized hands were folded on the table in front of him. He was dressed in the same tan suit and silk stock with its gold pin shaped like a pistol that he'd worn when Bond first met him.

Bond said easily, 'I rather doubt that.'

'Doesn't look too pretty to me.' Scaramanga took out a thin cheroot and lit it with a match which he flicked alight between his thumb and the nail of his third finger. The little flame danced under his chin. 'Your people send you all the way out here. You're almost two thousand miles from home and you think you can pull a fast one on a feller who can look inside your head like it's a trash can. You ask me, I'd say they don't give a damn about you.'

'I'm going to be just fine,' Bond said.

'You think so? They've been lying to you, Mr James Bond, 007, of the secret service. You think they care about you? Buddy, they've been swindling and manipulating you since day one. You're just part of a world system of colonial oppression and when you finally get that bullet in the back of the head, they won't even blink . . .'

Bond looked away. Scaramanga wasn't there, of course, and if he had been he wouldn't have talked like that. The stuff about colonial oppression, the swindling and manipulation, was pure Lenin even if it had been delivered in the familiar gangster drawl. The only person manipulating Bond was Colonel Boris. How did it even work? Bond drank some more of the tea. When he looked again, he was alone in the room.

At the same time, he tasted the bitterness of the chemicals that had been concealed by the sugar and knew that his drink had been drugged and that he had once again allowed himself to play into Colonel Boris's hands. Disgusted with himself, Bond felt the china cup slip out of his fingers and fall the improbable distance to the floor, where it broke, slowly, into fragments. The room spun. Bond dived forward, back into the abyss.

In the next few days – or hours, or minutes – he was interviewed by two identical Russian psychiatrists, mirror images of each other in white coats and glasses. Then by Colonel Boris, who was accompanied by the silent figure of Rosa Klebb, formerly of Otdyel II, the Operations and Executions wing of Smersh. He was beaten again, this time by a ferocious guard with a cudgel who didn't ask him questions but who let out a bark of laughter each time he landed another blow. He was chained to the wall and forced to stand for hours with no way to measure the passing of time. He was caged in a tiny metal box with no room to move. He was starved. He was force-fed. He tried to hang himself . . . or he was told he had tried to hang himself. He had no memory of it but when he was left on his own, he felt the deep welt across his neck. All these things happened to him quite randomly, with no sense of sequence. Bond was floating in a dark sea of pain. He could not tell when one torture ended and the next began.

Somewhere in what was left of his mind, he knew that they were trying to break him, that he would tell them anything to make this stop. M is alive. It's all a trick. He could shout out the words and they would release him. They might kill him but at least death would bring an end to all this. For the first time he allowed a worm of doubt to wriggle into his consciousness. How could he have agreed to this, to deliver himself back into the hands of people who had come close to destroying him a year ago? Curled up, suffering, Bond asked himself what he was doing with his life. Every time M sent him out on a mission he came back with life-changing injuries. There had been Mr Big, deliberately breaking the little finger of his left hand. Dr No burning him and electrocuting him in his pointless assault course. The vicious beating he had received from Le Chiffre. The merciless exhaust of Hugo Drax's Moonraker that had peeled off his skin. Was this to be his future, staggering from one assault to the next?

He'd had enough. If he could survive this and get back to London, he would stop. Given his profession, he must be close to retirement age anyway. Bond squeezed his eyes shut and imagined an alternative life for himself. Golf at the Royal St George's. Lunch at the Savoy Grill. Dinner and cards at White's. Maybe he would look up Honey Rider or Tiffany Case. And there was still the work he wanted to do on the Mark II Continental Bentley he had bought from a man who'd managed to steer it into a telegraph post: the new Arnott supercharger with its magnetic clutch was playing up again. Rolls-Royce had warned him against installing it and it irked him that, as always, they had been proved right. Perhaps it was time to take a spin across the Côte d'Azur to Saint-Tropez. Yes. There had to be a better life than this.

It was very warm in the room. Bond was back in bed and this time he was naked. He could feel the sheet defining the shape of his body.

It was a different bed and different walls. Someone had added blinds to the window. There was a shaft of moonlight slanting through, creating a square of black and white bars that fell on Bond, imprisoning him. He noticed a basket of fruit on the table – a different table – and somehow it reminded him of something. Outside, the almost eerie silence of the night was punctured by the sound of a dog barking, joined seconds later by several others. Listening to the sudden cacophony, Bond knew exactly where he was and what to expect next.

Sure enough, something stirred on his right ankle. Even as he acknowledged its presence and felt the familiar terror wash over him, it began to move, creeping up the inside of his shin, making its way inexorably towards his groin. It was an insect. A poisonous tropical centipede, three inches long. Bond didn't need to lift the covers to examine it even if he had actually been able to move his hands. He was experiencing – or re-experiencing – what had happened to him eight years ago in Kingston, Jamaica, on his way to Crab Key. Dr No had tried to kill him, first with a basket of poisoned fruit, then with the centipede.

Bond forced himself to breathe normally, to fight against the waves of fear. The insect isn't there, he told himself. It's a trick. The gentle tickling you can feel on the inside of your thigh, those two rows of soft, insistent feet? They don't exist. They're only in your mind. And what if it bit him? Would it kill him? Would his imagination do the creature's work for it, sending a signal to his heart to go into palpitations so that even if there was no actual poison it would still lead to ventricular fibrillation and death? Now that was an interesting thought. A man killed by his own bad dream.

He was sweating. He could feel the liquid trickling across his chest and thighs. He tried to move but either the drugs or his fear had pinned him down. It isn't there. IT ISN'T THERE! He could only scream – soundlessly – what he knew to be true while the centipede reached the smooth plateau of his stomach and continued its journey up into the brushland of his chest.

The centipede reached his throat.

And then the lights went on and Bond saw that the room was the same as it had been when he first arrived. The shutters and the fruit had gone. So too had any sense of the centipede, although the sheet was drenched with his sweat. How long had he been here? He raised a hand, surprised that he was actually able to move, and touched his cheek. He felt stubble that was close to becoming a beard. He knew instinctively that it was the growth of at least five days. How was that possible? His memories could only be a small part of what had actually happened. The centipede, Scaramanga, the liquid floor . . . if he had been here for five days, there must have been more. He realised that he wasn't feeling hungry or thirsty. So at some time he

had been given water and food. Why couldn't he remember that? What had they done to him?

'Are you feeling better now?'

'Yes . . .'

'Do you want to tell me the truth?'

'Yes. I'll tell you everything . . .'

A woman was standing beside the bed. Bond
thought he knew her. Wearing a clinician's white coat
over a dark suit. Fair hair tied back. Blue eyes. A small
body but an attractive one. He searched for her name
but couldn't find it and his sense of failure brought
with it a flood of emotions: shame, humiliation, help-
lessness, a need to humble himself, to do anything this
woman asked to make her forgive him. He opened his
mouth knowing that they had won, that he had no
choice but to make a full confession, that he had to tell
them the truth whatever the consequences.

But before any sound could reach his throat, he remembered Major Cunningham at The Park and heard
his voice once again.

'*They will have deliberately set out to cause you the
greatest anxiety . . . causing your own psyche to turn
against you. It will have created a form of menticidal
hypnosis which will have done much of their work for
them.*'

That strange little man with his tortoiseshell glasses

and the look of a college professor. C.C. He had prepared Bond for this. He had warned him what to expect.

Suddenly Bond understood the purpose of the magic room and he knew that this bloody woman, looking at him as if she was Florence Nightingale bringing him a bedpan and hot-water bottle when she'd just finished amputating his legs, was part of it. They had deliberately done this to him with drugs and with torture and with God knows what else, stripping away his defences, preparing him for this very moment. It was exactly how they had persuaded him to attack M.

The anger that surged through Bond had a healing effect. Like a half-drowned sailor, he grappled for a lifeline in the black ocean of his memory and found it. Of course he knew her. He had spent long hours with her the first time he had come here. What was her name? Bond remembered.

Katya Leonova.

Comrade Katya.

'What is it that you want to tell me?' she asked, sweetly.

He looked at her innocently. 'I killed M,' he said. He spoke quietly, almost in a whisper. 'It took me a long time to reach him but when they finally let me into his office, I used the gun you gave me and I killed him. They arrested me and they tried to interrogate me but I didn't tell them anything. I escaped and I was brought here. I'm glad to be here. I wish to join you in the struggle against capitalism and imperialism. I will do anything you ask.'

She looked at him for a long moment. 'Do you think you can get dressed?' she asked.

'Am I allowed to?'

'If you're strong enough.'

'Am I leaving this room?' Bond looked troubled. 'How long have I been here?'

'You've been here for a week, Comrade James. You weren't well. But you're a lot better now.'

'Yes. I think I am.'

'Then get up and prepare yourself. There's a razor in the bathroom and your clothes are in the wardrobe. I'll come back for you in half an hour.'

'Thank you.' Bond frowned. 'Where are you taking . . . ?' he began, then stopped himself. He looked ashamed.

'That's right, Comrade James.' The woman was pleased. 'You mustn't ask too many questions.'

'No. I'll just do what you tell me.'

'That's good.'

Bond smiled as she left the room. The bitch.

12
The Red Arrow

B ond did not believe in the romance of train travel.
The last time he had travelled on the Orient Express it had been in the company of a psychotic Smersh killer who had come within half an inch of shooting a bullet into his heart – and that experience had hardly come as a recommendation. Trains got you from one place to another and they did it slowly and never quite at the time you wanted to go. They were cramped and the food in the dining cars was usually inedible. As far as Bond was concerned, there was no view of a city more disappointing than the one seen from a train window, even assuming he could actually see through the glass.

And yet the great trains of the world had, without doubt, a certain theatricality. Even the names were instantly evocative: the Orient Express, the Mercury, the Streamliner, Le Train Bleu, each one a self-contained drama. And certainly, Moscow Station (the name of the station in Leningrad) presented itself as pure theatre from the moment Bond stepped out of the armour-plated ZiL-115 that had brought him there. He had seen very little of the city during the half-hour journey. It was eleven o'clock at night and the limousine's windows were fitted with darkened glass, which might have prevented anyone on the pavement from gaping at the VIP passengers but which also blocked most of the outside world. He had got the impression of wide streets with very little traffic, apart from trams that reminded him of the metal toys he had played with when he was a child. The buildings on either side looked European – French or Italian, nineteenth century – and the sodium flare of the street lamps gave them an unreal quality, as if they were no more than ghosts or memories of what had once been. There were statues at every crossing: soldiers, workers, horsemen and angels, each one vying to be more heroic than the last with swords, laurel wreaths or sickles held high above their heads. And here was the greatest hero of them all. Vladimir Ilyich Ulyanov, better known to the world as Lenin. Bond saw him half a dozen times standing in different parts of the city. A crowd of Lenins. It was strange to think that a large part of what he had been fighting against all his life had begun with this single man.

When the car stopped and Bond was allowed out into the cool night air, he found himself facing a palatial building which might have looked out onto a Venetian canal rather than a wide and very empty Russian square. A series of arches and colonnades ran across the front with a clock tower high above showing ten past eleven. Bond had travelled alone. Katya had told him she would meet him at the platform and now he was escorted by his driver through the vaulted entranceway and into the main hall where another bust of Lenin looked on in granite approbation. The platforms stretched out ahead and there, in front of him, stood the Red Arrow.

The mustard-coloured letters on the sides of the carriages spelled out its name in Russian: KRASNAYA STRELA. The carriages themselves had been painted an imperial red and then cleaned and polished to such an extent that the entire train might have just rolled out of the factory. Above, the roof was punctuated with open vents. The windows were square with curtains hanging on the inside, each one offering a glimpse of the same corridor as it ran the full length of the train, bathed in softly honeyed light. Crowds of people were carrying heavy suitcases and bundles of clothing towards their compartments, helped by unsmiling conductors in badly fitting military jackets. It was the first time Bond had seen ordinary Russians. They looked drab, their faces blank, their clothes various shades of black, brown and grey. But Bond did not judge them too badly. He had seen much the same at Waterloo Station during the rush hour.

The driver had not spoken to him yet but now he pointed and uttered what sounded like the only word of English that he knew. 'There!'

Bond followed his finger and saw Katya Leonova waiting for him beside a carriage near the front of the train. As he walked towards her, he forced a half-smile to his face. He had to seem pleased to see her. But not too pleased. Everything he did would have to be carefully measured. He couldn't even look at her the way he looked at other women. He had to let her think that she controlled his every thought and emotion. She pushed the buttons. He obeyed.

'Good evening, Comrade James,' she said when he reached her.

'Good evening, Comrade Katya.'

'So – we are travelling to Moscow, the greatest city in the great country which is to be your home. Are you ready for the journey?'

Bond spread his hands. 'I have nothing for the journey. No clothes to change into. No razor.'

'We have packed a suitcase for you and it's waiting in the compartment. We are travelling in luxury cabins. "*Lyuks*" in our language. You are in number three. I will be next door.' She switched to Russian and spoke briefly to the driver, who turned and left. It occurred to Bond that they were putting a lot of faith in him. After his treatment at the Institute, he might have decided to make a break for it and with the driver gone and Katya on her own, there was nothing to prevent him . . .

. . . except that he was on his own in a hostile country, unable to speak very much of the language and with nowhere to go. Suddenly Bond was struck by the enormity of what M had asked of him. He was completely in the hands of Colonel Boris and his poisonous assistant. Only they could lead him to Stalnaya Ruka and if anything went wrong, he would find himself at large in the world's largest prison – and serving what might well be a life sentence.

'The train leaves in a few minutes. Shall we go on board?'

'Can I carry your case for you, Comrade Katya?'

'No. I can manage.'

She had one case which she picked up and took with

her. Bond followed her the short distance to the door. As she climbed in, the dress she was wearing stretched tight and despite what he had been thinking a few moments before, Bond found himself assessing the shape of her bottom. It was a very pretty one. In fact, if Comrade Katya didn't take herself so seriously, and if she hadn't devoted her life to psychological torture, he might have found her attractive. What would she be like in bed? Strip off her clothes and would he be able to discover the woman underneath? That would be a challenge, to persuade her that she could surrender herself to him and that, just for once, it would be the patient who was in command. But then she had disappeared into the belly of the train and, putting the thoughts out of his mind, Bond climbed up himself.

There were just four cabins in the luxury class, which, Bond imagined, must be reserved for Communist Party apparatchiks or very important passengers. She had reserved two of them. Bond slipped into what might have been a whore's boudoir only in miniature. The furnishings were plush red with ornate, tasselled curtains and red cushions sitting on the bed which occupied most of the space. There was a banquette opposite. A narrow door led into a bathroom with a shower, a toilet and an abundance of heavy gold fittings. Bond wondered what he had done to deserve this treatment.

Or what he was expected to do. Certainly, it was a step up from the Institute. He noticed the single suitcase that had been left for him at the foot of the bed but before he had time to open it there was a movement behind him and Katya appeared.

'We will be leaving soon,' she said. 'It's too late for dinner but I will still eat something. You will join me.'

Was it an invitation or a command? 'That would be very pleasant,' Bond said.

'There is a dining car. We have a reservation.'

At exactly five to twelve, the station loudspeakers burst into life playing a piece of orchestral music that was both grand and funereal. At the same time, the Red Arrow broke free of its berth and slipped out into the night. Sitting in the surprisingly spacious dining car – red tablecloths, red curtains, red velvet seats . . . by now he'd got the general idea – Bond felt the vibration of the wheels and pistons beneath him. He watched the empty platforms roll back with a few sullen porters finishing for the night. Then Katya Leonova sat down opposite him.

'I've ordered zakuski,' she said.

'What's that?' Bond asked. It had been a long time since he was attached to the British Embassy and he had forgotten many of the words and phrases he had learned.

'You're going to have to learn the language if you want to stay in this country,' Katya said. 'It's a snack. Pickles, herring, black bread. I think it's enough for this late hour. And we'll have some vodka.'

She raised a hand and a waiter stepped forward with a bottle in an ice bucket and two glasses. He placed them on the table and Katya poured two measures: one for Bond and one for herself. 'You drink vodka,' she said. Again, it was a statement. She had read his files. She had read him. There was nothing she didn't know.

'Vodka martini,' Bond said.

'In Russia nobody mixes their vodka – unless it is with beer – but that is not something you would expect civilised people to do.' She raised her glass. 'Be careful, Comrade James. This is Krepkaya vodka. *Krepkaya* is the Russian word for strong and the vodka is fifty-six per cent alcohol.'

There was a little crucible of pepper on the table. Bond pinched a few grains and added them to the liquid, watching as they sank to the bottom of the glass. Katya looked at him askance. 'I'm just checking the purity,' Bond told her. 'Sometimes you get fusel oil on the surface and it's poisonous. But if the pepper sinks, it's all right.'

Katya frowned. 'Who told you this?'

'A friend who was working in the British embassy in Moscow.'

'Well, he told you wrong. There is no oil in good Russian vodka.'

'I'm sure. My friend knew nothing.'

The two of them clinked glasses and drank the vodka in a single gulp. 'We use vodka to create an atmosphere of trust and friendship,' Katya continued. 'The term we have for it is *dusha-dushe* or soul to soul. I hope this will be the beginning of a friendship between us, Comrade James.'

'I hope so too,' Bond replied. 'And in the spirit of friendship, perhaps we could stop calling each other "Comrade" all the time. We both know we're on the same side. It would be nice to think we could be a little more relaxed with each other.'

Katya considered what he had just said as if such an idea had never occurred to her before. Eventually, she nodded. 'Yes, James. I think that would be good.'

Bond made a mental note. It was the first time he had asserted himself and he had won. In the smallest possible way, he had begun to make the running.

The waiter came back with a tray of *zakuski* and while he set it down, Bond looked around him. Most of the passengers had gone straight to bed but three other tables were occupied. Diagonally opposite them, a couple of men were sitting face to face, drinking vodka. The train hadn't yet reached the outskirts of Leningrad but they had finished half a bottle. They looked like military men: KGB or OGPU. Bond recognised the empty eyes and unhealthy skin of men who spend too much of their lives in the shadows. They both had shaved heads. They were talking to each other in low, conspiratorial voices, occasionally glancing across the aisle at Katya.

She had her back to them so she wasn't aware they were there but Bond could see that they were evaluating her, swapping dirty schoolboy jokes that were all the more pathetic because they were both grown men. Bond thought of saying something but instead he found himself re-examining Katya. With those blue eyes and that straight blonde hair, there was something of the porcelain doll about her but the vodka had brought colour to her cheeks, and the more she relaxed the more desirable she became. Bond noticed her silk scarf and the leather belt around her waist. In contrast to her rather drab shantung dress, they were expensive, obviously imported. So no matter what she pretended, there was a feminine side to her and one that might need to be satisfied. *Dusha-dushe* indeed. Perhaps there was a soul here for him to glimpse.

Bond realised he too was staring at her and quickly broke the spell. 'May I ask you something, Katya?'

'Of course.'

'We're obviously going to Moscow. But why? What's going to happen to me when we get there?'

'You don't need to worry about these things, James. Everything will be taken care of. But I will tell you this. You did a great service for us in London. You struck at the heart of our enemy's *apparat* and in time you will be rewarded. However, first there is another assignment for which you are being considered. I say "considered" because no decision has yet been made. We need to be sure that you are capable and willing to do what is asked of you.'

'I will do anything,' Bond said, fervently. 'Haven't I proved myself already? Whatever you want me to do, I'm ready.'

'We'll see. Don't ask me any more questions. We have a week together in Moscow. It's a wonderful city. Let's try to enjoy our time.'

She would say no more. They drank one more glass of vodka together and then went to their neighbouring compartments. Bond noticed the two men watching them leave. Their bottle was now almost empty.

———

Three hours later, in the dead of night, Bond woke suddenly.

Instinctively, his hand reached for the Beretta under his pillow before he remembered that it wasn't there. Far below, he could feel the vibration of the wheels as they carried the train forward at eighty miles per hour and the whole compartment was shaking. He had not drawn the curtains but there was nothing to see outside. No lights. The sky was an inky black. What had woken him? Bond was already completely alert, playing back the sounds that he had heard, subconsciously, while he was still asleep. The sound of a door closing. And something else. A brief cry, immediately stifled.

Bond sat up, throwing off the bed covers. He had been supplied with pyjamas but the coarse fabric and prison stripes had disgusted him so he had slept naked. Quickly, he pulled on his trousers and shirt, then – barefoot – slipped out into the corridor.

A second cry, louder this time. Then a thud as something hit the wall that separated his cabin from Katya's. A brief, ugly laugh.

Softly glowing lamps lit up the full length of the train with the blackness of the night rushing past outside. There was nobody in sight. Bond heard something else: a few words spoken in Russian. He recognised Katya's voice. She sounded scared, pleading.

What should he do? It occurred to him that this might be some sort of test. He might not even have left the magic room. There was a horrible thought. This whole journey – the music, the vodka – could be some sort of hallucination. After all, Scaramanga and the centipede hadn't been real.

He had no choice. Carefully, he slid open the door to Katya's cabin and looked through the crack. There was a light on in her bathroom which illuminated a scene he couldn't possibly have imagined.

The two shaven-headed men from the dining car were with her. One of them was sitting on the bed. Katya was lying on her back, helpless. The man had torn open her negligee to reveal her small, perfectly round breasts. He had his hand on one of them. His other hand was clamped over her mouth. His partner was standing by the window, eagerly watching, waiting his turn. The sound of the engine, the night streaking past and the shaking of the room all added to the nightmare.

Bond threw the door back and charged in. The man who was on top of Katya looked up but too late. Bond lashed out with the heel of his hand, driving it into the man's face. He felt the nose break and saw the curtain of blood come down. He was already twisting towards the second man but stopped dead, seeing the glint of an automatic pistol, possibly a Stechkin, pointing at his head. Bond was low down, crouching in the narrow space next to the bed. The man he had disabled was bleeding profusely, out of action. But the man with the gun was unreachable. Briefly, he wondered if this was how it was going to end. Shot to death on a Russian train in the middle of nowhere.

But then the man with the broken nose spoke, a couple of sentences in guttural Russian. He straightened up, blood still gushing between his fingers and onto the sheets. His eyes stared savagely at Bond.

'He says they're leaving,' Katya said. She grabbed at her torn nightdress and pulled it over her. 'They don't want any more trouble.'

Bond had to let them go. In fact, if they wanted to leave that was fine by him. He had no intention of sacrificing his life for this woman. He stayed where he was as the man with the gun brushed past, his face filled with hatred, dragging his friend with him. They slid the door shut behind them and he and Katya were alone. At the same time, he felt the train lurch as the brakes were applied. It shuddered and came to a halt. Suddenly electric lights were blazing behind the curtains. He heard someone shouting outside.

'Are you all right?' Bond asked.

'Yes . . .' Katya had been terrified. The tears were streaming down her face. Her hair had fallen loose and her hands were folded over her breasts as if to protect herself from any further attack. She looked completely vulnerable, traumatised by what had happened. Bond was amazed by the audacity of the attack. The two Russians had been making enough noise to wake the dead. They had even given Katya a chance – two chances – to call for help. Was this how things worked in this country? Had they really believed they could do whatever they liked because they were in 'luxury' class and whatever happened there was nobody else's business?

'We can get the conductor . . .' he said.

'No.' She was still trembling. 'There's nothing he can do now. They'll have left the train.'

'Where are we?'

'I don't know. The train doesn't usually stop. They must have pulled the emergency cord.'

Bond opened the curtain and saw a country station, a single platform with the dark shadow of a ticket office or waiting room. He turned back to Katya. 'Who were they?'

'I don't know. I was asleep. They came into my room . . .'

She was shaking even more now. Bond sat down beside her, on the very edge of the bed. 'We should call the police,' he said.

'No!' She shook her head forcefully. 'We cannot involve you. Nobody must know you are here. It's an important part of the business.'

'Colonel Boris told you that?'

'Yes. Comrade Colonel Boris.'

Bond watched her, still crying quiet tears. He heard footsteps pounding down the corridor as the conductors tried to find out what had happened. 'Would you like me to stay with you?' he asked.

She stared at him.

'There's a second bed,' Bond said. 'I can fold it down. I don't think you should be left on your own.'

She seemed to take ages to make up her mind. Then she nodded. 'Yes. I would like that.'

'Is this criminal behaviour what you would expect in Russia?'

'No!' Despite everything, she was outraged. 'I've never known it to happen. Those men were animals. They'd been drinking. They didn't know what they were doing.'

Bond folded down the bed and ten minutes later the train pulled out of whatever station had become its unscheduled stop. He didn't know whether Katya was asleep or not but she was no longer making any sound. Bond lay on his back and reflected. For the first time, he wondered if the whole thing might now have been some sort of test, arranged by Colonel Boris before they had even got on the train. Could Katya have been part of it, seeing how he would respond to a moment of danger?

But that was impossible. The girl had been genuinely terrified. Bond had seen it in her eyes; there could have been no faking it. And at the end of the day, what was there to be gained? He would have helped her whether he was brainwashed or not. Colonel Boris would have learned nothing from what had just occurred.

And then, from out of the darkness, came the words. 'Thank you, James. I'm glad you were here.'

The two of them lay in their separate beds with a narrow space between them as the Red Arrow rocketed through the night.

13

Places of Intourist

It was Nikita Khrushchev, the premier of Russia, who welcomed Bond to the Hotel National. His image was on a banner that stretched across five of the hotel's six storeys, dressed in a suit with three medals across his chest and one hand raised, the index finger pointing, as if to say, 'This is your room, Comrade Bond. What time would you like breakfast?' The face, with its bald head and sagging cheeks, reminded Bond of the head waiter at Blades. It had the same eager-to-please features although, he decided, Porterfield wore better-tailored suits. An image of Lenin – drawn rather than photographed – hovered in the air above the premier's left shoulder and there were two words emblazoned along the bottom, blocking the view for a dozen rooms on the first floor: MIR NARODAM.

'It means "peace to the people",' Katya translated. 'Lenin stayed here with his wife,' she added, breathlessly. 'In Room 107.'

'Have you booked it for us?' Bond asked, casually.

'Of course not,' Katya said, ignoring the suggestion that the two of them might be sharing. 'Anyway, the room isn't used any more so neither of us will be sleeping there. We'll be on the third floor. In adjoining rooms.'

There had been a marked change in her behaviour since the attack on the train. When the two of them had woken up at half past six in the morning, she had slipped into the bathroom to get dressed and hadn't referred to the incident when they sat down to breakfast: black tea, rye bread, jam and doughy cheese pancakes or *syrniki* – another Russian word she offered for Bond to learn. None of the officials or the other passengers seemed aware that anything had taken place during the night. Another couple had taken the table where the two men had been sitting.

But Katya was definitely more relaxed. She allowed Bond to pour the tea. She smiled more. She didn't draw back when his hand brushed against hers. They were tiny details but Bond made a note of each of them. With the Institute 400 miles behind them, they were both beginning to shrug off the roles of doctor and patient. Bond was already wondering what sort of relationship might replace them.

There had been a car waiting for them at Leningrad Station and this time they had travelled together, their knees almost touching on the back seat. Katya's good mood was heightened by her arrival in the capital and already she was pointing out the churches and the government buildings, the parks and inevitable statues.

'That's the Bolshoi!' she exclaimed, as they passed the monumental entrance with its seven Olympian pillars. 'When I was nine years old, my father took me to see Galina Ulanova dance in *Swan Lake*. I will never forget that night. I dreamed of becoming a ballet dancer.'

'But instead you became a clinical psychiatrist,' Bond muttered.

'I danced when I was at school but I was never good enough. The theatre was bombed a year later. Do you like the ballet?'

It was a question Bond had never thought he would be asked. 'I can't say I've ever been.' He searched for an excuse. 'Isn't it a bit decadent?'

'Since the October Revolution, the Bolshoi has brought culture and entertainment to all the people of Russia. The theatre employs 250 dancers and the finest orchestra in the world. It's hard to believe that you have never seen Ulanova or Lepeshinskaya. You have much to learn!' She sighed. 'We may only have a few days together in Moscow but I will speak to Intourist and they will provide tickets. They have also arranged for us to see the Kremlin, the Central Lenin Museum, the Novodevichy Convent, the Museum of the History and Reconstruction of Moscow . . . There are so many places I want to show you.'

So the torture that had begun in the magic room wasn't over yet, Bond reflected. He glanced at Katya, recognising the unhealthy gleam in her eye. He had already seen it when she had first announced their departure to Moscow, the greatest city in the greatest country with the greatest hotels and the greatest all the rest of it. Did she really believe this stuff or was she merely saying what was expected of her? Already, Bond was beginning to think that, in the glorious Soviet Union it would always be impossible to tell the two apart.

Her enthusiasm carried them through the main entrance of the National and into a spacious reception hall full of gilt mirrors, antique furniture and oil paintings which, she explained, had been liberated from the tsar's palaces and the homes of the nobility. Guests were sitting on Louis XIV chairs, sipping tea served from ornate samovars. The dense, acrid smell of Russian tobacco hung thick in the air. The hotel had seen better days even if the staff and guests pretended not to notice. The wallpaper was fading and the carpets were wearing through but the reception desk manager with his waistcoat and Order of Lenin badge, the porters and the lift operator all went about their work with evident pride. Katya Leonova was greeted by name and treated with deference. Bond was completely ignored.

They were taken to the third floor and as the lift doors opened, Bond was confronted with another icon of Soviet life. A woman was sitting on a hard wooden seat, directly opposite the lift. She was well into her sixties, her face a picture of dark misery, her hands folded on her lap. She had the body of a retired weight-lifter, with bulbous arms and legs swathed in folds of black and grey with drab khaki stockings and heavy shoes. This was the *dezhurnaya* or Russian concierge. Bond knew that there would be women like her in flats and hotels all over Moscow, silently ruling over their miniature kingdoms.

Bond's room surprised him. He had visited the National a few times while he was attached to the embassy in Moscow. The rather grand bar with its wide-open spaces and quiet corners had been a favourite meeting place for journalists, diplomats, businessmen and anyone else with information to share. Bond remembered that many of them would be pouring their first vodka at ten in the morning. He had spent a few nights in a room on the fifth floor with a Lithuanian stenographer but he had never been inside any of the suites. This one was vast and lavishly appointed with a four-poster bed, French furniture and a richly patterned, deep piled carpet in much better condition than the one downstairs. They were certainly giving him the VIP treatment! A bathroom led off to one side and a second door communicated with the neighbouring suite occupied by Katya Leonova. Bond gently tried the handle. It was locked. Squatting down, he saw that the key had been left in on her side.

He went over to the full-length windows framed by curtains so heavy and elaborate that they might have been swept open to reveal Act One of *Swan Lake* at the Bolshoi. In fact the view was no less impressive. From where he was standing, he could see the ochre walls of the Kremlin on the other side of Mokhovaya Street with the tower and the huge clock rising up behind. The twisted domes and bright colours of St Basil's Cathedral were over to one side, the whole building sitting in an empty space like an illustration in a children's book. He knew that Red Square was just out of sight, a five-minute walk away.

The ground seemed to shift beneath his feet and he

was briefly aware of a sense of unreality. Yet again he wondered if he was still in the Leningrad Institute, imagining everything. Could Colonel Boris have done that to him? Could he still be inside Bond's mind, manipulating not just what he thought but what he saw and felt? Bond reached out and touched the window, the glass cold against his fingertips. He listened to the rush of the cars travelling past. He smelled the disinfectant that had been used to clean the room. One by one he checked his senses until he arrived at the inescapable conclusion. This was real. This was happening to him.

He was back in Moscow, twelve years older than he had been the last time he was here. What had changed since then? Very little, from what he had seen so far. The Russian capital still seemed to be sitting there like an unpleasant schoolboy, not caring that it had once again come bottom in the class. The buildings were as magnificent and as lifeless as he remembered. The streets had been cleaned and cleaned again with porcelain litter bins every hundred yards, and even the passing cars seemed to have been polished before they were allowed on the road, but all that effort failed to disguise the innate shabbiness of the place, the shop windows half-empty, the people in their headscarves and ill-fitting suits, hurrying to get where they were going but with no interest in where they actually were.

Moscow was a silent place, a well-oiled machine that had been turned on and left to run. Bond could live without car horns and sirens, but the stillness here had a dead quality about it. There were no children. The young lovers that he would have seen clinging onto each other on every corner of London or Paris had stayed at home. Or perhaps they'd never met.

This was what he had been fighting against for the last two decades but, looking out of the window, Bond had to ask himself if it had really been worth all the effort. As far as he could see, the communist system was defeating itself without his help. How else to explain the forlorn hopelessness of its capital? Even its leader, First Secretary of the Communist Party and Chairman of the Council of Ministers of the Soviet Union, had all the menace of a waiter or a bank clerk. When he had been alone during those long nights in the magic room, Bond had thought that it might be time to get out of the business of espionage, to move on with his life. Suddenly he saw that time had moved on without him and that perhaps it was already too late to make the choice.

He unpacked his bag, noting the poor quality of the clothes he had been given and which he would never normally have allowed to touch his skin. He took a quick look around the room and found electronic bugs in the bathroom, the skirting board, the cornicing and the lamp beside the bed. Although it annoyed him, he had no choice but to leave them intact. He washed his hands and brushed his hair. Then he went out to meet Katya in the corridor as arranged.

'Do you like the room?' she asked.

'It's magnificent,' Bond said. 'You're looking after me very well.'

'We value your services, James. Is there anything you need?'

'There's no soap or plug in the bathroom.'

Katya looked annoyed. The *dezhurnaya* was still in her place and she addressed a series of words to her in Russian. The elderly woman shrugged and although Bond couldn't understand her reply, she seemed put out that such minor details had even been mentioned. Eventually, Katya turned to Bond. 'She says she'll see to it while we're out.'

'Please tell her that I wasn't complaining,' Bond returned. 'It's a beautiful room.'

Katya translated what he had said but the woman responded only with a scowl.

The day's sightseeing began with a visit to the Kremlin and even before they had arrived Bond's worst fears had been realised. Katya Leonova had an encyclopaedic knowledge of the ancient citadel and worse still intended to share it, starting with the names of all twenty towers which she had learned by heart. There was a long queue to enter the Armoury (in this country, Bond knew well, there were even queues to join queues) but there was an Intourist guide at the door and the two of them were ushered in, unchecked. For the next hour, Bond tried to show enthusiasm for crowns and carriages, jewellery and serving plates, weapons, kaftans and silverware in quite execrable taste. But he had no interest in museums. The past could look after itself. Put it in a glass case, dress it up and shine lights on it, it still meant nothing to him.

After the Armoury, they walked across Red Square to the Lenin mausoleum, the low, marble and granite structure where the embalmed body of the former leader was on permanent display. This was, of course, a must-see on Katya's list and already she had tears in her eyes. She really was the perfect communist, Bond decided. She could be happy or sad but either way she would always be fanatical.

'Do you often come to Moscow?' he asked her.

She nodded. 'I used to live here.'

'With your parents?' She had mentioned that her father had taken her to the Bolshoi.

'We had a flat in the Lenin Hills, looking over the Moscow River and later on we were given a dacha nearby, in Serebryany Bor. Perhaps I will be able to take you there. As a child I used to go swimming and walking and mushroom-picking. We had a chauffeur and a nanny and we were very fortunate to have so much space but that was because of my father who was highly valued by the state. He was an academician at the Academy of Medical Sciences.' She paused. 'He worked with Comrade Snezhnevsky.'

'And who was that?' Bond asked.

'Oh, James! You really should have heard of him. You could say that he is the father of Russian psychiatry. He was the man who first recognised what he called "slow schizophrenia" which was a mental disease suffered by many dissidents after the war.'

'Were many dissidents ill?'

'They all were. That's why they were dissidents.'

'And your father worked with him?'

'Yes, although at the time he specialised in other mental diseases including drug addiction and homosexuality.' She moved on quickly. 'I was evacuated during the war. I spent five years in a village south of Leningrad.'

'Did your parents come with you?'

'My mother died when I was young. My father had to stay in Moscow. It was my grandmother's village and she looked after me.'

There was another long queue ahead of them and this time there was no Intourist official to wave them through. Bond wondered how long they would have to wait to see the dead man and how Katya would react if he suggested lunch instead.

'After the war was over, things were very difficult,' Katya explained. 'The Germans had destroyed so much. I hardly ever saw men in the villages around me because they were all dead. Twenty million people lost their homes. And then there were famines. The harvests failed and there was hardly any food in the shops. Soup and potatoes . . . that was all we ate. You could never find soap or shoes or all sorts of things. I had to wear my mother's shoes to go to school! But we never lost heart. Every day, at school, we would thank Comrade Stalin for taking care of us and we knew that if we worked hard, the motherland would be strong again and we would all be happy.'

'Stalin is no longer kept here, is he?' Bond asked innocently as they approached the mausoleum.

'No.' Her face fell. 'They moved him a few years ago. He's nearby.'

'Why did they do that?'

'I don't know. It's best not to ask about these things. Why are you asking me so many questions, Comrade James?'

The 'Comrade' was back. Bond realised it was time to retreat. 'I want to learn about this country if it's going to be my home,' he said. 'And I'm interested in you.'

She blushed. 'What do you want to know about me?'

'Was it your father who persuaded you to work in psychiatry?'

'I didn't need persuading. I was always interested in my father's work. I spent six years studying at the University of Moscow and after that I was employed at the Serbsky Institute for Forensic Psychiatry. That was very exciting for me. Comrade Snezhnevsky had been a director there.'

'So how did you meet Colonel Boris?'

'I was recommended to him. He asked me to join him at the Institute in Leningrad.' She was suddenly in a hurry to move on. 'I don't want to talk about my work. You're still my patient.'

'I hope I'll be more than that.'

'What do you mean?'

She was struggling to meet his eye and for a brief moment Bond saw the woman in her . . . alone and yearning for what every woman wanted. She was lonely. She needed to be loved. She was unmarried of course. He could imagine her sitting in a studio room in Leningrad, trying to lose herself in a copy of *Das*

Kapital or whatever rubbish she took to her bed. Bond felt a sudden desire to rip it all away and to devour her. The woman who didn't want him was always the one he most desired.

But he chose his words carefully. 'It's just that I'm very grateful to you, Katya,' he said. 'You were part of my treatment and I owe you so much for helping me see things more clearly.' He reached out and took her hand. 'I don't suppose . . .'

'What?' She looked away, afraid.

'I know it's stupid but do you think that one day, you and I . . . ?'

'James!' She tried to pull her hand away but he held on to it.

'Are you seeing someone?'

'No!'

'But there must be someone in your life, Katya.'

She faltered. 'Not any more. There was.'

'Well, there should be again. You're too damned attractive to be on your own.'

'James – you can't talk to me this way. It's wrong.' She broke free of him and walked briskly ahead. Bond smiled to himself and followed her in to pay his respects to the dead man.

14

The Finger of Suspicion

The next morning, Katya Leonova went out on her own.

It was only a short walk to the building on Sretenka Street but she felt uncomfortable walking there and worse still going in. She had passed it often enough and, like anyone living in Moscow, knew the organisation that it had once housed. She was a good communist. She had never spoken a word against her party or her country. But the address reminded her that she would never be completely safe. Even a woman like her, who had devoted much of her life to helping the state, could still make mistakes.

For example, there had been that moment, just a few weeks ago, when she had complained how difficult it was to buy stockings that did not wrinkle and itch.

How could she have forgotten herself, speaking like that in public? And then, in the company of two girl-friends she had listened to an illegal recording of the British band of musicians that called themselves the Shadows. Of course she had mocked them for being trite and decadent but even so she had secretly enjoyed what she had heard. And she had laughed at a joke about Comrade Khrushchev! She knew that, in the past, even these minor offences could have resulted in her arrest. She saw herself being dragged out of bed in the middle of the night, thrown into the back of a van and brought to a building like this for questioning. It was only what she deserved. But it was no wonder that she felt the grip of fear around her throat as she approached the main door.

She had spent thirty-six hours with the British spy but had told him that he would have to visit the State Central Museum of Contemporary History of Russia on Tverskaya Street without her. He had not looked pleased although he had quickly assured her that he had been very much looking forward to the museum with its unique collection of porcelain, posters, rare negatives and original historic paintings but that he would have enjoyed it twice as much if she could come too. Katya had to disappoint him. Although she couldn't tell him anything about her movements, she had received a note while they were having dinner at the hotel the night before, summoning her to a meeting with Colonel Boris at the old headquarters of Smersh. She was to report on her progress with Bond. His life or his death would depend on what she had to say.

And the truth was, Katya didn't know what to think. She could not deny that she had enjoyed the last two days (just as she was still unable to get the Shadows and the tune of 'Wonderful Land' out of her head). In fact, she had never met a man like James Bond even though his looks – the blue-grey eyes, the dark hair, the easy smile with just a hint of something cruel – reminded her a little of . . .

She had tried to put the name out of her mind but it was already too late. Bond was older but there was still something about him that made her think of Dmitry Serafimovich as he had been when she had known him five years before. He had the same coolness, or carelessness even, that came from a lifetime spent living in danger. She had been shocked when Colonel Boris had ordered her to accompany Bond to Moscow but already she felt comfortable with him. She was looking forward to seeing him later that day.

But – no. How could that be? Bond was the enemy. He came from a different world; one that was utterly alien to her. Sometimes he would talk about his old life in the West and she would get a glimpse of things she could never understand. Breakfast at a restaurant called Lutèce in New York. The cigarettes from Morland, the shirts from somewhere called Turnbull & Asser in Jermyn Street. The atmosphere in a casino at three in the morning. He did not complain that he had now left these things behind him and she was glad about that. After all, she had played her part in making him into the man that he now was. But she still felt that despite her efforts, part of him still belonged to the world he had come from and it was a part that would always be out of her reach.

So what was she to tell Colonel Boris about her progress with the British agent? *'I need to know that he is what he seems to be.'* That was what he had told her back at the Institute and the awful truth was that Katya had her doubts. If she was going to be honest, based on what she had observed so far, she would have to admit that there was a strong possibility that Bond was a fake. If this were the case, he would be killed.

Was she sure enough of her feelings to send him to his death? It was the moment she had been dreading. Everything depended on what she said in the next few minutes. Katya's mouth was dry. She was wearing her smartest suit from ODMO, the Moscow General Soviet House of Design. Simple, practical and, above all, modest . . . that was the Soviet way. She had no jewellery and little make-up. She had rehearsed what she was going to say many times. Was she ready? She raised her hand and adjusted the scarf around her neck. Then she went in.

Bond watched her from the other side of the road.

He had sensed there was something wrong when Katya had received a handwritten note at the dinner table the night before. In an instant, her good humour had been wiped away and suddenly it was the severe clinician in her white coat and glasses who was sitting opposite him. His attempts to cheer her up had fallen flat and she had refused his offer of a vodka in the hotel bar, instead insisting on bed and an early night. Then, at breakfast, she had told him that he would have to spend the morning on his own. That was when he had decided to follow her.

He had slipped out of his room, avoiding the sullen gaze of the old woman, the *dezhurnaya*, who never seemed to leave her seat. While Katya had taken the ancient lift, he had jogged down three flights of stairs, arriving at the ground floor as she left the hotel. The reception area was almost empty, with the desk manager deep in conversation on the phone. Bond knew that he was supposed to stay in his room. Katya had made it clear that he could not wander through Moscow unescorted but this was a risk he was ready to take. He had come to Russia to get close to Colonel Boris, who in turn might lead him to Stalnaya Ruka, but he was running out of patience. At the Institute, Colonel Boris had spoken of an assignment but since then there had been no sign of him. Katya had told him nothing. If he was caught, he would say he had wanted some fresh air.

It seemed his gamble had paid off.

Bond knew exactly where he was. Back in London, M had told him that the new organisation had based itself in the offices once occupied by Smersh and that was where Katya had brought him. So she and Colonel Boris were actively working for Stalnaya Ruka! Bond imagined her on her way to the eighth floor and wished that he could find a way to go after her. But that would be risking too much. He would just have to work on her when he saw her again later that day and perhaps get some information out of her. The sooner he got her into his bed, the better. In the meantime, he might as well continue towards the bloody museum that she'd lined up for him. Marxism–Leninism. The one sure way to this woman's heart.

He was already moving when a man appeared at

the front entrance of the building, making his way out onto the street. Bond stopped at once, recognising not just the shaven head, the dull eyes and the same cheap suit that he had been wearing the last time they met but the strip of adhesive over his broken nose. Bond knew that he had been responsible for that.

It was the man from the Red Arrow, one of the two KGB thugs who had attacked Katya in the middle of the night. He had just emerged from the same building that she had entered before and now, watching him walk down the pavement, Bond knew that it couldn't just be a coincidence. He had to be working for Stalnaya Ruka or for Colonel Boris, which meant that, just as he had suspected at the time, the supposed assault had been faked.

But for whose benefit? His or hers?

There were three people in the room on the eighth floor when Katya Leonova entered. Colonel Boris was seated with his back to a pair of windows, both of which had recently been barred. Katya noticed that the metal was new, the welding still raw. The man on one side of him was very old, bald, dressed in a well-tailored suit. He looked terminally ill, holding a cigarette in the claw of his hand and coughing as he inhaled. The woman on the other side was much younger, about Katya's age. She was wearing the tunic and trousers of a KGB officer, complete with gold buttons and medals. Her hair was tied back and seemed to have drawn her face with it. She was examining Katya with pinched, hungry eyes.

'This is my assistant, Comrade Katya Leonova,' Colonel Boris introduced her. 'As I told you, she is a highly trained psychiatric analyst and was very helpful to me when we first treated Bond at the Institute. She has spent a great deal of time with him since his return to Russia. She is here to answer any concerns you may have.'

The old man gestured towards one of the many empty chairs around the table. 'Please, sit down, my dear.' His voice suited his appearance. It was that of a dying man. 'My name is General Grubozaboyschikov, but you can call me General G. And this is Lieutenant General Kirilenko. We have a great interest in what you have to say.'

'What is it you want to know, Comrade General?' Katya took a place on the opposite side of the table, as far away from the three of them as she could get.

'What are your observations of the man, Bond? How has he been behaving himself?'

'I'm not sure . . .' Katya was at war with herself. Part of her wanted to protect Bond. But all her training, everything she had learned, warned her that she could only do so by hiding at least some of the truth.

'You don't need to be afraid of us,' Irma Kirilenko said. 'Just tell us what you think.'

'I think that he is confused,' Katya said at length. 'He wants to be a good citizen. He wants to serve the motherland. But I have noted certain schizophrenic tendencies. He is still struggling to leave behind his former self.'

'What do you mean?' General G asked with a hint of annoyance.

'Only that he makes jokes, Comrade General.' She thought back. 'When I told him that Comrade Lenin had stayed at our hotel, he asked if he would be sleeping in the same room. This showed disrespect. And on the train, he talked of a friend who worked in the British embassy here in Moscow and it struck me as strange that he should think of such a man – or anyone employed by our imperialist enemies – as his friend.' She struggled to find another example. 'It also seemed to me that he was unimpressed by the Polytechnic Museum. I showed him a car built before the glorious revolution as I thought it would be of interest to him but his remarks were quite disparaging.'

'What of his day-to-day behaviour?' Colonel Boris asked, rather testily. Katya was afraid that she had disappointed him and carefully retreated from her earlier position. 'He has been exemplary in his dealings with me,' she said. 'He has said on many occasions that he will do whatever we ask of him and that he is happy to serve the motherland.' She paused. 'I believe him.'

'What has he said about his commanding officer?' General G asked. 'The man he killed in London?'

'He has not spoken a word about it,' Katya replied. 'But nor would I expect him to.'

'Quite right,' Colonel Boris agreed. 'When he was in London, Bond behaved exactly as he had been programmed. I interrogated him about the death of his superior myself.' He raised a languid hand. 'He was not ashamed of what he had done. On the contrary, he was quite satisfied with the way he handled the matter even though he had been forced to wait several months.'

'So why won't he talk about it now?'

'Because there is no need to. There is also the question of his own self-preservation. At some level in his subconscious, Bond is aware of the trauma of what took place. M was clearly a father figure to him. It is the parent who forms almost the whole environment of a child during the first year of its life and it was M who performed very much the same function for Bond when

he became a spy. In destroying the father, he has destroyed a large part of himself. Instinctively, he avoids
the subject in much the same way as a man who has
been severely burned will not wish to discuss the fire.'

'You believe we can rely on him?' General G had cut
to the point. His question was directed at Katya.

Katya gazed at the old man. She knew that this was
the moment when Bond lived or died. She waited for
as long as she could. Then she answered, with certainty. 'Yes, Comrade General. I think the Comrade
Colonel has turned him into a perfect instrument and
that he is trying very hard to become an educated and
cultured citizen and to be of the greatest service to his
adopted country. To that end, he will do anything that
is asked of him.'

'Thank you, Comrade Leonova.'

It was a dismissal. Katya glanced at Colonel Boris
who nodded almost indifferently. She got up and left
the room.

Colonel Boris waited until she had gone, then addressed the two others. 'Are you satisfied?'

General G turned to Lieutenant General Kirilenko,
who drew a document out of her leather attaché case.
She laid it on the table. 'We have new and disturbing
information to share with you, Comrade Colonel,' she
began.

'Please enlighten me.' Colonel Boris did not look concerned but he reached into his pocket and removed an inhaler which he placed on the table beside him.

'First, are you aware that Mr Bond left his hotel this morning without the necessary authority?'

'Where did he go?'

'He is outside this very building – or was a few minutes ago. It appears that he followed your assistant. This would suggest an independence of spirit that I, for one, find disturbing.'

'Not necessarily. Bond is completely docile. He could have followed her like a dog.'

'Then let me move on to a much more serious business. I recently had a telephone conversation with an agent working in our Central Office in Havana. The call was by way of an interview. This individual is being considered as our next director for the Caribbean. The position has become vacant due to the unfortunate death of the former director, a man by the name of Hendriks. He was killed three weeks ago in Jamaica.' She spoke like the recorded message on an Ansafone, blandly laying out the facts at exactly the right speed. 'We spoke for an hour and it was during this time that he mentioned something which I did not believe to be possible but which, if true, casts grave doubt on everything you have told us, Comrade Colonel.'

'So what did this man say?' Colonel Boris asked.

'That he had heard that Mr Hendriks had been shot dead by a British agent, the same person who murdered Francisco Scaramanga, a freelance assassin who had provided his services to us on many occasions.'

'And the name of the agent?'

'James Bond.'

There was a lengthy silence punctuated only by the double hiss of the atomiser which Colonel Boris had directed towards the back of his throat. The faintest scent of lemongrass escaped into the air.

'That is not possible,' he said. 'Bond was in London. The agent you spoke to must be mistaken.'

'Naturally, I challenged him on the matter and I have made further investigations. Scaramanga is most certainly dead. That much is clear. But who in fact killed him? It would seem that there may have been an error of communication. The man who was posing as Scaramanga's assistant but who was actually a British agent called himself Mark Hazard, and this was the name that was sent to Moscow and which appeared on the death warrant which was subsequently issued.'

She held up a hand before Colonel Boris could interrupt. 'However, it now transpires that before he died, Hendriks had sent Havana a description of this man, with particular reference to the scars on his body and his face. They identified him as James Bond.'

There was a long silence.

'Nobody from Havana Central actually saw this man, Mark Hazard,' Colonel Boris said.

'No.'

'Was Hendriks able to send them a photograph?'

'No. But his description was very precise.'

Colonel Boris addressed himself to General G. He could see that Lieutenant General Kirilenko had already made up her mind. If she was allowed to have her way, she would have Bond executed immediately. And he, doubtless, would be next. But the lemongrass, insinuating itself into his hippocampus, kept him calm. 'With respect to Comrade Kirilenko, this is absurd,' he said. 'She is suggesting that Bond has managed to fool me – and for that matter to fool Comrade Leonova whose professional opinion you have just heard. Let me assure you that it would have been physically impossible for Bond to have harmed a Russian agent following his treatment at the Institute. And for that matter, if it wasn't Bond, who do you think killed M? Or are we to believe that all that was arranged for our benefit too?

'The essential point here is that nobody in Havana

saw Mark Hazard. Comrade Kirilenko admitted as much herself. It was why they were unable to confirm his identity to Moscow. They did not even see his picture. There are many agents with scars. Are we seriously going to accept this extraordinary conclusion based on a series of Chinese whispers?'

'I agree with the colonel,' Kirilenko said, but there was an edge to her voice that told him she had something else up her sleeve and that this wasn't over yet. 'That is why I have arranged for a witness to come here to Moscow. He was actually part of the group who met with Scaramanga at the Thunderbird hotel in Jamaica and he came into contact several times with Mr Hazard, or whoever he was. He was also on the train when Scaramanga died.'

'Who is this man?'

'His name is Hal Garfinkel. He lives in Chicago and works with the Teamster Union. He also has connections with the American mafia and other criminal organisations. As luck would have it, he is currently in Paris but my department has reached out to him and invited him to Moscow.'

'You've bribed him?'

'There was no need to. Mr Garfinkel is interested in exploring business opportunities in this country. He also has a predilection for very young girls. We were able to satisfy his requirements on both counts and will arrange for him to come face to face with Bond so that the matter can be settled at once.'

'And when is Mr Garfinkel arriving in Moscow?' Colonel Boris asked.

It was General G who answered.

'He will be here tomorrow.'

15

Dark Angel

'All right, Katya,' Bond said as the waiter served what passed for a luxurious breakfast in a five-star Moscow hotel. There were three fried eggs on his plate and a spoon but no knife or fork. Not for the first time, he found himself thinking of his flat in Chelsea and his wonderful housekeeper, May. 'We're not going to any more bloody museums,' he announced. 'I've had enough of tourism and anyway if I remember rightly it was Lenin who called tourists "the decadent excrescence of a corrupt and doomed economic system". I couldn't agree more. The sun is shining and I think we deserve a day off. Let's find somewhere to go for a walk and a swim and afterwards we can have a picnic. Maybe you can drop into one of those *beryozkas* of yours and buy us some decent food. But I'm telling you, the only eggs I'm going to eat today are caviar.' He pushed his plate away. 'And stop pouting at me like that! You know everything about Marx and Stalin and the Communist Party and the history and traditions of the Soviet Union. You can't possibly want to see any more.'

Katya looked around her, terrified. 'James! You shouldn't talk like that,' she whispered. 'You don't know who's listening. And we have tickets to the Exhibition of Economic Achievement.'

Bond knew he had to be careful. Push Katya too far and who knows what she might report back to Colonel Boris. But at the same time, he was becoming increasingly impatient. It seemed like he had been in Russia for an eternity even if he knew that the drabness and grim authoritarianism of Moscow had the effect of making the hours seem like days. Somehow, he had to get closer to Stalnaya Ruka. Katya wasn't saying anything but she had reported to them only yesterday. She must know something of what they were planning. For a week and a half he had played the part of the acolyte, in awe of his newly adopted country, but that had got him nowhere. Now he was going to take the upper hand – and to hell with the consequences.

'I'm meant to be educating you,' Katya scolded him.

'And you've succeeded. I've learned a great deal.

But you also said you hoped we would become friends. Maybe we owe it to ourselves to have a little more time just with each other if we're going to make that happen.'

She considered. 'Well, I suppose it wouldn't hurt to take you to Serebryany Bor. We could take the trolley bus from Gorky Street and I could show you Sovietskaya Square on the way. There's a fine monument to Yury Dolgoruky.'

'The founder of Moscow,' Bond said.

She beamed at him. 'You remembered!'

'Of course.' Bond had seen a painting in one of the museums they'd visited. The twelfth-century princeling had been looking remarkably pleased with himself, which was perhaps why he'd stuck in Bond's mind.

At any event, he had passed the test. Katya relented and the result was the first normal day Bond had experienced since he had arrived in Russia. Serebryany Bor was a huge woodland park to the north-west of the city with an artificial lake built into a bend of the Moscow River. People came here to get some fresh air; to swim and have picnics or to walk among the pine trees. It was an unusually warm spring day and the beaches were crowded with whole families out with their children and Bond was particularly taken by the sight of antique matrons with cabriole legs, paddling in their nightdresses. He asked Katya about this and she reluctantly admitted that swimming costumes were in short supply.

She had brought lunch – black bread, sausages and cheese – from a shop displaying exactly those products as wax models in the window, and they found a shady corner of the wood in which to eat on their own. Katya was more relaxed than he had ever seen her. She had kicked off her shoes and was lying on a bed of pine needles, her bare arms folded across her breasts. One strand of her hair had come loose and it unlocked the rigidity of her features. She looked pretty and Bond was almost ready to forget that she worked for Colonel Boris, that she earned her living putting needles into people's brains and that she would have him killed if she realised that he was lying to her.

'Tell me about England,' she said, taking him by surprise.

Bond was wary. 'What do you want to know?'

'I've never been there. Will you miss it?'

'No.' Bond searched for the words she wanted to hear. Unemployment, child poverty, race riots, the imminent collapse of capitalism and all the rest of it. But he couldn't bring himself to do it. 'I'll tell you about it over dinner,' he said.

'Where are we having dinner?'

'I don't know. You're the one with the money. I didn't even have the four kopeks for the trolleybus. But if Colonel Boris is paying, he can take us somewhere expensive. I want to eat caviar with ice-cold champagne. Russian champagne is too sweet but I'm told the Abrau-Durso '58 is acceptable. Do you think you can manage that?'

She looked at him coolly. 'I'll see what I can do.'

She was as good as her word. That evening, after they'd both showered and changed, she took him to a restaurant that Bond knew by reputation but had never visited. Aragvi, in Tverskaya Street, was an unimpressive-looking place, opposite the mayor's office and next to a tiny park. But it was famous for its Georgian cuisine and for the high prices that made it inaccessible to the majority of Soviet citizens. Katya had dressed up for the evening in a slim-fitting black silk dress, with a matching kimono jacket and a simple string of black pearls. Bond, in his borrowed clothes, looked Russian, which was both the best and the worst that could be said about him.

After the tranquillity of their day at the park, Katya was in an excitable mood as they climbed up the three steps from the street and entered through the glass doors. 'They say that Beria himself designed and built this restaurant,' she told Bond. 'Stalin's son – Vasily – used to eat here. Can you imagine that! You're going to have to try their *khinkali*. They have a special train that comes in from Georgia with ingredients every day.'

A pianist in black tie was playing Cole Porter as they were shown to a table in the corner of the main room. Bond noticed a few eyes turning his way and remembered that Aragvi had always been a favourite haunt of the KGB. When an agent was being sent abroad, they would host his farewell dinner here and at one time Station M had tried to get one of their people onto the staff to spy on the proceedings, only to find that the waiters were, exclusively, ex-KGB officers too. He wondered if the pianist was also a spy. The room was about three-quarters full but Katya had deliberately chosen a table far enough away from the others so that their English conversation would not be overheard.

Katya gave the order, directed by Bond. She began with 500 grams of caviar, beluga, from the *Huso huso* sturgeon in the Caspian Sea and with its large, buttery pearls easily the best variety available. As it arrived, Bond reflected that he had once heard it described as the most expensive aphrodisiac in the world. Casanova had devoured quantities of the stuff between conquests. How typical that in this almost completely joyless country, it should be cheaply available: the local *gastronom* would be selling it for less than a tenth of London prices. Bond remembered being told that at the embassy in Moscow you could tell the new arrivals because they always made a beeline for the caviar bowl. The older hands would search for fresh fruit and vegetables, which were much harder to find.

And what to accompany it? They ordered two glasses of champagne but it was too sweet so they moved on to vodka. The pianist was playing 'Take Me Back to Manhattan'. If only, Bond thought.

The waiter had brought a half-bottle in an ice bucket and Bond watched approvingly as Katya threw back three glasses one after the other. She drank more with the main course. *Khinkali* turned out to be dumplings stuffed with minced lamb which they ate with their fingers. They also ordered a spicy chicken stew and *khachapuri* – bread topped with melted cheese. The food was every bit as good as Katya had said.

'So are you going to tell me something about yourself?' Bond asked. He poured two more tumblers of the icy, viscous liquid.

'I've already told you enough.'

'Nonsense. You told me about your father and how he got you into psychiatry. Where are your parents, by the way? Are they here in Moscow?'

Katya looked downcast. 'No. My mother died when I was twelve years old,' she said in a low voice. 'She killed herself.'

'I'm sorry.'

'She was unhappy. She came to my room the night before. I was in bed. She said that she was going away and the next day she went to the railway station and . . .' She drank more vodka. 'My father always said that it was an accident, that she fell, but I knew the truth. I knew I was never going to see her again and when I was told what had happened, I wasn't even a little bit surprised.'

'Where is your father now?'

'I don't know. I don't want to talk about him.' She brightened up. 'I loved our day at Serebryany Bor with the sun shining and everyone out enjoying themselves. I wish life could always be like that.'

'Maybe it can,' Bond said. Katya didn't reply so he pressed on, wondering where this might go. 'Why are you on your own?' he asked.

'I'm not. I have plenty of friends.'

'You know what I mean. Why don't you have a boyfriend?'

She blushed. 'That's not the sort of question you should ask a Russian girl.'

'Too late, I'm afraid.'

'Well . . .' She searched for an answer. 'It's my work, I suppose.'

'That's nonsense. I saw the way those young orderlies were looking at you – and with good reason. You remind me of someone I used to know. Her name was Loelia Ponsonby and she was my secretary . . . a damned good secretary too. She used to say that she was married to the job but it was a one-way relationship. The job never bought her flowers or gave her a good time and by the time she finally walked out on it, it had stolen her best years. Anyway, I thought the Communist Party encouraged love and marriage.'

'It may do now but that wasn't always the case. Lenin saw marriage as a sort of slavery. He said it was the best weapon to stifle the desire of the working class for freedom. He wanted a union of affection and comradeship which would allow women to be free to take part in the revolution.'

'What about family?'

'The country is our family.'

Bond was exasperated. Just when he thought he was getting somewhere, Katya fell back on the tired slogans with which she'd been indoctrinated. It was his own fault for bringing politics into the conversation. Then he remembered what she had told him when they were walking in Red Square. 'But you did have a boyfriend once,' he teased her.

'Who told you that?'

'You did. I asked you if there was someone in your life and you said there had been.'

'That was a long time ago.'

'What was his name?'

It took her a few moments to answer. 'Dmitry.' The single word fell heavily from her lips and she drank again.

Bond could see that he was finding a way through her defences and he pushed harder. 'Did you love him?'

'Yes.'

'Tell me about him.'

'Why do you want to know?'

'Because I want to know about you.'

She examined him carefully as if she didn't completely trust him but Bond could see the beginnings of tears forming in her eyes. This was something that she had never talked about. He knew she wanted to. 'If I tell you about him, will you leave me alone?' she asked.

'I only want you to be happy, Katya.'

'You know nothing about me, my country, my family, the way I was brought up.' Bond had done what he intended. He had got her drunk. The alcohol was playing havoc with her emotions: she didn't know whether to be angry or resigned, cold-blooded or broken-hearted. She was all of them at the same time.

He put his hand on hers. 'Tell me about Dmitry.'

The food was forgotten as she told her story. She spoke so quietly that she might have been talking to herself and in a way she was. It was fortunate that the pianist had taken a break. In the brief silence, the pain poured out.

'He was the man I was going to marry. I knew that the moment I first met him at Moscow University although we were both so very young. The university was a huge place but it seemed that everybody knew Dmitry Serafimovich. People called him Dima. Or Serafim. He was studying the arts: literature and poetry. He wanted to be a poet and he certainly looked like one. He was like Lord Byron. He had the same black hair which he wore very long, and deep brown eyes, like an angel. I thought he was the most beautiful man I had ever met.'

'How did you meet him?'

'A friend of mine took me to a poetry recital. Dmitry read two poems that he had written himself. They were both about peasant life before the war and about the summer harvest, how strength will always be found in the soil of the motherland. He was given an ovation that lasted three minutes although nobody in the audience had really understood the true significance of his work, what he was writing about. If they had, perhaps they'd have been more careful. But that was the thing about Dima. He was talented. He was going to be famous. Everybody knew that. But there was so much about him that they didn't know. He was a dark angel. He had his secrets.

'My friend lived in the same apartment block as him and introduced me to him. From the moment we began talking we both knew what was going to happen. There could be no doubting it. We were worlds apart – I was in the Science Department and I didn't know anything about poetry and literature – but we felt comfortable together as if we'd known each other all our lives and soon we were seeing each other every day.'

'How old were you?'

'I was nineteen. He was twenty-three. Is there any more vodka?'

Bond lifted the empty bottle and signalled to the waiter. 'Did you live together?' he asked.

'That wouldn't have been possible. But we spent as much time together as we could. He told me that his parents were dead. They had both been killed in the war and he had been brought up by an aunt in Moscow. He had no brothers or sisters. I was the first girl he had ever gone out with. We used to walk together in Serebryany Bor and he would always have a notebook with him. He would sit in the shade of the pine trees and write whatever came into his head. I was thinking about him this morning when I was with you.'

'I'm not sure that's a compliment.'

'But it is. You are like him in many ways. Maybe not good ways.' She turned her glass in her fingers, looking into it for inspiration. Suddenly the anger was back. 'It's impossible to explain this to you. You have no understanding of Moscow in the fifties. Life at the university. What it was like to be young at that time.'

'I won't understand if you don't tell me,' Bond said.

She nodded. 'There had been many hardships because of the war. Twenty-six million people had lost their lives! Can you even begin to imagine such a number? Seventy thousand villages had been completely destroyed. Moscow was crowded with refugees trying to begin a new life. You would see children in the street, begging at stations, even selling themselves to get food to eat. For everyone there were privations and shortages. But I had complete faith in Comrade Stalin who would lead us to a better future. We had won the war, hadn't we? If we just worked hard enough and made enough sacrifices, everything would be all right. That was what I believed.'

The second bottle arrived. The waiter plunged it into the ice bucket.

'Dmitry was doing brilliantly. He was attending evening classes at the Literary Institute and all his professors spoke highly of him. He had even had a poem published in *Novyi mir* – can you imagine? It was the most prestigious literary journal in Russia. Better still, they offered him a job in the poetry division. How we celebrated that night! And at three o'clock in the morning, walking beside the river with a full moon in the sky, he asked me to marry him. That was the happiest night of my life.

'We never told anyone. We couldn't. I wasn't even sure my father would give permission. But it was agreed between us. Nobody was going to tear us apart.

'That was what I believed, what I hoped, but as our time at the university drew to a close, I became anxious. Dima was too independent. He didn't seem to understand the rules or if he did, he ignored them. For example he had refused to join the Komsomol because he said it was corrupt and run by careerists. I knew that he was meeting with independent student groups without authorisation from the university and that he was reading foreign literature and philosophy.

Once, I saw him with a copy of *America* magazine. It was full of propaganda about the West but when I asked him about it he just laughed and said that it was nothing to do with me. I tried to warn him. Everyone knew that the KGB was active in Moscow University. There were some students who were not students at all but who would become your friends to find out who you were seeing and what they were saying. We knew that many of the rooms were bugged and NKVD informers were everywhere. You could be arrested just for reading a seditious poem. Or meeting a foreigner without permission. Or so many things. You had to be careful about what you said and especially who you said it to but Dima didn't care. He thought he was invulnerable.'

She reached out with her glass and Bond filled it for her. The pianist had returned and was playing something soft and classical but it seemed to him that all the sound in the restaurant, including the gossip of the other diners, had receded, like the atmosphere before a storm.

'One day I was alone in his room and I noticed that a drawer in his desk was open although most times it was locked. I looked in it and noticed several pages of writing, in Dima's hand. I could see at once that it was a poem and I began to read it. I was curious why he hadn't shown it to me before. I had got into the habit of reading everything he wrote.

'Well, I soon found out why. What Dmitry had written was shocking. It was an attack on Stalin, on the party, on the entire history of the last twenty years. It described the suffering of the *kulaks*, which was the name we gave to the agricultural workers who spoke out against collective farming fifteen years before the war. It was true that many of them had been arrested and sent into exile. Some of them were executed. But I had always been taught that this was a necessary process. Nothing could be achieved without struggle and this was part of it. Dmitry did not see it this way. He described Stalin as a murderer. The words were there in black and white.'

'Did you tell Dmitry what you'd found?' Bond asked.

'I had to. I was going to be married to him. We couldn't have secrets from each other.'

'What did he say?'

'He told me the truth. I should have seen it all along but perhaps I'd been too busy with my own studies and too blinded by my feelings for him. He was an enemy of the state, a conspiracist. What he had written was what he believed. Stalin was a monster. The Communist Party had betrayed the people. The English and the

Americans were not our enemies. Once he had started, he couldn't stop. He told me his whole life had been a lie. His parents had not been killed in the war. They were themselves *kulaks*, enemies of the state, who had been arrested for anti-patriotic activities and sent to a special settlement in Siberia when Dmitry was two years old. They had both died there; his father shot, his mother from pneumonia. But before they left the village, they had managed to smuggle their only child to safety. He was sent to Moscow to live with a woman who was a friend of the family but not a blood relative as he had claimed.

'Worst of all, he had lied on his *anketa*. This is the questionnaire that every Russian must complete before going to university or getting a job. Hiding the truth about his family, the fact that his parents had been exiled, was unthinkable. If the authorities had known, he would have been arrested immediately. Certainly he would never have been admitted to Moscow University and any position on *Novyi mir* would have been out of the question.'

'Were you angry with him?'

'How could I be angry with him? I loved him! But I didn't understand him. He was so proud of himself. He said that he had always wanted to tell me the truth and that we could not be married if we were not completely honest with each other. He said that he knew I loved him and that he loved me equally. He wanted me to share his secrets, to be part of his life. He was confident that I would agree.'

'And did you?'

Katya gazed at him sullenly as if Bond and his ignorance were somehow to blame for this long confession. 'I had always been brought up to believe that there was nothing shameful about doing what was right. When I was in the Young Pioneers, we always talked of Pavlik Morozov. We had his photograph in our assembly hall. He was the thirteen-year-old boy who had denounced his own father for corruption. He had reported him to the GPU and later on he was murdered by his family. He was a hero! We had to follow his example. If I heard one of my friends or another student saying something negative about the teachers or complaining about the government, it was my duty to report it immediately. I had no choice.'

'Is that what you did?'

Katya shook her head, unable to find the words. She emptied her glass. 'To report him would be to lose him,' she said eventually. 'I couldn't imagine my life without him. My dark angel with his laughter and his moods and his beautiful words.'

'So what did you do?'

'I didn't know what to do. I was being torn apart. I became ill. I couldn't sleep. By not telling anyone what I had discovered, I had become a criminal myself. I stopped seeing Dmitry. I didn't go anywhere near him. I left the university early and went home. I thought that maybe if I was far enough away from him, I'd be able to forget about him but of course that didn't happen. I thought about him all the time, day and night.' She paused. 'I also thought about my duty.'

She fell silent. Bond waited for her to continue, quietly dreading what was to come.

'In the end, I went to my father for advice. I told him what had happened and what Dmitry had admitted and asked him what I should do. His reply was unequivocal. Of course I must report Dmitry. I had already endangered myself by delaying so much. And not just myself. His own position could be threatened if I was arrested. I tried to argue with him but he wouldn't listen. He said that if I did not accept my obligations, he would have no choice but to report us both. I've already told you. My father was a senior figure at the Academy of Medical Sciences. He had many contacts within the party. By confiding in him, I had already denounced Dmitry, even if that had not been my intention.'

But perhaps it had, Bond thought. Easier to tell her

father than to walk into the offices of the KGB or the MVD or whatever.

'I cried. I pleaded with him. I told him that Dmitry and I wished to be married. I became quite hysterical and in the end my father promised me that he would use all his influence to ensure that Dmitry would not be imprisoned or sent into exile. The authorities weren't heartless, my father said. Dmitry was young. He had made a mistake. He would be treated with kindness.'

'So what happened?'

'I did what he told me to. I told them about Dmitry.'

'And?'

'He was removed from the university immediately and placed under arrest. Nobody ever spoke about him again. It was as if he had never existed. But my father had not lied to me. Dmitry was not exiled or imprisoned.' Katya took a deep breath. 'Instead, he was sent to a *psikhushka*, a psychiatric hospital. The authorities had been persuaded that he should be treated for what was clearly an abnormality of the mind. He was not a criminal. He was suffering from a mental disorder. After all, only a mad person would deliberately act in a way that was clearly against his own well-being. Dmitry had demonstrated this not just by his anti-patriotic writing but by confessing everything to me.'

'Did you ever see him again?'

'I saw him just once, a year later. I had asked many, many times to be allowed to visit him but it was only then that it was finally allowed. I saw him for just five minutes. It was enough.

'I hardly recognised him. His beautiful hair had been shaved all the way to his skull. His eyes were unfocused, they said from the electric shock treatment he had received. He could not speak. He was wearing a long bed jacket with bare feet. His leg was twitching. I tried to talk to him but he did not know who I was. He opened his mouth but all that came out was a sort of animal cry. I got up and walked away. I couldn't bear it.'

'And this was what your father thought would help him?'

'My father did what he thought was right!' Katya exclaimed defiantly and then burst into silent tears. She reached for the vodka glass but her hand was trembling and knocked it over, the liquid soaking into the tablecloth. Bond gazed at her, helpless, shocked by the sudden breakdown, the loss of control.

'Can you take me back to the hotel?' she asked, finally. 'The meal is paid for. I don't want any more.'

The restaurant was a ten-minute walk from the National and Bond managed to get her back with his arm around her waist, her head resting on his shoulder. She was sobbing uncontrollably and despite everything, he felt ashamed of himself, knowing that he had purposefully brought her to this point. She quietened down as they entered the reception area and they travelled up to the third floor together, taking the lift. Bond was relieved to see that the old woman who usually stood guard had gone home. Her chair in the third-floor corridor was empty.

Bond led Katya to her door but before she got there she turned and brought her hands up, holding each side of his neck, staring at him with a desperation he had never seen before.

'Please,' she said. 'Can you love me?'

Bond leaned forward and kissed her on the lips. Then he swept her into his arms and carried her into his room, kicking the door shut behind him. He threw her onto the bed and undressed her, the silk sliding off the slender body underneath. She was wearing a bra and a half-slip and Bond saw that they were obviously, expensively French, flesh-coloured and trimmed with white lace. She reached out to him and he grabbed hold of her wrists, then lowered himself onto her, crushing her into the mattress. Bond was not interested in seduction. They both knew what they wanted. It was going to be quick and brutal.

Even so, he was surprised by the passion, even the

ferocity with which Katya made love. Her father's cru-
elty and her own gullibility had destroyed any chance
of happiness in her life and it was as if she had chosen
this night finally to make amends. Just a few days before
she had reminded him that he was her patient but that
would never be true again. Writhing on her back with
her legs clamped around him, she had forfeited all the
control she'd had over him. From now on he would be
in command.

Later, lying in the darkness with Katya asleep in his
arms, Bond reflected on what had happened; the story
she had told him and this, the inevitable consequence.
Briefly, he was overcome with an emotion he had never
felt before. It was self-disgust. He had only bad feelings for this young, pretty, wicked girl whose neck he
could snap right now with one turn of his wrist. He
hated her for what she had done to him when he was at
the Institute. She had almost destroyed him as surely
as she had destroyed her dark angel, Dmitry.

But he needed her so he had provided her with what
she had demanded. Would she now lead him to Stalnaya Ruka? He hoped so. Suddenly Bond wanted this
business to be over. He wanted to be back in London,
in his own bed and in his own clothes, leaving this
dreadful, merciless country far behind.

16
A Knock on the Door

With the sunrise and the start of another day, Bond experienced a change of heart.

Katya was lying asleep beside him with her head on his chest and one arm stretched out over his shoulder. She looked beautiful, at peace after her frenzy of the night before. Perhaps Bond had been unfair in his judgement of her . . . and of himself.

First of all, what had happened had been spontaneous. He hadn't planned it. He had poured alcohol into her to get information from her, not to get her into his bed. He hadn't quite turned into M's gigolo.

And thinking about it, he was forced to recognise that in many ways she was as much a victim as he was. He had been brainwashed over a period of many months. She'd had the same treatment all her life: as a child in a school that celebrated informers, in the blasted Pioneers with her white shirt and red scarf, prancing round the Russian flag, bombarded by mind-deadening slogans from dawn to dusk, shredded by her father and the pieces sent to Colonel Boris, who would have reassembled them in a design of his own. She'd never had a chance.

Looking at her now, lost in the innocence of sleep, he could almost forgive her for her part in what had been done to him. He examined the quarter-moon curves of her eyelashes, the strands of fair hair sweeping unevenly across her forehead, the pulse in her neck beating softly, echoing her heart. It suddenly struck him how young she was, how many years there were between them. Did he hate her? Was that what she deserved? It helped that only fractured memories of what had happened to him at the Institute remained. He had Sir James Molony to thank for that. It was Colonel Boris who had given the orders, Colonel Boris who had (in the indelicate words of Dr Joost Meerloo) raped his mind. Bond decided that he would very much like to kill Colonel Boris before he left Russia. He wondered if he would get the opportunity.

Katya stirred and opened her eyes. She smiled. '*Dobroe utro,*' she said. Bond understood the two words. Good morning. 'I drank too much,' she added.

'Does that mean you regret what happened between us?'

Katya reflected. 'No.' She placed her hand on his chest, the fingers splayed. 'I'm glad.'

'Did Colonel Boris ask you to get close to me? Do I have him to thank for last night?' Even as he spoke the words, Bond was annoyed with himself. The thought had arisen, uninvited. He hadn't meant to express it so brutally.

'That's a horrible thing to say,' Katya recoiled and would have got out of the bed if he hadn't caught hold of her wrist.

'I'm sorry, Katya. You're right. I thought last night was wonderful. It's just that sometimes I don't know what I'm thinking anymore. I don't know what Colonel Boris wants with me. I don't even understand why I'm here.'

'I told you when we were on the train. You have been chosen for an assignment.'

'But what assignment? And when you say I've been chosen, who exactly by?'

She sighed but seemed to have forgotten his hard words. 'I don't know, James. You can decide not to believe me if you want to but they haven't told me.' She paused. 'You're being sent to East Berlin.'

The news came as a shock to Bond. He remembered

M briefing him at The Park – how long ago had that been? Stalnaya Ruka were planning '*something big, a single event that would completely smash the balance of power between East and West*'. Was it going to happen in East Berlin? Well, that was a big step forward – and one in the right direction. He was moving closer to the free world, brushing up against the very edge of the Iron Curtain. At the same time he wondered what could possibly be demanded of him in the capital of the so-called German Democratic Republic. And why him?

'When am I going?' he asked.

'Soon, I think.'

'Will you be coming with me?'

'I hope so.' She rolled over so that now she was on top of him, her knees straddling him. 'I don't want to talk anymore,' she said. 'I want you to make love to me again and then we will shower and have breakfast and after that we'll go out.'

'Whatever you say, Comrade Katya.' Bond reached out to her. 'But no more bloody museums.'

Meanwhile, just outside the Sadovo-Samotechnaya, the fourteen-lane ring road that encircled the old heart of Moscow and which had always been known to the staff of the British embassy as 'Sad Sam', Hal Garfinkel had also just woken up, in a luxury suite at the Hotel Leningradskaya. The real-estate magnate and union man could hardly believe his luck as he looked around the magnificent room still displaying the grubby souvenirs of a night he would remember for some time. First, there was the ice bucket with one empty champagne bottle lying beside it and another, still half full, jutting out of a pool of melted ice. From here, his eye travelled to the glass bowl of caviar (how much had he managed to get through?) with blinis and chopped onion, to the ashtray with three crushed cigar butts and the vanity mirror still loaded with half a dozen lines of cocaine. Clothes, crumpled and entangled, lay on the carpet where they had been thrown. And on the other side of the room, lying on the Louis XV giltwood and Aubusson tapestry sofa, the naked girl was still asleep. She had told him, in her broken English, that she was thirteen although he suspected that she was at least two years older. Once he had finished with her, he had kicked her out of his bed. Hal Garfinkel liked to sleep alone.

He was sixty, overweight with flesh that sagged around his neck and, unusually for an American, very bad teeth. Despite his power and his contacts back in Chicago, the only way he was going to get a girl like that was if he paid – but everything that he had enjoyed last night, including this room with its snazzy furniture and godawful wallpaper, had come free of charge with the compliments of the USSR. He had known from the moment he had been approached at the Tour d'Argent restaurant in Paris that this trip wasn't just about opportunities in real estate. That was the thing about the commies. They were as venal and as unprincipled as anyone in the world. What he admired about them was that they didn't care if you knew it.

Last night, just before dinner, the Kirilenko woman had told him the true purpose of the visit. The man who had called himself Mark Hazard but who had been identified as a British secret agent, James Bond, was here in Moscow! Garfinkel smiled at the thought of seeing him again. Quite apart from the raw terror of that final train journey on the Lucea–Green Island Harbour railway, with Leroy Gengerella getting his brains blown out right in front of him, that visit to Jamaica had cost him dear. The lawyer's fees and bribes paid to judges and contacts in the Justice Department had totalled almost half a million dollars. Otherwise, he'd be doing time in Sing Sing with Scaramanga's other associates. Sam Binion and Louie Paradise, for example. It would be a while before those two were playing with their grandchildren.

All he had to do was meet Bond and verify that he

was the same man who had been working as Scaramanga's assistant at the Thunderbird hotel. It would be easy. He had seen Bond several times at close quarters and had heard him talk. His hosts had assured him that he would be in no danger. A single nod of the head and it would all be over. Bond would be taken somewhere and shot. Perhaps they'd even let him pull the trigger.

The telephone rang, disturbing the girl on the sofa, who turned over and drew up her legs. Garfinkel answered it. 'Yes?'

'Mr Garfinkel?' He recognised the monotonous voice of Lieutenant General Irma Kirilenko. 'Have you slept well?'

'Yes, thank you.'

'We will be coming to your hotel in thirty minutes. It is a short drive to the destination.'

Garfinkel was about to answer back but the phone had already gone dead. Thirty minutes! He'd intended to have the girl again and then take a hot shower. Now it would have to be one or the other . . . unless, of course, he did both at the same time.

'Go into the bathroom,' he commanded. 'Wait for me there.'

The girl did as she was told. Garfinkel threw off the bedclothes to reveal his own naked form. Then he followed her in.

'**You still** haven't told me about England,' Katya said, drowsily.

'Let's not talk about that now . . .'

'I want to know.' She nudged him with her fist. 'You were going to tell me last night but you poured vodka into me instead.'

They were still in bed. Quite soon the kitchens would close and they would be too late for breakfast but neither of them was in any hurry. Katya was very calm. The passion of the night before had given way to a vulnerability and a softness that Bond had not seen in her before. Even so, her question worried him. Was she still testing him? How would a traitor, a recent convert to the cause of communism, answer her?

'Life is difficult in England,' he said, formulating his words carefully. 'I only learned that when I came here. For a start, there are millions of people in poverty. The workers spend their whole lives worrying if their wages will keep up with prices while at the same time the gap between the rich and the poor grows wider every year. If you walk down the streets of London, you'll see expensive cars and shops full of luxury goods. But the ordinary people can't afford them . . .'

'You're only telling me what you think I want to

hear,' Katya cut in. 'Explain to me why you love your country. Or do you dislike it so much now that you can't find anything good to say about it?'

'All right. If we accept that there are failings and, for the sake of argument, ignore them, there's plenty to admire, starting with the fact that Britain won the war against what looked like impossible odds, and until Stalin signed his mutual assistance treaty in July '41, we were alone. It was British inventiveness that defeated the Nazis: radar, chain command, the Spitfire, the bouncing bomb. It was British resilience that kept us going through the horrors of Norway, Dunkirk, the Blitz.

'Perhaps we look back too much but that doesn't mean we've stopped looking forward or slowed down. The Colossus computer, the world's first commercial jet liner, the first accurate atomic clock. Carbon fibre which is set to revolutionise manufacturing. Even these new desktop calculators. They've all been developed in Britain since the war.

'We are a beautiful country, as beautiful as anywhere in the world. Walk in Regent's Park after the grass has been cut. Drive through the orchards of Kent. Have lunch at the Ritz. Take a boat on the Thames on a summer afternoon. Go racing at Ascot or watch the cricket at Lord's. Play a round of golf at St George's. Listen to the protesters at Speakers' Corner. Tune in to the BBC. Until you have done these things you will have no idea what it is to be British.'

'Would I be happy if I lived there?'

'Are you happy here?'

'Of course.'

'If you were unhappy in England, you'd be allowed to say so.'

'I'd be happy if I was with you.' She stretched towards him and kissed him on the cheek. 'And now I need to get ready for breakfast. We have a busy day ahead.'

'I'm told the State Museum of Agricultural Development is interesting.'

'How did you know we had tickets?'

She slipped out of bed and he watched her as she crossed the room, picking up her clothes, seemingly unaware of her nakedness. She slipped into the dress she had worn the night before and went over to the door. 'We're going to have to hurry if we want breakfast,' she said.

'I'll see you down there.'

She opened the door and left.

Bond waited a few minutes after she had gone, then got out of bed himself and padded into the bathroom. The one good thing you could say about Russian hotels was that they had a plentiful supply of hot water, bursting out of the taps at high pressure.

Maybe that was something he should have added to his encomium to England: the truly dreadful plumbing. Standing with a towel around his waist, he shaved using the Mosshtamp safety razor with which he had been supplied. It resembled a miniature garden rake and treated his skin as if it were a spread of gravel that needed shifting. Then he got dressed and lit the first cigarette of the day.

There was a knock at the door.

Could it be Katya? Surely, she hadn't been gone long enough and anyway she had said she would meet him downstairs. Bond glanced at his watch. It was ten to nine. Room service? The black-stockinged chambermaids, coming to strip his bed? With no sense that he was in any danger, Bond crossed the room and opened the door.

Ten minutes earlier, Hal Garfinkel had arrived at the hotel in an official ZiL. There were two other passengers as well as the driver, KGB men, both armed. They had not introduced themselves by name and had viewed the American with quiet distaste. Lieutenant General Kirilenko had not come herself but had sent instructions which had been translated into broken English. The men would escort Garfinkel to Bond's room on the third floor of the Hotel National.

He would knock on the door and if he identified the occupant as Mark Hazard, the man who had worked as Scaramanga's assistant, he would nod and the two KGB men would take over. Bond was to be incapacitated and brought to the headquarters of the KGB in the Lubyanka Building for interrogation.

They entered the hotel and the receptionist nodded at them. Bond was in his room. With Garfinkel following behind, they took the stairs to the third floor and walked the short distance down the corridor. Garfinkel stepped forward and knocked. The door opened.

He found himself facing a slimly built man with a black comma of hair sweeping down over his eye. There was a scar on one side of his face. He was wearing black trousers and a loose-fitting jersey. He looked puzzled.

'Yes?'

'You're Mark Hazard. We met in Jamaica.'

Behind him, the two KGB men's hands slid towards their guns.

'No. I think you're mistaken.'

'You called yourself Mark Hazard but you're actually James Bond. You killed Scaramanga. You damn nearly killed me.'

'I'm afraid I don't know what you're talking about. My name is James Bond. But it's been a while since I

was in Jamaica. I've never heard of this man, Scaramanga, and I've never seen you before in my life.'

Garfinkel looked closer. At first, he had been sure
he was talking to the same man who had greeted him
at the Thunderbird hotel and who had organised the
drink and the dancers, but now he wasn't so sure. The
scar was wrong, for a start. It was too short and on
the wrong part of his face. This man had brown eyes.
He was much older than the assistant he'd met in Jamaica. He didn't even have the same voice.

He faltered. 'Hey – I'm really sorry. I heard you
were staying here and I thought we could catch up.
But I can see now that I'm mistaken. Forgive the
intrusion.'

'Not a problem.' The man closed the door.

Garfinkel turned to his escorts. 'Well, that was a
complete waste of time,' he declared. 'It's not him.'

Bond had heard the entire exchange from the bathroom where he had been standing with a gun pressed
against his neck. He was still reeling from the moment
he had opened the door and seen the *dezhurnaya*, the
woman who ruled over the soap and the bathplugs on
his corridor, aiming the same gun at him with a finger
on her lips, warning him to be silent. She had grabbed
him by the shoulder and led him into the bathroom

while a second man took his place. It was this other man who had spoken to Hal Garfinkel.

Now, finally, as the outer door closed, she lowered the gun and quickly busied herself, turning on the taps and the shower.

'Who was that?' Bond whispered, knowing that the rushing water would conceal the sound of his voice.

'His name is Hal Garfinkel. You met him in Jamaica. He was brought here to identify you. The man who spoke with him teaches English at Moscow University. He will leave in a minute. You do not need to worry about him. He is very reliable.'

For a moment, Bond wondered if he was back in the magic room. It was hard to make sense of any of this. The old woman with her butcher's arms and her lugubrious face spoke fluent English with a Russian accent. She was armed and knew what she was doing. It was clear that she had just saved his life. 'And who are you?' Bond demanded.

'My name is Margarita. I am to say that your friend, Mr Tanner, sends you his best regards.'

Mr Tanner. Bill Tanner. M's chief of staff. This was getting more extraordinary by the minute.

'We do not have much time,' Margarita went on, also keeping her voice low. 'I have been reporting on you since you arrived in Moscow. We have a covert listening device in the office of Lieutenant General Kirilenko and you were lucky that she was there at her desk when she gave the orders for Mr Garfinkel to be brought here from Paris. We worked out who he was and realised that he was being used to identify you.'

'So they suspect I'm lying to them. What's given me away?'

'I can't tell you that, although Kirilenko is aware that you followed Katya Leonova from this hotel to the building on Sretenka Street. That may have been enough to make them lose faith in you.'

Bond was annoyed with himself. He had taken every precaution leaving the hotel. The reception area had been empty and, as far as he could see, there had been no one looking out for him once he'd left. Yet still he had given himself away, following Katya unaware that he was being followed himself.

The *dezhurnaya* must have sensed his irritation. 'It is possible that they had contact with their Havana Central. It might just have been bad luck.'

'I still took an unnecessary risk.'

She ignored this. 'Do you have any information about Stalnaya Ruka?'

'Only that whatever they're planning, it looks like I'm going to be part of it. And any day now they're sending me to East Berlin.'

'I'm glad you told me. We'll keep an eye out for you.'

'It's good to know I'm not on my own.'

Bond heard the door of the room open and close as the man from Moscow University let himself out. Margarita glanced at him, then reached out to turn off the taps. Bond stopped her. 'Just tell me one thing,' he said. 'Who are you really? Why are you helping me?'

She looked at him without emotion. 'My grandson was a student in Budapest,' she said, simply. 'He was killed in the November uprising.'

The Hungarian Revolution of 1956. More than 2,500 people had been killed when Zhukov, the Russian defence minister, had sent in the troops.

'What I do now, I do for him.'

Bond nodded. Margarita silenced the taps and they left the bathroom together.

Katya Leonova was standing in the room, staring at them, her face white with shock. Bond saw that she had come through the communicating door to her own room, unlocking it from the other side. Perhaps she had intended to surprise him. How much had she heard? Margarita had not yet concealed her gun. There was no possible reason for her to be in his room. Whatever story Bond might come up with, it would do no good. He could see it in her eyes. She knew the truth.

17
Target Practice

'It seems that we were mistaken, Comrade Colonel.'

'So I understand, Comrade General. The American was quite certain that this was not the assistant he met in Jamaica?'

'Absolutely. He says that the man who called himself Mark Hazard was younger, with differently coloured eyes and a lower voice. There was a passing resemblance but nothing more.'

'I assume the matter is closed then. The American has returned to Paris?'

'Unfortunately not. Apparently, he suffered a massive heart attack in the car on the way to the airport and did not survive the journey.' There was a pause in which many things were left unsaid. 'Comrade

Lieutenant General Kirilenko did not approve of him. She said that he was debauched.'

'She could have given him to me for reprogramming.'

'She preferred a more immediate response.'

The conversation between Colonel Boris and General Grubozaboyschikov took place that same morning. The two men had met at Uspensky Cathedral, converted into a museum after the revolution. They were sitting side by side on a bench, beneath a sixteenth-century fresco of the Last Supper, and it might have been said that, with his long, fair hair and complete composure, Colonel Boris could quite easily have joined the disciples at the table. But neither of the two men had the slightest interest in their surroundings. Nor, when they spoke, did they look at each other. To anyone watching, they would seem to be strangers; two visitors, stopping for a rest.

'I assume, then, that the operation is going ahead as planned,' Colonel Boris said.

General G nodded. 'Yes. Three days from now it will all be over and we will be living in a new Russia. You have the candidate?'

'Yes. Bond is being brought to me this afternoon. I will assess his capabilities and report back to you.'

'Good.' There was something else. General G was uncomfortable. 'I'm afraid that, despite everything,

Comrade Lieutenant General Kirilenko still has her doubts,' he said.

For the first time, Colonel Boris allowed his irritation to show. 'She thinks that Bond is counterfeiting, that he has managed to trick me? I told you when we last met, Comrade General, that is inconceivable. What evidence does she have now?'

'There is still the question of his unauthorised departure from the hotel.'

'He followed my assistant.'

'He spied on her. You should also be aware that the two of them have now become lovers.'

'She is only doing as I instructed her.' Colonel Boris was undisturbed. 'The best way to get into a man's inner thoughts is to have an intimate relationship with him. Bond will be able to hide nothing from her.'

'And you trust her?'

'Completely.'

General G shifted in his seat. He looked Colonel Boris in the eye. 'Look, this is very awkward,' he said, his voice catching in his throat. 'I have – and always have had – total faith in your judgement. But Comrade Kirilenko still needs to be persuaded. She has suggested we give Bond one last test before he leaves Moscow. A killing.' He took out an envelope and handed it across. 'If Bond were prepared to kill one of his own, an extremely effective and highly regarded intelligence agent currently attached to the British embassy here in Moscow, for example, that would be a clear demonstration of where his loyalties lay and I'm sure it would be more than enough for Lieutenant General Kirilenko.'

Colonel Boris opened the envelope and read the two pages of typewritten notes he had been given. After a short silence, he nodded. 'Yes,' he said. 'I can see that this will work very well.'

'You have no concerns?'

'None at all. You want me to explain to him what must be done?'

'That would be simplest.'

'Then that is how we will proceed.' Colonel Boris folded away the notes and stood up. 'It seems to me that Lieutenant General Kirilenko has an unnecessarily suspicious nature,' he said, looking away into the distance. 'When this operation is accomplished, you perhaps might allow me to adjust it.'

General G frowned. 'I don't see why not.'

He stood up. The two men went their separate ways.

Katya Leonova had not spoken since they had left the hotel. She and Bond were now crossing the Moscow

River on the Krymsky Bridge on their way to Gorky Park. One of Stalin's monolithic towers blocked out the sky behind them, a crouching beast of brickwork and glass that watched their every move. Ahead, Bond could see boathouses and pavilions that appeared more welcoming. The sun had gone in and the river was a murky grey.

She stopped, halfway across. 'I always knew,' she said.

'What did you know, Katya?' Bond pressed on hurriedly. 'You shouldn't jump to conclusions. What happened this morning at the hotel . . . There's a simple explanation.'

She held up a hand. 'Please don't lie to me, James. You've had plenty of time to invent some elaborate fantasy but you'll just make it worse.' She looked out over the water. 'I deal with the patients of Colonel Boris all the time. You can tell when he's finished with them because they've lost something. They may smile at you, laugh at your jokes, argue with you or break down in your arms but there's always something missing. It's as if something of their identity has been taken away.

'Even in Leningrad, in the magic room, you weren't like that. I knew you were different but I persuaded myself that you weren't lying to me because I liked you. But I was wrong, wasn't I. All the time you've been pretending.'

'Not all the time.'

'Last night?'

'Katya, you're a beautiful girl and last night happened because we both wanted it to. It had nothing to do with Colonel Boris or anyone in the world except for you and me. This is a nasty business we both find ourselves in. But let us at least cling on to the good parts. You could have had me arrested before we even left the hotel so I'm hoping that you understand that the feelings between us are real and neither of us wants to hurt the other.'

'So tell me, then. Did you kill M? Why did you come back to Russia? And why was that woman – the one pretending to be a *dezhurnaya* – what was she doing in your room?'

They had come to the crux. Bond had wondered if Katya would ask him directly what he was doing in Moscow and as they had walked from the hotel, he had been trying to work out how to respond. He had thought he might deny everything and throw a few Marxist platitudes her way but she had already made it clear that wouldn't work. As far as he could see, he had no choice but to tell her the truth. And what then? If he believed she was going to run off to Colonel Boris, he would have to kill her. It wouldn't be so difficult. One hand on her head, the other caressing her chin, then the sudden twist that would break her neck. She wouldn't feel anything. If anyone saw, he would say she had fainted.

Could he do that? Would he?

'I tried to kill M,' he said. 'But that was quite a few months ago and I didn't succeed. I was treated at a hospital outside London, a place called The Park, and everything that Colonel Boris had done to me was reversed. After that, I was sent to Jamaica, to deal with a man called Scaramanga. It was my way of proving myself.

'M's funeral was faked and I was sent back to Russia because it turns out that Colonel Boris is involved with a group called Stalnaya Ruka. They're planning an event that could change the balance of world power. My job is to find out what it is and, if I can, prevent it. That's the long and the short of it, Katya. I didn't expect to spend time with you and I certainly didn't expect to fall in love with you, certainly not after what you helped do to me.'

She turned round and, to his surprise, Bond saw that she was on the edge of tears.

'I didn't want to do that,' she exclaimed. 'Not to you, not to any of them. I never asked to work at the

Institute. I was drawn into it. You don't understand how much power Colonel Boris has – over me and everyone around him. He's the devil!' The first tear drew a line down her cheek. 'He has no heart at all. He will destroy any human being for his own pleasure, just because he can. He made his assistant, Ilya, jump out of a window and kill himself. There was another boy, called Sergei, who drank petrol and lit a match. And Dmitry . . .'

'He knew Dmitry?'

'It was his hospital where Dmitry was sent. He made the rules. I couldn't help any of them, just as I couldn't help you.'

'And now . . . ?' This was what Bond had been hoping to hear.

'I won't tell him what I know. I promise you. I don't care if you're the enemy because when I think about what we've done . . . maybe we deserve enemies like you.' She took out a handkerchief and wiped her eyes. 'I've heard the name but otherwise I know almost nothing about Stalnaya Ruka. Colonel Boris has often talked to me about the authority of the Communist Party and how it should be more dominant. He told me he was going to change history. He didn't say anything more than that but maybe I can help you if you'll let me. He trusts me. Maybe he'll tell me more.'

She paused, her eyes brightening. 'He said that he was sending you to East Berlin and I gave you that information even though I shouldn't have. And I can reassure him that everything's all right, that you're still under his control. But there's something I want in return.'

'What's that, Katya?'

'I want you to take me with you when you leave. I want to do all those things that you talked about. Walk in Regent's Park and go racing at Ascot. I want to go to pubs and shopping and all the other things you didn't talk about. All of it! I hate what this country has done to me and what it did to Dmitry. Why should I live somewhere that only makes me want to die?'

'You want to defect?'

'No. I just want to be with you.'

Bond let out a low whistle. 'Well, I'm not sure how we'll arrange it but I'll talk to my people as soon as I'm in East Berlin. Do you know when we're leaving?'

'Very soon. I'm to take you to Colonel Boris this afternoon. He's not in the city. He wants you to come to the woods just outside.'

'Do you know why?'

'I'm sorry . . .'

'Well, I doubt he's inviting me to a picnic.' Bond drew her into his arms. 'Of course I'll take you with me, Katya. My country's not perfect. I never said it was. But I can't wait to show it to you. I know you're going to love it.'

'Just be careful, James. Colonel Boris will see right through you. Those eyes of his! There are parts of Russia where they say that his condition – heterochromia iridum – is the sign of black magic. They believe that one eye has been taken away and replaced by a witch. That's how he is.' She clung to him. 'Don't let him hurt you.'

'I'm not afraid of Colonel Boris. Not any more.' He kissed her lightly on the cheek. 'How do we get to these woods?'

'They're sending a car to the hotel.'

'Then let's head back and find out what he wants.'

The official car had driven Bond and Katya deep into the Khimki Forest, to the north-west of Moscow. With the sun just beginning to set and the whole area empty, the forest had an ancient feel, a sense of permanence. They were following a rough track through hundreds of twisted oak trees beneath a canopy of leaves so thick and vibrant that the very air had turned green, and although it had only taken them thirty minutes to get here, Bond could easily have believed that they had lost themselves completely in the great sprawl of the Russian countryside. And yet, he wondered how long it would all survive. Sheremetyevo International Airport was close by and even as they rolled forward, the silence was shattered by the roar of an Ilyushin turboprop airliner coming in to land. With a fast-growing airport on one side and the open arms of a city on the other, the forest, for all its natural beauty and antiquity, would surely one day become extinct.

Colonel Boris was waiting for them in a clearing with the sparkling water of the Moscow Canal just visible on the other side of the undergrowth. There were three men with him. They had set up a table and, about a hundred yards away, a series of targets had been arranged along the branches of a tree. These ranged from a couple of bottles to an apple to an egg and even a bronze three-kopeks coin, hanging on a thread. A semi-automatic sniper rifle lay on the table. Bond recognised the very latest gas-operated Dragunov SVD. Paired with a PSO-1 scope boasting ×4 magnification, stadiometric rangefinder and infrared detector, the completed assembly was probably the most sophisticated weapon in the world.

'Good evening, Comrade James.' Colonel Boris was wearing a loose-hanging coat and an ivory-coloured tight turtleneck jersey. Bond found himself examining his eyes, the blue one and the grey one and, remembering what Katya had said, wondered which one of them was original and which had been replaced by the witch. 'How are you? How have you been enjoying Moscow?'

'It is a wonderful city, Comrade Colonel. Comrade Katya has been looking after me very well.'

'So I understand.' Was there something lewd in his eyes as he glanced at Katya, an awareness of what had passed between them? 'You have been comfortable at the hotel?'

'You have been more than generous to me.'

'I hope you've been behaving yourself.'

'Not all the time, Comrade Colonel.' Bond paused, as if unsure of himself. 'There is something I need to report to you.' He twisted like a schoolboy in front of the headmaster. 'I regret to say that I left the hotel without permission. Comrade Katya knew nothing of this. I disobeyed her instructions and followed her.'

'And why did you do that?'

'I don't quite know, Comrade Colonel. I suppose I was wondering where she was going. It was wrong of me. I'm ashamed.'

'Do you know where she went?'

'To an office building. A clinic, perhaps. I didn't ask.'

Colonel Boris seemed amused. Bond hoped that he would report back to Lieutenant General Kirilenko that his patient had made a full confession, unprompted, and had suitably demeaned himself. 'Well, I think we can forget about that,' he said. He gestured at the table. 'Are you familiar with this weapon?'

'It's a sniper's rifle,' Bond replied. 'Developed by Yevgeny Dragunov, a superb engineer. We have nothing like it in Britain.'

'Have you ever fired one?'

'No, Comrade Colonel.'

'Would you like to?'

'May I?'

Bond picked up the rifle. He noted that the box magazine was already loaded with ten full-power 7.62 × 54 mm bullets sitting in the usual zigzag pattern. For a brief moment he wondered what would happen if he turned the gun on Colonel Boris and shot him and his three men there and then. Might that bring an end to whatever Stalnaya Ruka were planning? It was very tempting. The world would be considerably improved without the presence of the colonel and it would also give him great personal satisfaction. But he couldn't do it. There was too much risk involved and anyway he hadn't been sent all this way just for personal revenge.

He balanced the rifle in his hands, admiring the skeletonised stock and carefully trimmed-down barrel, both designed to save weight. For once, there would be no faking his admiration for Russian technology.

It was a beautiful weapon, accurate to a fraction over one minute of angle at a hundred yards. A real killer's delight.

Was that to be his job for Stalnaya Ruka? A simple assassination?

'Begin with the bottle,' Colonel Boris suggested.

It was the largest of the targets but it was still very small, so far in the distance. All the objects looked a little bizarre, suspended above the ground as if left behind after a schoolboys' picnic. Bond attached the magazine, then lay on his stomach on the soft earth, supporting the rifle with one hand, the stock pressed against his chest. He sighted the bottle on the other side of the clearing, aimed, fired . . .

. . . and missed.

He suspected that Colonel Boris might have done it on purpose, adjusting the telescopic sight to undermine his confidence. Either that, or the Dragunov aimed too low. Bond made the necessary adjustment and fired again. He smiled with satisfaction as the bottle was blown apart.

'The next bottle,' Colonel Boris instructed.

Bond fired two bullets in succession, removing the neck and then exploding the rest of it. Without being asked, he shredded the apple, vaporised the egg and finally sent the coin spinning into the canal.

The Dragunov rested comfortably in his hands. There had been almost no kickback. He had felt the lethal machinery enjoying its work. He glanced out of the corner of his eye and saw Katya standing a distance away, her face solemn. It occurred to him that they were on the same side now, both playing their parts, and that although Colonel Boris had demonstrated he could control minds it was fortunate that he could not read them.

'I see you've lost none of your skills,' Colonel Boris remarked.

Bond stood up. 'So who do you want me to kill?' he asked. He laid the gun back onto the table. 'It's not going to be you, you grinning maniac. At least, not today.' These last words were in his head but he left them unspoken.

'We do have a target for you, Comrade James.' Colonel Boris snapped his fingers and two of his men came running forward with folding chairs which they set up on the forest floor.

'Is Comrade Katya going to come with me?' Bond asked, hopefully. 'She has been very kind to me.'

'You will see her later.' Colonel Boris gestured as they both sat down. It was as if they were about to have a picnic together rather than arrange a man's death. 'As I told you when we were in Leningrad, I have an assignment for you,' he continued. 'It is a *konspiratsia* of the gravest importance and you have a vital role to play.' He paused. 'Unfortunately, there are those amongst my associates who have their doubts about you. They have asked for some proof of your loyalty both to me and to your new home.'

'I will do anything you ask of me, Comrade Colonel.'

'That's what I hoped you'd say.' He allowed his eyes to rest on Bond's. 'Have you heard of Zephyr?'

At once Bond's nerves were taut. This was what he had been dreading. He had already given away a lot of what he knew to Colonel Boris the first time they had encountered each other, before he was sent to kill M. He had been unable to help himself and his only consolation had been that most of the information was already out of date. To be interrogated now, however, when he was in full command of his senses, was another matter. If he lied, Colonel Boris would know. If he told the truth, who could say how much harm he might do?

'I know the name,' he admitted.

'The code name, you mean.'

'Yes.'

'And his true identity?'

'He is one of the cultural attachés at the British embassy. At least, that's his cover. He is actually an SIS officer and one of their most respected operatives.'

'Have you met him?'

'No, Comrade Colonel.'

'Would you recognise him?'

'I'm afraid not, Comrade Colonel.'

It was true. Bond had never seen the man who called himself Zephyr but he still knew him by reputation. It is said that intelligence officers abroad are either hunters or farmers, which is to say they recruit new talent – possible informers and defectors – or they manage them, working as their handlers. Zephyr had been supremely successful in both roles. He had managed to create a spy ring that extended to Leningrad and Kiev, at the same time filtering out the KGB plants and double agents who had been sent to unmask him and to infiltrate his organisation.

'I think it's fair to say that Zephyr is the greatest threat to Russian security at this present time,' Colonel Boris continued. 'We have long wished for his elimination. And now it seems that an opportunity has presented itself.' The two disparate eyes examined Bond as if from different perspectives. 'We have managed to intercept a message and know, with certainty, that Zephyr will be in Moscow tonight at one o'clock. He is meeting a new recruit to his network of bandits and negative elements in the main hall of the Komsomolskaya metro station, next to the Koltsevaya line. The metro station is currently closed for repairs – some of the mosaic work is being restored – but a service door at the far end, opposite the Yaroslavsky railway station, will be unlocked to allow entrance.

'Zephyr has not yet met the man he hopes to corrupt and turn against his country. The name of this traitor is Vadim Ivanov and he is employed in the NKVD, the People's Commissariat for Internal Affairs. You will take his place and this is what you will do – and you must follow these instructions to the letter. Do you understand?' Colonel Boris didn't wait for a reply. 'You will be driven to the metro station shortly before one o'clock. You will be supplied with a semi-automatic pistol. You will locate the door and walk down to the platform where Zephyr will be waiting. He may greet you and ask your name. However, you will not speak to him. You will simply shoot him in the heart. Do you understand these instructions, Comrade? I am being quite specific. A single bullet into the heart. Then you will leave the same way that you came. The car will be waiting to take you back to your hotel.'

'I have one question,' Bond said.

'You may ask it.'

'What has happened to the man that Zephyr is supposed to be meeting, Vadim Ivanov?'

'We have arrested him. He is being interrogated prior to his execution.'

Bond nodded. 'That makes it safer for me.'

Colonel Boris examined him curiously. Bond could feel the calculations going on behind the eyes. 'You have no hesitation in killing one of your own countrymen?' he asked.

'I killed several of my own countrymen before I came back to Russia, including my superior officer.'

'That's true. But this man is of great value to your former employers.'

'That only makes it more important, then, that he should die.'

'Exactly.'

Colonel Boris stood up. Respectfully, Bond did the same. 'My driver will take you now. This test was not of my devising but I have every confidence that you'll pass with flying colours. Remember what I've said. If you utter so much as one word it will be considered that you have failed and I cannot answer for the consequences. Otherwise . . . good luck!'

'Thank you, Comrade Colonel.'

'Goodnight, Comrade James.'

18

Death Beneath the Chandeliers

The nights are never kind to Moscow. With nowhere to go, the traffic disappears and the streets seem to parade themselves, mile upon mile of empty concrete glinting uselessly in the flare of the sodium lights. The great monuments and buildings, no matter how proud of themselves in the day, stand there like old men in the darkness, their windows black, their doors bolted fast. No lovers meet. No revellers make their way home from jazz clubs or restaurants. The best you will hope to see are clusters of soldiers or policemen, muttering to themselves as they make their presence known because the population needs to be watched and guarded even when everyone is asleep. Otherwise, nothing moves. The entire city takes on the psychopathy of the graveyard; pleased with itself because it will be there for ever, unaware that it is actually already dead.

It had begun to rain as Bond got out of the back of the ZiL, a thin drizzle driving in from the east. It clung to every surface, giving the pavements an oily sheen. Bond could feel it seeping into his cheaply made trousers and jersey, chilling his skin. Water trickled down the side of his face. There was a driver and a security man in the front of the car but neither of them intended to leave their seats. The security man wound down the window and handed Bond a gun. Bond recognised the square, all-steel body of a 9 mm Pistolet Makarov, or PM as it was always known to the Soviet police and military who had been using it since the fifties. From the weight, he could tell that there were eight bullets slotted into the magazine with its fast-heel release. It was an old-fashioned but reliable weapon, fine for close quarters. He slid it into his trouser pocket.

A single bullet into the heart. That was what Colonel Boris had said. There was to be no conversation. Bond was simply to walk up to a man who was waiting for a contact he had never met and kill him. The reward would be entrance to Stalnaya Ruka and the opportunity to put an end to whatever they were planning. He would be extracted from East Berlin and he would go home. Mission accomplished.

But could he do it?

Quite apart from his huge operational value, Zephyr was attached to the embassy, working at the same level as himself. He would have friends and colleagues, perhaps a wife and children. How would Bond live with himself if he murdered an innocent man simply to protect himself? There was no saying it would even work. This whole thing could be another one of Colonel Boris's tests designed to look into Bond's mind, and even if he passed the test, he could find himself discarded, sent back to Leningrad. It might have been their plan all along. One British agent kills another in a Moscow metro station. There's a public outcry, an international scandal. A whole operation is exposed and subsequently shut down. Bond is executed. Suddenly he could feel the sweat mingling with the rain on his forehead. He was in a potentially disastrous situation. The consequences could be unimaginable.

A single bullet.

The man in the passenger seat was glaring at him. Bond turned and walked across a wide, empty space towards Komsomolskaya metro which stood there in front of him, more like a museum or a temple than a stop on a subway system. Six pillars with elaborate mouldings held up a great slab of marble or concrete with the name of the station carved in Cyrillic text. A succession of glass and wooden doors, firmly sealed, stretched out behind. Bond continued round the side, feeling very exposed in the wide space. He found what he was looking for some distance down, at the back: a single, ordinary-sized door, open, with the dull glow of an electric light behind.

This was clearly not an entrance that the public ever used. It led into a service corridor with crates partly concealed by dust covers, paint pots and stepladders stacked up against a wall. The air smelled of metal and cheap disinfectant. A series of doors, all of them closed and placed at exact intervals, stretched out ahead. Bond could feel the weight of the gun pressing against his thigh and took it out again, checking that the safety lever was disengaged. As he walked, he felt the floor vibrating beneath his feet and heard the rumble of a passing train. Dust danced in the air. The station might be closed but it seemed that at least part of the Koltsevaya line was still in operation. He waited until the train had gone past, then listened carefully. As far as he could tell, the area was deserted . . . but why would there be anyone around at one o'clock in the morning?

He continued on his way. The walls were painted an unpleasant shade of green with dozens of pipes and multicoloured cables, strapped in place, running in parallel lines. He could sense the grime all around him. He felt it on his fingers and he smelled it too. Naked light bulbs hung above his head so that as he walked forward, his shadow leapt ahead of him, then retreated. Perhaps it knew something he didn't. One of the doors was open and he looked into a drab kitchen with a table and half a dozen chairs, an ancient sink, a kettle, an assortment of mugs. There were various sheets of paper – safety instructions and duty rosters perhaps – pinned onto a cork board. The corridor opened out and now he saw a flight of steps leading down. Colonel Boris hadn't given him directions but this had to be the right way. It was an underground station. He headed underground.

The further down he went, the darker it became. There were no electric lights shining and although Bond was briefly tempted by a bank of switches at the foot of the stairs, he couldn't risk turning them on. Ahead of him he could make out another door, with a strip of light bleeding through beneath. He continued towards it, found the handle and pressed down. The door opened. Bond passed through.

He was in a hallway of some sort, with a second

door, half-open, ahead of him. The light he had seen was coming from here. He had the Makarov in one hand. He pushed the door fully open with the other. He knew immediately where he was. He had passed through this station many times when he was last in Moscow. Only the Russians could have built a subway system so beautiful that it would become a tourist destination in itself, and Komsomolskaya was one of its most precious jewels.

The platform – which looked more like a hallway in an impossible French chateau – continued for such a distance that if it had been above ground a plane might have landed here. There was a series of colonnades on either side, behind which the two train tracks ran in opposite directions, along outer walls of honey-coloured marble. A series of huge glass and metal chandeliers ran the full length of the station, the light from the artificial candles reflected in the polished floor. A pure white bust of Lenin, carved in alabaster, stood at the end where Bond had entered and the great man seemed to be gazing at the architecture as if in approval. He was framed by a massive archway, its architrave made up of twisting golden leaves with a hammer and sickle at the centre. There were decorations everywhere, the vaulted ceiling interrupted by elaborate panels that contained intricate mosaics made up of thousands of tiny tiles. Halfway down, some scaffolding towers had been erected where the artwork was being repaired. But there were no workmen here now. As far as Bond could see, he was alone.

No. At the very far end, a man was sitting on what looked like a wooden, folding chair. He must have seen Bond come into the station but he didn't make any move. It had to be Zephyr. Bond slipped the gun back into his pocket and began to walk at an even pace towards him, following the line of colonnades, trapped between the two railway lines. No other trains had appeared. Perhaps the service had finally shut down for the night. He could hear his feet measuring out his progress. Even walking at a reasonable pace, it would take him a minute or two to reach the end.

Gradually, Zephyr came into sight. He was wearing a suit and a tie with pink and blue stripes which Bond recognised as the colours of the Garrick Club in London. He was sitting with one leg crossed over the other and his hands folded in front of him as if the station doubled as his private office and meeting here in the middle of the night was the most natural thing in the world. Now Bond could make out his features. He was in his thirties, with carefully groomed hair, an aquiline nose and a thinly drawn beard; the appearance of a man who looked after himself. About twenty yards separated them. The man was in no hurry to make a move. He waited for Bond to arrive.

Bond had already decided what he was going to do. There was no easy way out of this. All he could do was choose the least dangerous option and if the result was his own extinction, at least he would have some consolation, knowing that he hadn't caused too much harm.

Another ten steps. He stopped in front of Zephyr.

'Vadim Ivanov?' Zephyr asked.

'Yes.' With that single word, Bond had disobeyed Colonel Boris's instructions and committed himself to the course of action he had decided upon. 'You're Zephyr?'

'That's right.' The man from the embassy had a deep, cultivated voice. He chose his words carefully. 'You wished to see me.'

The moment had come. Bond committed himself. 'I've come here to warn you,' he said. 'The Russians know who you are and what you're doing here in Moscow. They've sent me to kill you. If I'd done what they told me to, you would already be dead.'

Zephyr unfolded his legs. His hands fell to his sides. 'You are not Ivanov,' he said. 'Who are you?'

'My name is James Bond, 007. I'm an agent with

the secret service. We have very little time. I need you to trust me and to do everything I tell you. Your life, and mine, depends on it.'

'Go on.'

'You cannot be seen leaving this station. You cannot be seen again until you hear from my superiors in London. I will tell the Russians that I shot you and that I concealed your body . . .' Bond looked around him. '. . . inside the tunnel. As far as I can tell, this whole thing could be over in forty-eight hours. Whatever happens, you're no longer safe in Russia. You have to lie low for a while and then get out at the first opportunity. I'm sure there are diplomatic channels or whatever that can achieve that. Do you understand?'

'Yes.'

'You'll tell no one about this meeting?'

'Of course not.'

'Then that's it. I'm leaving now.'

'Thank you, Mr Bond. And good luck with what it is you're doing.'

Bond nodded. He had done everything he could; saving Zephyr, protecting himself and not endangering his mission. He turned and walked away.

It was the chandeliers that shouted out their warning. They were placed in such a way that, just then, his shadow was stretched out in front of him and, happening to glance down, he saw the second shadow closing in, rapidly, from behind. He twisted round, instinctively crouching low, shifting into the combat stance, just in time to glimpse a silver blur of metal scythe through the air, inches from where his neck should have been. It was a Russian army knife, lethal, with a vicious razor-edged blade tapering to a clip point. It was being held by the man who had identified himself as Zephyr.

But already Bond knew that he had been tricked. The Garrick Club tie should have been enough to alert him. It was typical of the KGB mindset, that they should think that a British cultural attaché should belong to an expensive club. And the Garrick of all places! A talking shop for old actors and writers. Playing back the conversation, he remembered how slowly and carefully the man had spoken to him, disguising any traces of his Russian accent. And that construction of his. 'Good luck with what it is you're doing.' Not 'whatever'. His English was good but not that good.

Bond had doomed himself the moment he had opened his mouth and but for a stroke of luck, a trick of the light, he would already be dead. He leapt back, every sense alert. In just a few seconds, everything about 'Zephyr' had changed. His face was contorted into something between a snarl and a smile. His hair had come loose, a thick strand hanging over eyes which gleamed with pleasure. He was standing with his legs apart, balancing on the balls of his feet, his every movement fluid. Bond could see that he was facing a professional who had been thoroughly trained, who not only knew what he was doing but who was supremely confident in the outcome of the next few seconds. This was a man who had killed many times.

Bond still had the gun. He drew it from his pocket and fired the single shot that would have finished this already if he hadn't been so bloody cautious. He couldn't miss. The two of them were just a few feet apart and, perhaps out of deference to Colonel Boris, he had aimed for the heart. The sound of the detonation echoed in every direction. Bond smelled cordite. It should have been over but it wasn't. It took him a few precious seconds to process what he was seeing. Zephyr was unhurt. He was smiling. He lashed out a second time. Bond jerked back but not fast enough. The edge of the blade slashed across his arm. At the same time, Zephyr swivelled round on one foot and, using the other, delivered a turning kick that crashed into his chest, hurtling him backwards. He lost his grip on the gun, which flew out of his hand and slid across the platform, disappearing underneath the nearest archway.

It was useless anyway and had been from the start. The bullets were blanks. He should have already guessed. This whole thing had been set up. Walk in, fire, prove that he was what he said he was, make the appropriate apologies and leave. It could have been so easy. Instead, Bond was alone and unarmed, facing a professional assassin who presumably had orders to execute him the moment he revealed he was an agent working for the British.

Bond clasped hold of his arm, allowing the blood to seep through his fingers. He wasn't badly hurt but it wouldn't do any harm to convince his opponent otherwise. At the same time, he dredged through his memory for anything that might help him. He had been trained in close-quarter combat when he was in Naval Intelligence and had read the manuals written by Major W. E. Fairbairn, who had created his own fighting system – Defendu – as well as helping to design one of the deadliest fighting knives used by the British special forces during the war. What first came to mind was not helpful. '*In close-quarters fighting there is no more deadly weapon than the knife – and the unarmed man has no defence.*'

Zephyr was waiting for him to make his move, knowing that he didn't have one. The Russian was still smiling, utterly confident.

'Twenty thousand dollars, paid into any account in the world. I can arrange it.' Bond spoke the words, knowing that they weren't true and wouldn't be believed. But he was buying time and that cost nothing at all.

Zephyr answered him in Russian, not even pretending any more. Half a dozen words. Bond understood only the contempt.

A knife fight is all about distance. Bond and the Russian were still sizing each other up. The further away Bond kept himself, the more time he would have to react to any move. He kept his eyes on the other man's hands. That was also in the manual. Hands were signposts. They would warn him what was coming.

The Russian tried another jab, the blade spitting towards his chest. Bond sprang back then twisted away as the follow-through narrowly missed the edge of his shoulder. He was running out of time. One mistake was all it would take and the longer this went on, the more likely that was to happen.

'*There is no fair play, no rules except one: kill or be killed.*' Again, the words from twenty years ago came into his head. This wasn't a duel. It wasn't even a fight. It was a killing and Bond had to do anything in his power to prevent it. He couldn't run. The moment he turned his back, he would lose any tiny advantage he still had. What then? Throw dirt, gravel, coins, whatever was in his pocket. Distract the other man just long enough to disarm him. That was what he had been taught.

Still pivoting, moving all the time, Bond took stock of his surroundings. The chandeliers cast their golden light on the killing ground. It was hopeless. Apart from the gun – about fifteen feet away, close to the edge of the platform – there were no weapons, no loose pieces of scaffolding, no tools left behind by the builders that he might have been able to use. He was horribly exposed in a wide, empty space with nothing to help him. The Russian knew it too. He lashed out twice more, the point of the knife pricking Bond's shirt above his chest, drawing a thin line of blood.

Bond made his move. During the last encounter, with his eyes fixed on Zephyr's, he had been easing off one of his shoes. It helped that the shoe was a poor fit, loose and cumbersome. His heel had come free and as the Russian closed in again, he kicked out, not even trying to make contact. The idea was that the shoe would come loose and hit the other man in the face, giving Bond the vital few seconds he needed to move in and end this. With a sense of shock, he saw that it hadn't worked. Zephyr had either seen what Bond was doing or he had expected it. He batted away the shoe with his left hand and let out a brief, guttural sound that was, unmistakably, laughter.

That was it. Bond had nothing left.

Unless . . .

He looked left and right, allowing fear and defeat to show themselves for the first time in his eyes. He seemed to notice the Makarov – as if he had forgotten it was there. Perhaps it had misfired. Perhaps he had somehow missed. Neither of these two things were possible but they were the thoughts that he was now communicating. If he could just get hold of the gun once more, he could make good. Bond seemed to come to a decision, one born of despair. He launched himself across the platform, throwing himself to the ground and reaching out to grab the weapon with one hand. The Russian had seen the move and was already coming after him. Bond twisted onto his back. The Russian stood over him. As far as he was concerned, the British agent had acted like a simpleton. He had gambled everything on possession of the Makarov, still not realising that it was useless to him. He was lying on his back. He had no more moves to make.

Zephyr dropped down, positioning himself perfectly for the kill. If his weapon of choice had been a gun, he could have finished it there and then but the knife demanded closer contact. His knee slammed into

Bond's stomach, forcing the breath out of him. The knife came slanting down towards his throat. Bond reached up with his left hand, catching hold of the Russian's wrist. He knew it was going to be over very soon. He was winded. The Russian was heavier than him and gravity was against him. Inch by inch, the blade edged down. It had a journey of just six or seven inches before it would cut into Bond's larynx. Victory danced in Zephyr's eyes.

Inch by deadly inch, the tip of the knife drew nearer. Zephyr was pressing down with all his weight, his eyes ablaze, enjoying these last few moments. There was nothing more the British agent could do. He had foolishly thrown away any advantage he might have had, going for a gun that he didn't realise was useless to him, with seven blank bullets in the magazine. He pushed harder. Bond knew that he couldn't hold back the knife for more than a few seconds. The strength was draining out of his arm. At the same time he heard a distant rumbling coming from the tunnel somewhere behind him as another train approached, rushing out of the darkness like his own death. The Russian grunted with exertion. This was it. This was the moment. Bond stretched out with the gun and pulled the trigger.

A bullet is a fairly simple device although the name

is misleading. A gun is actually loaded with a cartridge which consists of a metallic case filled with gunpowder with a primer at the bottom and a piece of metal – the bullet – lodged in the top. The firing pin hits the primer. The powder ignites. And the explosion of gas forces the bullet to fly out with extraordinary force. If the gun being used is a Makarov, it will travel at a speed of approximately 1,000 feet a second, and this is what will kill you.

A blank cartridge has no bullet. The end of the metal casing will be blocked with a wodge of paper or cotton. There will still be an explosion. But – as Bond had seen for himself just a moment ago – there will be no projectile, nothing to incapacitate the target.

But that doesn't mean that a blank cartridge is harmless.

Bond had been holding the Makarov so close to the Russian's face that the tip of the muzzle was almost touching his nose. When he fired, the gas exploded out, blasting up his nostril and into his brain. That in itself might have been enough to kill him. Bond saw the shock in the Russian's eyes as his consciousness was blown away. The hand with the knife went limp. But Bond only had this one opportunity. He wasn't going to leave anything to chance. As the train burst into the station, the soft thunder becoming a roar, he crossed his wrists, forming a defensive barrier, then curled his feet into the Russian's stomach, lifting him up over his head and throwing him in a limp somersault onto the line. He didn't see what happened next. He was aware only of a series of flashing lights, a streak of brightly coloured metal, the rush of wind and then a horrible metallic screaming. The driver had seen what had happened or perhaps he had felt the impact and had pulled the emergency brake. But he had not acted quickly enough. The train plunged into the tunnel, carried forward by its own velocity, and Bond found himself alone on the platform with the red tail lamps in the far distance, glaring at him from the darkness.

A few minutes later, with his shoe back on, his injured arm cradled across his chest and with the look of a beaten dog, Bond made his way back out into the open air. The rain had eased off but the roads and the pavements were glistening beneath a sheen of water too thin to reach the drains. The car that had brought him here was still waiting, the two men sitting in the front, but Colonel Boris had also chosen to make an appearance, presumably to check that everything had gone according to plan. He was standing in the car's headlights, his coat flapping around him.

He saw Bond and frowned. Bond realised that he should have walked out with the man who called himself Zephyr, the two of them having a good laugh together, by now the best of friends. Either that, or he should have been dead.

'What happened?' Colonel Boris demanded.

Bond answered with humility. 'I did exactly what you told me, Comrade Colonel,' he explained. He held out the Makarov, gripping it with just two fingers so there could be no threat. 'I met Zephyr and shot him in the heart.'

'And?'

'I'm very sorry to have to inform you that the gun misfired. I couldn't possibly have missed at that range so I can only assume the weapon was faulty.'

'So what did you do?'

'There's no need to worry, Comrade Colonel. I took care of it. I threw Zephyr under a train.'

Colonel Boris stood there, staring. Bond nodded politely and limped towards the car.

19

The Inhuman Element

Katya was horrified by Bond's injury. The knife wound wasn't deep but in the twenty-minute car journey from Komsomolskaya the blood had seeped through his shirt sleeve, and by the time he arrived in her arms he looked like a casualty of war. The driver had not taken him to the Hotel National but to the edge of Moscow, back to Serebryany Bor, not far from where he and Katya had walked just two days before. It was Katya's surprise for their last night in the city. She had prepared a light supper with vodka and more caviar, even though it was two o'clock in the morning. There was a fire burning in the brick stove, casting a glow across the room and fighting off the chill of the post-midnight hours. The dacha was traditional, fashioned out of wooden boards and almost a perfect triangle in shape, dominated by a roof that slanted down on both sides. It was tucked away in the pine trees, reached by a rough track with no signposts. Add a covering of snow and it would have reminded Bond of the chalets he had stayed in as a child at Chamonix . . . not that that place had many happy memories for him. It was where his parents had died.

She had bathed and disinfected the wound, which ran almost six inches from his elbow down to his wrist. Bond wondered if it would create yet another scar to add to the collection his body had amassed over the years. He really was a walking encyclopaedia of injury. After they had eaten and drunk a little, she had taken him to a bedroom at the very top of the house and made love to him carefully, finally curling herself into him on his 'good' side and lying there with her head on the pillow next to him.

'Promise you won't leave me behind,' she whispered.

Bond stirred uneasily. 'Should we be talking here?' he asked.

'I brought us here because we can talk without being overheard.' She drew closer to him. 'I've had enough of my life. I want it to be over.'

'What do you mean?'

'I mean – this life. I told you, when I was a girl, I

never wanted any of this. I'm not a wicked person, James. Do you believe me?'

'Of course.'

'I will change my name. In England I shall call myself Kate Leonard. I will never speak my mother tongue again. I shall become a housewife and I will look after the man I am married to.' She smiled, drowsily. 'I know it won't be you, James. You don't have to worry. I'm not going to pretend that anything between us would ever be permanent. I know it's not in your nature. You have to keep moving and fighting the enemy. Because that's what you do. There isn't a woman on this planet who could ever satisfy you. But I hope we'll stay friends. You will come and visit me and we'll remember our Moscow nights and we will never talk about them to anyone else. They'll be our secret . . .'

She fell asleep.

But Bond stayed awake for a long time, watching as a million black pine needles took shape against the slowly brightening sky. He was thinking about what Katya had said and about everything he had observed since he had arrived in Russia.

On at least three occasions, Bond had seriously considered leaving the secret service. He had actually written a resignation letter to M although that had been occasioned by a sense of boredom and futility and, wisely, he had never sent it. He had thought he was going to be fired just before he was sent to Japan and had welcomed it. And a long time ago, at the nursing home at Royale, there had been a conversation with René Mathis, his friend from the Deuxième Bureau. After everything he'd been through with Le Chiffre, Bond couldn't see the point of going on but Mathis had mocked him. *'Don't let me down and become human yourself.'* Bond had often remembered the parting words that had been thrown at him that day. He thought about them now. What had Mathis been saying? That his line of work had infected him with some sort of inhuman element which meant he could never be satisfied by ordinary life but that instead he would have to spend the rest of his days racing around the planet, chasing monsters, until the inevitable bullet finally rewarded him with its own definition of peace?

It was a depressing thought, made worse by his time in Moscow and Leningrad. Everything he had seen – even Katya with her lost opportunities – had brought home to him the impossibility of the task he had set himself. Evil in this country wasn't just a group of men talking in a room – Smersh or Stalnaya Ruka. It wasn't one madman hanging out in Crab Key or another planning to steal all the gold from Fort Knox. It was a huge machine, a sickness that had corroded itself into the souls of a hundred million people and at the end of the day they were the only ones who would ever be able to rid themselves of it.

Bond still had complete faith in M, in the secret service and in the rightness of what they were doing. But lying there in the dacha watching the light making its way in through the double-height windows, he found himself once again questioning his part in it all. The criminals and conspirators he had been fighting against all his life were becoming superannuated as time moved on, and another decade, younger and brasher than any that had gone before, imposed itself. Things had seemed so much simpler in the years immediately following the war. And secret agents, the men and women supposedly on the side of 'good', were becoming more ambiguous. Bond might have a licence to kill but that wasn't the same as an absolute right.

Was this the time to get out once and for all? Could he imagine climbing out of bed in the morning without a fresh cut running halfway down his arm and a bullet wound still throbbing in his stomach? There had to be a life where he could walk down a street without wondering if he had placed himself in a sniper's sights. Surely, he could find a job that would pay him enough to support his, admittedly, extravagant lifestyle and which wouldn't bore him to death. Perhaps that was what it came down to. What he called *acidie* . . . that sense of living on the edge of a world that was forever out of his reach.

Bond needed death, or the threat of death, as a constant companion. For him, it was the only way to live.

That same morning, in his Moscow apartment, Colonel Boris sat down and typed a short letter to General Grubozaboyschikov on paper stamped with the address of the Institute in Leningrad. A messenger with a motorbike waited outside to deliver it.

He knew that it was dangerous to commit himself to a written communication. When this operation was over, it would still exist. For the rest of his life it could be used to incriminate him. But even if he had been given the general's home telephone number, it would have been unthinkable to speak to him over an open line. For his own security, Colonel Boris had to inform the other members of Stalnaya Ruka of what had taken place. He would choose his words carefully – and the fewer of them the better – but he was quite sure that there was no other way.

Dear Comrade General Grubozaboyschikov,
   I must inform you of events that took place
at Komsomolskaya metro station in Moscow

last night. You will recall that, in the light of Comrade Lieutenant General Kirilenko's suspicions, we had agreed that one more test was required before the British agent, James Bond, could be considered worthy of our trust. Although Bond had demonstrated to my own complete satisfaction that he was suited to the task at hand, I was content to go along with your, and the committee's, decision. I was quite certain that he would succeed with this final assignation, the murder of a supposed British agent known as Zephyr.

Bond did succeed. But not in the manner we had expected.

The man he met at Komsomolskaya was not, in fact, Zephyr but Ivan Aranov, the very agent we had chosen for the operation in East Berlin and who Bond had, unknowingly, replaced. I believed Aranov to be an excellent choice for this test. He had spent two years in London and spoke first-class English. His instructions were simple. He was to allow Bond to shoot him with an automatic pistol which would in fact be loaded with blank cartridges. But if Bond broke faith, if he spoke even one word, then Aranov would eliminate him. It seemed that we could not lose, whatever the outcome. If Bond did as he had been ordered, if he proved that he was prepared to kill one of his own, then we would know he could be trusted. If he failed, then he would die and Aranov would once again take over the assignment.

Comrade General, before I explain what occurred, may I say that Bond was always, for me, the superior candidate of the two. I personally witnessed his marksmanship which is remarkable whereas Aranov was never entirely comfortable with firearms (as evidenced by his decision to carry a knife into Komsomolskaya metro). Moreover, the one remaining instance of Bond's possible untrustworthiness, his decision to leave his Moscow hotel without authorisation, was resolved when, with no compulsion, he made a full confession of what he had done to me. A citizen who is prepared to denounce even himself is a citizen to be valued above all others and I remain convinced that we have found the perfect weapon in Bond.

Furthermore, we have what might be termed an insurance policy. I referred, at our last committee meeting, to a trigger planted deep in Bond's consciousness. As I demonstrated with the deviant Ilya Platonov who threw himself to his death, there can be no resistance once this trigger has been activated. Bond will obey me. He has no choice.

And now to the matter at hand.

Bond did meet Aranov. As instructed, he attempted to shoot him in the heart with the 9 mm pistol with which he had been supplied. It was at this point that I regret our plans took an unexpected turn. In the belief that the gun was faulty, and unaware of our true aims, Bond attacked Aranov and killed him with his bare hands. Aranov was thrown beneath a train. My people removed what was left of his body.

Comrade General, although like you I regret the loss of a good man, I must impress upon you that as far as Bond is concerned, he has killed a highly regarded British agent and the fact that he did not hesitate, that – on the contrary – he proceeded to kill his opponent in such a ferocious manner, only emphasises his suitability for the task ahead.

It is therefore with complete confidence that I suggest to you that Bond is flown to Schönefeld this morning as agreed and that the operation which has been so many months in the planning should proceed without further delay.

Sincerely,

Colonel Boris

Bond woke up late.

He slipped out of bed, leaving Katya asleep, and tiptoed downstairs, wondering if there would be any coffee in the kitchen. As he went, he took in his surroundings, wondering if this was the dacha which she had talked about on their first day together in Moscow and which had been given to her family by a grateful nation. It was larger inside than he had expected, solid rooms filled with solid furniture. The dark wood floors, the bookshelves with their leather-bound volumes and the thick curtains with their over-elaborate valances seemed to suck out much of the light. For what was supposed to be a holiday home, it was surprisingly gloomy.

A creaking staircase had led him into the main

living room with a grand piano standing in the corner. It was a Becker, made in Russia. Bond went over to it and gently pressed a few of the keys. It was in tune. So who played? Somehow, he couldn't see Katya there, hammering out Tchaikovsky and Rimsky-Korsakov (there was sheet music with compositions by both of them). As the question entered his mind, it occurred to Bond that there was something strange about the room. There were no photographs on display: not one. Russians place a huge importance on family life and keeping a record of past generations is second nature to them. If this was a family dacha, Bond would expect to see framed portraits of parents, grandparents, great-grandparents, aunts and cousins on every shelf and yet the top of the Becker was completely bare. He looked more closely at the polished mahogany lid of the piano and saw that there had been pictures there. The cut-out slots were visible in the dust. So they had been deliberately removed before he came here. Why?

Bond hadn't intended to pry but suddenly he had to know the answer. He glanced at the bookshelves, the nesting tables, the drinks cabinet. He peered inside a maritime chest that turned out to be storing old blankets. Finally, his eye fell on a wooden armoire, painted with leaves and flowers. A brass key with a velvet tassel protruded from the lock. Bond opened the door

290 · ANTHONY HOROWITZ

and saw at once that he had found what he was looking for. There were at least a dozen photographs stacked up inside, one on top of another, face down. Uneasily, he began to go through them. First came the grandparents, then a bunch of children – they were probably adults now – in sailor suits. He found a picture of Katya, looking stiff and awkward, holding some sort of diploma. So he was right about the dacha. It belonged to her family. Next came a photograph of a younger Katya with an Alsatian dog. Each photograph was heavily framed, almost like a church icon.

The last photograph, surrounded by dark red leather, told him everything he needed to know and much more. Looking at the image, he felt a sickness in his stomach like nothing he had ever experienced. He wished now he had never come here. He wished he had not opened the armoire.

'James . . . ?' Katya had come down the stairs in her bed clothes. She had seen what he was doing. She knew what he knew.

Bond turned round, holding the photograph of Katya, aged about seventeen and looking innocent in a summer dress, standing on a beach, holding hands with Colonel Boris in white trousers and long-sleeved shirt. In the picture, there was even a family resemblance between them. Bond looked from the image to her.

Perhaps it was what she had been doing in the last years that had changed her or perhaps it was what had been done to her. But she no longer looked like her father.

'Colonel Boris . . .' Bond couldn't finish the sentence. The words refused to leave his throat. 'Why didn't you tell me?' he asked.

'I couldn't.' She looked terrified. Did she think he was going to kill her? At that moment, Bond could quite easily have done so. 'I wanted to. But I didn't want you to think . . .'

'What? Think what exactly, Katya?'

'Please, James. Don't be angry with me.'

'Angry?' He wasn't. He was too disgusted – with her and with himself. 'He's your father!'

'Yes. But it's not the way you think it is. He never treats me like a daughter. I work for him. We're always formal when we're together. I hate him! He killed my mother. She was so unhappy living with him, she killed herself. And ever since then, he's used me. He doesn't care anything about me. He doesn't care about anyone!'

'Does he know we're here?'

'He knows everything.'

'He arranged everything. Even those people who attacked you on the train! They were working for him. They made enough noise to make sure they woke me up and the whole idea was that I would rush in and rescue you. The aim was to bring us closer together. Did you know about that?'

'No.'

'I don't believe you, Katya. You did everything he told you.'

The last time he had accused her, she had denied it. Now she looked ashamed. 'It was what he wanted. Yes. He had to be sure about you and he thought if we were close . . .' She drew a breath. 'But I didn't sleep with you because it was what he wanted. I love you, James.'

'Like you loved Dmitry?' Right then, Bond didn't care how much he hurt her. 'So when do you hand me over to the colonel to have my brains fried in his lunatic asylum like your last boyfriend? I take it that's the plan.'

'No! How can you say that!' She stared at him, her eyes wide. 'I know the truth about you!' she gasped eventually. 'I saw you with the *dezhurnaya* in your room. I know the reason why you're here. If I told my father you'd be shot. You'd already have been shot.'

Bond threw the photograph towards the sofa. It missed and hit the floor, the glass splintering. He moved towards her, his face a mask of cold fury. He reached out and grabbed hold of her, one hand closing around her throat. 'Listen to me, Katya,' he snarled. 'If you tell them what you know, you'll be dead too. You've known about me for three days but you've said nothing. You want to defect! You denounce me and I'll do the same to you and we'll both end up in different wards of the same hospital . . .'

'I'd never do that!'

'You can't do that. You're in this up to your neck, just like me. But this is what's going to happen. I'm going to East Berlin. I'm going to find out what Daddy and his friends are planning. I'm going to stop them. And then, somehow, I'm going home.

'You can come with me. I promised you that and I won't go back on my word. But the moment we set foot in the West, you'll never see me again. You can become "Kate Leonard" and live in the Home Counties and marry a stockbroker and play bridge and forget all about this hellish country of yours. But you can forget me too.' His hands were tightening. Katya struggled for breath. 'Your father almost destroyed me and you helped him do it. And every time I look at you, I will think of him and as far as I'm concerned, no matter what you say, you're as bad as each other. Not just bad. Unspeakable! So that's the arrangement. Take it or leave it.'

Bond heard the sound of an engine. The black ZiL

had drawn up in front of the house. As he watched, its doors opened and two men got out. They were the same two men who had brought him here.

'Well?' he demanded.

'You're wrong about me.' She was crying now. She was still wearing her nightgown. Her hair had come loose. The tears were streaming down her face. She looked a wreck but Bond's only thought was that the two men couldn't see her like this. 'I've put my entire life in your hands,' she said. 'I thought you understood. Nothing I've ever done has been my choice. But I chose you.'

'Do we have an agreement?'

There was a knocking at the door.

'Yes! I'll say nothing. I promise. I'll go with you.'

'Not with me, Katya. No. That's over. Now go upstairs and get dressed. I'll let them in.'

'James, please . . .'

'Do as you're told, for God's sake. Or do you want to get us both killed?'

Katya sobbed. She took one look at Bond then went back to the stairs. Bond waited until she had gone, then walked over to the door.

PART THREE

Berlin Symphony

20

General Malevolence

Airports around the world are much the same but some are worse than others and East Berlin's Schönefeld was the very worst of all.

The Ilyushin IL-18V turboprop airliner that had brought Bond from Moscow didn't so much land as fall out of the swirling cloud and rain so that the last few minutes of the flight became a grim funfair ride with most of the passengers clutching their armrests in fear. It amused Bond that the thickset security man who had accompanied him from Sheremetyevo was more scared than any of them. He hadn't spoken a word throughout the entire journey but at the last moment, as the almost invisible runway stretched out to receive them, he muttered a silent prayer. The wheels hit the surface and the spray exploded outwards in white clouds, obliterating the windows and the body of the plane. The engines screamed out in reverse thrust. The curtain of water fell back. And then, suddenly, they were slowing down with the lights of the terminal on one side and release just minutes away.

Bond and his attendant were the first to leave the cabin. They'd been sitting at the very front . . . not that Interflug, the national airline of East Germany, offered anything that resembled first class. In fact, Bond would remember the flight for the most uncomfortable seats, the worst food and the most unfriendly air hostesses he had ever encountered. All the crew (including the pilots) would be staunch communists, of course, chosen more for their ideology than their charm or competence. The German Democratic Republic would not risk putting anyone in the air if there was the remotest chance of their deciding not to come back. Freedom was just the other side of a wall. Trains, cars and lorries had all been used to break through but planes were the most obvious choice.

Bond had glimpsed the twisting grey line of the Berlin Wall as they circled over the city; the single cruellest act of an utterly heartless regime, imprisoning two million people, separating families, carelessly destroying lives. The irony was, of course, that it was also communism's greatest failure, a physical testimony to the inadequacies of the system it was trying to protect. It had been built to stop people – thousands of them – leaving for a better life. Well, Colonel Boris had done him a favour bringing him here. As he stepped onto the tarmac, Bond reflected that he was barely an hour's drive from the West German border. The only trouble was, he was on the wrong side.

They walked across to the main terminal, a long, narrow building made of white concrete and glass. Glancing up, Bond saw the silhouetted figures of soldiers patrolling the roof, machine guns over their shoulders, their long coats being whipped up by the wind. He passed the inevitable statue, this one a concrete piece of nastiness with rockets (yes, the Russians had been the first into space) sketched out in bas-relief, shooting across its surface with a clenched fist above. Ahead of him, posters displayed the names of airlines he had never flown and hopefully never would: Lot, Air Cubana, Tarom. The rain was lashing into his face. After only a short walk, he was already drenched.

And then they were inside the grim, utilitarian air terminal surrounded by huddles of people queuing for their flights or waiting while scowling desk clerks examined their paperwork. The scene reminded Bond that he had no ID papers himself. But as they approached the passport control and another unsmiling official making the most of his kingdom of two square feet, his minder produced a sheaf of letters and documents, stamped and signed, and after a brief exchange in German, they were waved through.

They had no luggage. They continued towards the street which was barely visible on the other side of a bank of glass doors and windows with the rain still streaming down. The security man held the door open and Bond passed through, colliding with another passenger who had been entering. For a moment the two of them were almost chest to chest. Bond saw small eyes, ginger hair, a blotchy face twisted in anger. '*Arschkeks verfluchter!*' The swear words were spat at him and then the man had gone.

Bond smiled at his handler. 'Welcome to East Berlin,' he muttered.

The Russian ignored him.

An ugly car – a white Trabant Universal – was waiting by the pavement. Bond climbed into the back while the Russian sat next to the driver. The seats were hard. The car itself, manufactured from recycled cotton waste and resin, was a dustbin on wheels. Bond sat back and looked out of the window as they set off across what was left of the city.

About half of it had been destroyed during the war as part of the *Strafe*, the greatest act of revenge ever meted out to an enemy population. West Berlin had been restored with remarkable speed but the East lagged far behind, with death and chaos hanging heavily on the air. Bond gazed at the meagre and sham-looking streets. As they continued on their way, he saw a smattering of new buildings that had been put up with typical Russian bad taste and workmanship but it seemed to him that there were whole blocks, acres and acres, that needed knocking down, with shattered brickwork and useless, sprouting wires. Round every corner they came upon great piles of rubble – *Monte Klamotten* as they were called. Rubbish mountains. Everything was asphalt. There was no colour to be seen. It was the middle of the afternoon but the street lamps were already on, fighting uselessly against the shadows and the rain.

As in Moscow, the traffic was sparse and after half an hour they pulled up outside the ruins of a building on Wilhelmstrasse, three storeys high, its brickwork scoured by bullet holes. To his surprise, Bond knew where he was. He had been to Berlin before the war and he had stayed at the Hotel Adlon, famous for its opulence, the first choice for Hollywood film stars and world politicians. Bond remembered the restaurants, the coffee houses, the smoking rooms, the barber's shop with its black and white tiled floor and elaborate brass mouldings, the quartet playing Strauss in the great lobby with its marble columns and potted plants. The hotel had survived the war but there had been a fire in 1945 and this sad, forgotten ruin was all that remained. Was it even open for business? The driver had got out of the car and was urging him to move. Glad to be out of the rain, Bond followed him inside.

The building was a ghost, empty and silent. Bond had come in through what looked like an old staff entrance and he allowed himself to be escorted down a corridor to a double door which opened into what must have once been a ballroom. A few rags of silk wallpaper clung to the walls. A chandelier that had partly collapsed in on itself hung awkwardly from the ceiling. The polished wooden floor was now covered with dust. A trestle table had been set up in the middle of the room, with a man sitting behind it. Bond recognised the bald head and the unhealthy features immediately and knew that he had arrived at the heart of Stalnaya Ruka.

General Grubozaboyschikov. Formerly of Smersh. Now chief executive of Stalnaya Ruka. The reason he was here.

Grubozaboyschikov had two men standing behind him, thugs in suits. Bond had no doubt that they would be armed. The general himself looked up from the

documents he had been reading and examined Bond
with bleak, hostile eyes.

'James Bond,' he said.

Bond walked forward and stood in front of the
table, his arms behind his back.

'Do you know who I am?' the general asked.

'Yes, of course, Comrade General.'

'I don't suppose you ever thought we would meet.'
The voice, rattling in the old man's throat, sounded
more diseased than ever.

'It's a great privilege to meet you, Comrade General,' Bond said. He was careful to display no emotion,
simply uttering the words he was expected to say.

'Is it?' General G was unconvinced. 'You have
caused me a great deal of annoyance, Mr Bond. More
than you could ever believe and it would give me pleasure, enormous pleasure, to kill you right now, where
you stand. I would like to do it slowly and painfully. I
am not by nature a violent or a sadistic man but where
you are concerned, I believe I might surprise myself.'

He stood up and walked round the table.

'As it is, you have been chosen for a higher cause and
it seems I must restrain myself. There is work to be
done just a few hours from now. It will change Russia
very much for the better and restore to the motherland the power that has been seeping away from us for

so long. I suppose we can both reflect on the strange irony that has made you the perfect weapon for this event.'

'I am sorry for my past misdemeanours, Comrade General.' Bond struggled for the right words as he tried to dissect what General G had just said. 'Colonel Boris demonstrated to me – forcefully – how I had been deceived by my capitalist paymasters and I am ashamed. Anything I can do to make amends for my actions in the past, I will do without hesitation. I will give you my life if you ask for it.'

'It may well cost you exactly that.'

Bond looked down. He said nothing.

General G stood opposite him, a short distance away, carefully examining the man who had been his nemesis for so many years. 'I have chosen to come here personally,' he began, 'to explain to you, in detail, what must be done tonight. I have maps and diagrams which you must memorise and which will be destroyed after you leave.' He pointed to a bulky Kometa-201 tape recorder, squatting on his desk among the papers. 'We will listen to music together. Do you like Beethoven? It is of no importance. All that matters is the timing, which must be precise. A great deal of thought has gone into this operation, Mr Bond, and it is indeed a quirk of fate that the final moments will all depend on you. Tonight you are going to kill the man who stands in the way of everything that will make this country strong. You are used to killing. It has been your livelihood. But the man in Seat 12 is no ordinary target. Tonight, you are changing history.

'However, before we can discuss the details of what you must do, there is one small piece of business between us which you might like to think of as a final test of your loyalty and subservience. That is how you may see it but, I will confess, for me it is far, far more. It is something I have looked forward to for a long, long time and which, in my darker moments, I have even dreamed about. You will permit me this self-indulgence. I think I have earned it.'

Word by word, General G had brought himself to the point of no return. His voice had not risen in pitch but there could be no mistaking the ugliness, the sheer malevolence that coursed through him and lent him strength. Suddenly, without warning, he lashed out with a single foot. Bond was standing with his legs slightly apart and received the full force of the kick between his legs. General G was wearing heavy black boots which he had chosen deliberately. He was in his seventies but this single act of violence had ten years of suffering behind it and his aim was horribly accurate. Taken by surprise, Bond lurched forward, all

the breath punched out of his body, the blood draining from his face. Almost any other man would have
collapsed to the ground but Bond was superbly fit
and after all the attacks that had been made on him
through his lifetime, his threshold of pain was remarkably high. He stood where he was, gasping for breath,
but still standing.

General G stared at him as if baffled that he was
still on his feet. Then he kicked Bond in exactly the
same place a second time. Bond could have taken eva-
sive action. He could have blocked the attack. But he
knew that it was out of the question, that he had no
choice but to take the full force of the old man's rage
until, one way or another, it was over. The foot made
contact with the soft *wumph* of leather against flesh
and Bond cried out, his whole body contorting. His
breath burned in his throat. Despite the coolness of
the room, sweat poured down his face.

A third blow was enough. It landed with perfect
precision in the softest part of his body and this time
Bond crashed down, retching and gasping as he twisted
on the floor. Still he did not speak. Nor did he make
any move as General Grubozaboyschikov took another
step forward and leaned down over him. Bond wasn't
even sure he would have had the strength for any coun-
termeasure right then. His stomach was heaving. He

groaned and spat out blood. He must have bitten his tongue. His face, streaked with sweat, lay in the dust.

The general smiled, satisfied with what he had done.

'You are a strong, healthy man, Mr Bond,' he exclaimed. 'In two or three hours you will have recovered and this will be no more than a painful memory – though one, I hope you will agree, you have deserved.'

Bond grunted, inarticulate.

'I would have done more. I would have taken a knife to you. But you have to be in the right physical shape for the task that lies ahead.'

He took one last look at his victim. Then he leaned down and spat full into his face. The saliva splattered over Bond's nose and cheek but he didn't try to wipe it away.

General G straightened up. 'Take him away and allow him to clean himself up,' he commanded. 'When he is ready, bring him back to me.'

The two men picked Bond up under the arms and dragged him across the floor and out of the ruined ballroom. Bond was aware of the walls of the corridor sweeping past on the other side of a red mist of pain. His heart was pounding. It was almost impossible to catch breath. About halfway along, they came to an open door which led into a bathroom with a cracked basin and a filthy toilet missing its lid. One of the men turned on a tap and brown, brackish water spluttered. He muttered something in Russian. The other man laughed.

It took Bond several minutes to find the strength to stand up. He washed himself as best he could and examined his face in the speckled glass of the mirror. One of the men rapped at the door and barked out a command, again in Russian. Bond steadied himself and felt in his pocket for the slip of paper that he had been carrying ever since he had left the airport. It had been pressed into his hand by the ginger-haired man who had collided with him and sworn at him. A perfect piece of spy craft. The brush contact. Bond realised that a whole team of East Berliners must have been waiting for him ever since they had known he was being brought to their city. The information would have been passed on to them by the *dezhurnaya*, Margarita, in Moscow. There was an address, written in capitals: 28B ALBRECHT-DÜRER-STRASSE.

That was where they would be waiting for him. His way out.

Bond tore the paper into tiny pieces and scattered them inside the cistern of the toilet, fully aware that he would have been unable to flush them away. They disappeared into an inch of rusty water. Then he straightened his shirt, ran a hand through his hair, and went to his final meeting with General G.

21

The Man in Seat 12

The Berlin State Opera was everything a nineteenth-century opera house should be: grand, stately, aloof and utterly disconnected from the world around it. There were no barbed-wire fences here, no machine guns, no Stasi interrogation cells. Bond had only been to an opera once and that had been when he was following a Norwegian double agent in Paris in the early fifties. He'd had to sit through three hours of tedium, watching a lascivious but incompetent duke trying to bed his valet's fiancée on the night before their wedding, and it had been enough to persuade him never to return. The Berlin State Opera had been bombed not once but twice during the war, and the second time it had been almost destroyed. Bond was glad that the Allied pilots evidently shared his view.

At least there was to be no singing tonight. The auditorium was hosting a concert by the Berlin Symphony Orchestra with works by Russian and German composers including Beethoven, Tchaikovsky and Rimsky-Korsakov. They were starting with one of the greatest classics of all time: Beethoven's Fifth Symphony.

The opera house, a massive, pink temple to the arts with Greek columns and Prussian statues that had somehow found their way here from the Napoleonic wars, was only five minutes on foot from the Hotel Adlon. After Bond had been given his full briefing by General Grubozaboyschikov, he had changed into the suit that had been provided for him and, accompanied by one of the Russian minders, had walked down the most famous boulevard in Berlin: Unter den Linden. At seven o'clock in the evening, it was almost empty with just a handful of drab, makeshift shops. The new lime trees were skimpy and stark.

The rain had eased a little but still fell in a dreary, grey streak, splattering into the puddles that had formed in the many potholes. Bond was grateful for the bad weather. The audience, closing in on the State Opera, was in a hurry, packing together to get into the building as soon as they could. Many of the spectators were carrying umbrellas. Others were bunched up, their faces half-concealed by hats, scarves or the lapels of their coats. There were guards and soldiers all around the entrance but any sort of identification would be almost impossible – and as far as Bond could see, no one was asking for ID cards.

He had a ticket for the last row in the third, and highest, tier in this 1,300-seat auditorium. It would get him into the building but he would have to listen to very little of the concert. He had been told that the bullet had to be fired exactly four minutes and forty seconds into the first movement of the symphony. General G had been very precise, playing him the opening several times on his tape recorder so that Bond could recognise the separate passages. It just depended on what tempo the conductor chose for tonight's performance.

They reached the three main doors that led into the opera house. This was the moment when Bond would part company from his Russian attendant. Theoretically, as soon as he was inside, he could make his way out of one of the fire doors and disappear, but there was still one piece of information he needed. He knew that his target was the man in Seat 12. He had been shown photographs that revealed the exact position of his target. But he still didn't know who it was. If he returned to England without finding out, he would have achieved precisely nothing. There was every chance that Stalnaya Ruka would simply wait a few months and try again.

'Good luck.' The Russian had not said a word to him since his arrival at the hotel. Now he muttered the two words with a ponderous accent and not much sincerity.

'*Spasibo, tovarich,*' Bond replied, cheerfully.

He took out his ticket and went in, moving slowly. He was still breathless from the beating he had received. Even so, the general had either been too old to hurt him very much or he had been careful to restrain himself. Bond had not been disabled. He could walk without limping. He could aim and shoot.

It was only once he was in the entrance hall that he became aware of the heightened security. There were uniformed soldiers at every doorway, at the intersection of every corridor, at the bottom and top of every stairway. But they were largely ceremonial. More sinister were the obvious KGB men, tense and uncomfortable, standing blank-faced, their eyes dissecting the crowd. They couldn't have looked more out of place. It was as if the gorillas had been let out of the zoo. He examined the audience. There were plenty of men wearing medals making their way to their seats. But the most important visitors didn't need to advertise themselves. Bond could tell who they were simply by the way they walked, imperiously, arm in arm with their wives, expecting the crowd to separate and let them pass. These were the bigwigs from the Communist Party and the security services with tickets and doubtless an invitation to interval champagne, care of the state.

There was a clock on the wall showing twenty past seven, ten minutes until the concert began. Bond knew exactly where he was going and when he had to be there. He showed his ticket to an attendant and was nodded through to the main staircase. He began to climb up.

A bell chimed, warning the rest of the audience that the concert would soon begin. Bond made slow progress with the crush of people ahead of him but once he had passed the entrance to the stalls he was able to move faster. By the time he had reached the top tier, he noticed that the carpets had become thinner and the wallpaper drabber and it amused him that even in this socialist paradise, they still had to let you know when you had reached the cheaper seats.

He arrived at the top floor of the building and, taking advantage of a gap in the crowd, glanced through one of the open doorways into the huge horseshoe of the auditorium itself. It was a formidable sight. In front of him, and far below, the orchestra was beginning to assemble on the stage: the female players in cocktail dresses, the men in black tie. Already a few of them were tuning up, the woodwinds and the strings fighting each other across the elongated space. About half the audience – 700 people – had already taken their seats but Bond noticed an area in the first circle, diagonally opposite to where he was standing, which was conspicuous by its emptiness. He counted along until he came to Seat 12. Yes. It was exactly where General G had shown him.

He looked up. The entire ceiling was dominated by a splendid cupola, apparently modelled on an eighteenth-century palace in Potsdam. There were eight segments, with a massive chandelier hanging from the centre. The chandelier was surrounded by portholes which offered views to every section of the auditorium. General G had described this too.

More audience members were brushing past him and, with a rueful smile, as if he had forgotten something, Bond made his way along the outer corridor with its benches covered in red plush. He followed it to the end where a series of windows, set low in the wall and reaching almost to the floor, looked out over a badly bomb-damaged cathedral just opposite. St Hedwig's. The second of these windows was un-locked as he had been told it would be. Bond waited until another bell rang out and the remaining audience surged through the doors. Nobody was looking his way. Quickly, he opened the window and, shutting it behind him, stepped out into the rain.

He was at the very back of the opera house with a pink wall rising about ten feet above him. He had been warned that there would be more guards stationed on the roof and, peering round the corner, he spotted them immediately: two young men in the far distance, huddled together, wet and miserable. They couldn't possibly see him from where they were and it seemed that they couldn't be bothered to patrol. Presumably, they were waiting for the music to start so that they could leave and Bond only wished he could do the same. Quickly, he found what he was looking for. A drainpipe ran the short distance to the next roof, the highest point of the Berlin State Opera building. Bond climbed up. This was the moment when he would be most visible from the street, although the clothes he was wearing were slate grey, the same colour as the surface. Hopefully, with the rain still falling, he would blend in.

There were four access panels built into this final, slanting roof. All of them had been shut tight with brand-new padlocks. Bond drew out the key he had been given, inserted it in the nearest lock and turned it. There was a click and it sprang open. The lock had been well oiled. He glanced over his shoulder one last time, then swung the hatch open and levered himself in. At once, he heard the orchestra, tuning up. The sound, louder now, was coming from several openings in the floor, directly below. Bond was standing in a wide, empty expanse, between the ceiling of the auditorium and the roof, with so little space between the two surfaces that he was forced to crouch. A series of chains stretched upwards, connected to metal stanchions. There was a sunken area in the middle of the floor with eight portholes. This was where the light and the sound of the instruments were coming from. The largest chain ran through the centre.

Bond knew that he was standing exactly above the chandelier which was suspended beneath him. He had already noticed the portholes when he had glanced into the auditorium. He could see the entire audience from up here. But nobody could see him.

He edged forward, uncertain that the floor would bear his weight. But presumably technicians came up here. If the chandelier ever needed repairing, this was where they would gain access. He reached the edge of the sunken area with its ring of portholes and lowered himself onto his stomach. Reaching down, he found the wooden box which he had been told would be waiting for him. It was invisible below the lip, concealed beneath a piece of dark tarpaulin. He became aware that the orchestra had stopped tuning. Everything was suddenly very silent. He pulled off the tarpaulin and opened the box. Inside, he saw the Dragunov semiautomatic sniper rifle that he had used in the forest outside Moscow . . . or one that was identical to it. He knew that it was already loaded. This time, the scope would have been perfectly adjusted. He heaved the weapon towards him and took his position, his legs stretched out behind him, the barrel of the rifle slanting down towards one of the portholes. In the auditorium, the lights dimmed and went out.

A swell of applause spread through the audience as the conductor, silver-haired and dressed in black tie, entered the stage area and walked in front of the orchestra. Bond watched him through the scope, unable to prevent himself admiring the Soviet engineering. Even at this distance he could see the man's heavy eyebrows, the slight indentation above his lip. The conductor shook hands with the lead violinist then took his place on his podium. But he did not raise his baton to begin the concert yet. He was waiting for someone and a minute later they appeared, another burst of applause sounding out, louder and more sustained, echoing in every corner of the auditorium. The conductor turned and bowed; not accepting the applause for himself but acknowledging the man at whom it was directed.

Tilting the Dragunov, Bond followed his eye-line up towards the first tier and settled the scope on Seat 12 . . .

. . . as Nikita Khrushchev, First Secretary of the Communist Party of the Soviet Union, Chairman of the Council of Ministers, successor to Stalin and the most powerful man in Russia, raised a hand to the audience. The guest of honour had arrived.

22

The Finger on the Trigger

Khrushchev sat down. The audience settled itself. The conductor raised his hands – and moments later, the symphony began. Was there anyone in the world who had not heard those first thunderous chords and who would not recognise them instantly? For Bond, who had little knowledge of classical music, they were intimately connected with his work during the war. Short-short-short-long. In Morse code, this is the letter V and, starting in 1940, the BBC had played the opening notes of the symphony before all its European broadcasts. V for victory in English. V for *victoire* in French. V for *vrijheid* – or freedom – in Flemish. There was even the further coincidence that this was the Fifth Symphony . . . with the letter V for five in Latin.

The whole secret of Stalnaya Ruka had been re-vealed to him. As Bond had first suspected, Gen-eral G and his cohorts had nothing to do with Soviet security. They had created an organisation that was entirely independent and – indeed – renegade. Their aim was to assassinate Khrushchev and to replace him with anyone who might move the country closer to the ideology of Stalin which, they believed, had been left behind. Stalnaya indeed. They wanted a leader with steel in his heart.

From reports that he had read in London, Bond knew that Khrushchev had made enemies ever since his so-called secret speech eight years earlier, criticis-ing his predecessor. His more liberal approach, char-acterised as 'the great thaw', had further undermined confidence in his leadership. There had been his mis-handling of Cuba and even Berlin, his fractious rela-tionship with China. Intelligence services in Europe and America had been quietly awaiting his downfall but none of them had ever foreseen this. The fact that the conspirators were connected to the Kremlin, with a direct phone link to the first deputy prime minister, was almost beyond belief. Alexander Shelepin risking his life to rid the Soviet Union of the man who had been its leader for the past ten years? It was beyond treason. It was tantamount to another revolution. The result might be chaos, confusion, anarchy. Certainly, General G had been right when he said he was going to change history.

The music was still playing. To Bond it had become background noise, the repeated rhythm ricocheting through the orchestra, dark and ominous, suggesting what Beethoven's biographer had called 'fate knocking at the door'. Well, this was fate for sure. The fate of a whole country might be decided in the next few minutes.

Bond already knew that he wasn't going to kill the First Secretary. That much was certain and he would be mad to think otherwise. There was nothing to be gained from a political assassination and there could be no conceivable reason to do the work that Stalnaya Ruka had demanded of him. His only course of action was to get back to England with the knowledge of what had been intended. The secret service would use their contacts in Moscow to expose General G, Kirilenko and all the rest of them. The result would be immediate arrests, a great deal of soul-searching and, above all, massive destabilisation. The Russians had perfected the art of self-flagellation. They would turn on themselves with a vengeance and for the next few years they would be too busy with the internal investigation to worry about the rest of the world. Well, that would be worth something anyway. Enough to justify his being caught up in all this.

It was time to leave. Bond had the address in Berlin, a safe house where he could hide until his extraction had been arranged. How would the secret service get him home again? There were tunnels from East to West, built at great risk in the unstable ground beneath the city, but Bond suspected he would be smuggled out with fake documents or perhaps in the boot of a car belonging to a minor diplomat from a 'friendly' country. These embassy cars were never checked at the border crossings.

Bond took one last look at the man in Seat 12 who was listening with rapt attention to the performance and who had no idea that there was a single twitch of a finger between his enjoyment of the music and the end of his life. That was enough. He swung the scope away, briefly taking in the other spectators in the VIP section of the first tier. They were sitting in the shadows, barely visible in the light reflecting upwards from the stage, but he thought he recognised the Minister for State Security and the First Secretary of the German Democratic Republic. Of course, anyone in office would want their share of the limelight with their supreme leader. He smiled grimly, feeling the power of the world's most accurate sniper rifle in his hands. God! With automatic fire, he could take out the whole lot of them.

He adjusted the scope one last time.

And froze.

Colonel Boris had also been invited into the VIP section. He was sitting at the very back, three rows behind. But he wasn't listening to the music. His head was raised, his gaze fixed on the chandelier and the man hiding behind it. Of course Colonel Boris knew he was there. Bond saw the strange eyes boring into him, magnified eight times by the PSO-1 scope. And it was as if the colonel knew that, right then, he was being watched. For a moment, the two of them were locked together. An eternity seemed to pass and then, slowly, deliberately, Colonel Boris raised his finger and touched his cheekbone, just below the blue eye.

Bond knew the signal even without recognising it for what it was. Colonel Boris had pressed the trigger which he had planted deep in Bond's subconscious long ago and there was nothing Bond could do as months of torture and the most sophisticated techniques of menticidal hypnosis exploded inside his brain. At that moment, he felt a massive disconnection, a sense of falling as if from a precipice with nothing to prevent him plunging into a carefully manufactured oblivion. He was helpless. He no longer had any thoughts of his own.

What he was experiencing was what the Nazis had searched for in their own experiments and what they called *Gleichschaltung* . . . a sudden and overpowering levelling of the mind. Everything that had happened to him in the past few months, including the failed assassination of M, the weeks at The Park with Sir James Molony, Jamaica, Scaramanga and his return to Moscow, were gone. Right then, he had no identity. He had become the creature that Colonel Boris had made of him. He must do everything that he had been told, obeying the orders he had been given without question. Just like Ilya Platonov, who had thrown himself out of a window in Moscow, Bond would have willingly shot himself in the head if that had been his instruction. But it was not his death that was demanded. He knew exactly why he had been brought here. Gritting his teeth, barely breathing, he brought the Dragunov back onto the Russian leader.

The bald, wrinkled head came into focus. Khrushchev was wearing wire-frame glasses. His eyes were half-closed. Bond already saw the bullet flashing over the audience, drilling into its target. Unable to stop himself, he prepared to take the shot. He could hear

Beethoven's music, gentler now, somewhere in the far distance, trying to tug him back into the real world. No. It was only reminding him of the instructions he had been given a few hours before. A brief cadenza, played on the oboe. Then the orchestra would rise to another climax. There would be a drum roll that would disguise the sound of the shot, giving him a few precious seconds to get away before the audience panicked. Bond didn't try to fight. There could be no resistance. He was simply waiting for the exact second, defined by the music. General G had played it to him at the hotel. He was ready.

And yet one tiny part of his mind still screamed at him, telling him that nothing had been decided, that he had a choice. For months, ever since he had left The Park, Bond had been in control of his own thought processes. He had played the part of a traitor in London. He had fooled Colonel Boris in his own institute in Leningrad. He had survived the trap at Komsomolskaya station and found his way to the heart of the conspiracy. Had he come this far simply to surrender at the last moment?

How could he do it? How could he break free?

He shifted his position and felt the familiar pain from the bullet wound he had received in Jamaica. It was hurting less now. Finally, it had begun to heal.

But it was enough to connect him with what had happened, who he really was.

Bond knew what he had to do. There was no other way. Still holding the gun, he reached down and pressed one hand into the wound, prising it open, forcing his fingers into the flesh where it had been pierced by Scaramanga's bullet. He reeled back as the nerve ends screamed out. Taking a breath, he pushed harder, feeling the tissue part. The pain was instant, all-consuming and intense, but it was *his* pain. He had invited it. And being so primal, in the very core of his being, it surged through him, brutally overwhelming the more fragile mechanisms of his mind. In the rush of pain, Bond remembered everything that had happened: from the attack on M to the death of Scaramanga. The mental chains shattered and in that single, exhilarating moment of freedom, he swept the gun back up, pressed the scope against his eye, aimed and fired.

The single bullet spat through the darkness as the orchestra reached its crescendo and the drums thundered out their deafening climax. It hit Colonel Boris in his blue eye, killing him instantly. Bond saw the body jerk backwards, a spray of brain matter hitting the wall behind him. The body crumpled.

Bond had hurt himself badly. His own wound was

bleeding again. But he was in full command of his senses. It was as if he had managed to plunge into a shower of ice-cold water. He had not just killed the man who had come closer than anyone to destroying him. He had finally extinguished him, casting him for ever out of his thoughts.

Bond dropped the sniper rifle and he was already making his way across the cavity in the roof and back to the hatch that opened onto the outside when the first screams rang out and the orchestra shuddered to a halt. He didn't look back. He reached up and hauled himself up onto the roof, out in the rain. Briefly he reoriented himself, taking in the damaged cathedral, the main square far below. As he swung himself back down the drainpipe, he saw the two soldiers running towards him, alerted by the sudden disturbance inside the building. One of them fired at him but he was already out of sight, protected by the far side of the wall, and the bullet ricocheted harmlessly off the brick-work, high above his head. He didn't run. Instead, he crouched low, waiting. The first soldier came hurtling round the corner and Bond leapt up, seized hold of his rifle and used it like a battering ram, forcing him over the edge of the roof and sending him crashing down to the courtyard behind the opera house. The second soldier was right behind him, fumbling for his weapon. Bond had kept hold of the rifle and used it to knock him into unconsciousness with a single blow.

Bond found the window that had given him access to the roof. It was still unlocked. He drew it up and climbed back in just as the third-tier doors burst open and the audience, a confused mass of frightened people, rushed into the corridor. If there was safety in numbers, Bond knew he could at least partly relax. Suddenly he was one among hundreds and although there were KGB men everywhere (fewer, though, than in the lower tiers), there was very little they could do. It was already too late to organise barriers or to demand people's ID. The audience was out of control. A shot had been fired. A man – not the First Secretary, thank God – had been killed. The gunman was still in the building. They just wanted to leave.

The staircases were jammed with people shouting and pushing. The doors leading out to the street were opening on all sides. Bond allowed the human deluge to carry him down to ground level and out into the fading light. He was careful to clutch his jacket, pressing it against the open wound. Every movement caused him a jolt of pain and he knew that he would need medical attention before he went anywhere. 28b Albrecht-Dürer-Strasse. The address was seared into his mind. He needed to find it, get help and then get out.

He emerged into Bebelplatz, the great square where the Nazis had once held one of their largest ceremonial book burnings. The KGB men were shouting now, trying to hold the audience back, but for once nobody was listening to them. More armed soldiers were running into the theatre but they had no idea who or what they were looking for. The howl of sirens resounded over the eastern sector of the city. Bond headed south as he had been instructed, passing St Hedwig's and continuing across the wider Französische Strasse. There was a cluster of derelict buildings on the other side, one of them with its entrails – staircases, lights, broken walls – disgorging themselves into the street. He plunged into an alleyway that ran along beside it. General G had told him exactly where it led.

Bond knew that he was taking a major risk. He had been told that a car would be waiting for him in the quiet square at the end of the alley, with a driver ready to take him to a safe place – but could he be sure that General G would not renege on his side of the deal? Maybe it would help them if Bond fell into the KGB's hands. But then again, they needed to keep him safe. Put simply, he knew too much. He had all the names of the conspirators. Furthermore, the driver would not yet know if the assassination attempt had been successful or not. Certainly he would be unaware that

Colonel Boris had been killed. Bond had decided that they would have to keep him alive at least until General G and the other members of Stalnaya Ruka knew what had happened. And right now he was hurt. The flat in Albrecht-Dürer-Strasse was some distance away. He needed the car to get across Berlin.

And there it was, ahead of him. It was another Trabant, a more basic model, parked in the far corner of the square and partly concealed by a broken marble fountain. The flagstones in front of him were cracked and pockmarked with weeds. None of the surrounding buildings seemed to be occupied. They were two storeys high, each one identical to its neighbour, packed together in long rows. The doors were closed, most of the windows shuttered, perhaps permanently. Bond couldn't see a glimmer of light anywhere. Nor did there seem to be a driver in the Trabant. That suited him. It had always been his intention to drive away on his own.

He took two steps forward. A door to one of the empty buildings suddenly opened.

Katya Leonova walked out.

He had not seen her since Moscow and, despite what he had promised her, he had not really expected to see her again. She was wearing a cream-coloured raincoat, double-breasted, tied with a belt. At this distance, and in the dying light, it was impossible to make out her face but she looked like a ghost of her former self, solitary and pale. She must have seen him. She was deliberately making her way towards him, walking straight across the square close to the empty fountain. To his surprise, Bond realised that he was glad she was there. There was a part of him that, despite everything, had regretted the way they had parted company in Moscow. She had, after all, been true to her word and hadn't betrayed him and – it had occurred to him – throughout his career he had never left a relationship on a sour note, not even with Gala Brand, who had left him for another man.

He had wanted to see her again. Katya's father was dead. The long shadow he had cast over his life was finally extinguished. Perhaps there might be some hope for 'Kate Leonard' after all.

She was waving to him. That was what he thought and he was about to wave back when he saw the fear in her face and heard her calling out to him.

'Go back, James! It's a trap!'

She was moving faster towards him, in the centre of the square.

'I love you, James. I love you!'

She smiled. She had spoken her last words. She had said everything she wanted to say.

The machine-gun fire came from three directions, from different windows in separate buildings on the ground floor. Bond watched helplessly in horror as Katya was torn apart in front of him. Gigantic holes appeared as gashes in her raincoat, bright red blood splattering out as a stream of bullets entered her flesh. For a few moments she kept moving even though she must already have been dead. Then her body twisted. She fell to the ground and lay still. Bond felt the world twist around him. He had seen death many times, but never this violent, never this obscene. He thought of Teresa Draco, Tracy, the woman he had briefly married. He had always held himself responsible for what had happened to her and the same was true now. There was one difference. He had been kind to Tracy. He had made her happy.

Katya had died knowing that Bond had rejected her. And despite that knowledge, she had come here and sacrificed herself for him.

Bond gazed across the square, with the stench of cordite reaching out to him. The car was still parked there, beyond his reach. The body lay silent, a pathetic bundle of clothes and blood. He muttered something incomprehensible, then turned round and staggered back onto the main street, never feeling more on his own as he made his way across a dark and hostile Berlin.

23

No Way Out

The doctor in the flat in Albrecht-Dürer-Strasse spoke no English, but this didn't prevent him from keeping up a running commentary as he treated Bond's injury.

'I am going to have to stitch this together. I have no anaesthetic. I'm afraid it's going to be painful.' As he searched in his bag for suture thread, he continued muttering: 'I don't understand how you managed to do this to yourself. It's an old wound. It shouldn't have opened.'

As well as Bond and the doctor there were two men and a woman in the single room which contained a sofa, two armchairs, a kettle and a sink, a Bakelite telephone and little else. They were all speaking in low voices, nervous of being overheard, anxious to be out

as quickly as they could. The woman was in her fifties, dark-haired, uncomfortable. Bond had thought
she might be a nurse but she had been in the flat before
the doctor was summoned by telephone and hadn't offered to help him with the procedure. One of the men
had introduced himself as Otto – no surname – and
seemed to be in charge. He was tall, distinguished, with
curling grey hair and quiet eyes, dressed in an old coat
with an astrakhan collar. The other was the ginger-
haired man who had bumped into Bond at the airport.
He was the most nervous of all of them, bouncing on
the balls of his feet, constantly going over to the first-
floor window and looking out into the street.

Bond was lying on his back on the sofa, his jacket
off and his shirt pulled open to reveal his bare stomach.
He gritted his teeth as the doctor bent over him and set
to work. Meanwhile, Otto spoke rapidly, explaining
what they planned to do. He had already introduced
himself as an agent operating in East Berlin, known to
British intelligence although working with BOB, the
Berlin Operations Base, a network of agents run by
the CIA. He told Bond that he had already spoken to
his American contacts about what had happened and
that Bond's presence in the city had been known from
the moment he arrived. For the next few minutes,
Otto kept up a continuous monologue in near-perfect

English. It was possible he was trying to keep Bond's mind off what the doctor was doing to him.

'They're already saying that the detonation heard at the Berlin State Opera was a falling arc lamp and that nobody was hurt or killed. The Stasi aren't going to admit that anyone took a shot when the First Secretary was in the building – or that a man was hit just a few seats away. By the end of the week, I think you'll find that there will be no evidence that Colonel Boris ever existed. At least, not for the general public. The security machine won't stop looking for the man who killed him. They're looking for you now but this flat isn't known to them. You're safe for the time being.

'As for Stalnaya Ruka, they're finished. It won't take the Kremlin very long to work out who was behind the attack and we'll make sure that the correct names are brought to their attention. I think the Lubyanka is going to be very busy over the next few days. If General Grubozaboyschikov is sensible, he'll probably take his own life – if he hasn't already. I don't know what was going on in his head. It was a crazy scheme. Khrushchev won't last much longer anyway. The Russians don't execute their leaders any more. Not like the good old days. But he'll be gone in a year. Everyone knows it. They think he's weak, which is the worst thing you can be in Russian politics.

'Of course, there would have been an uproar if he'd been publicly assassinated. It would have been considered an outrage, a personal attack on the motherland. General G and his friends were creating the perfect circumstances for a hard-liner to take over, someone with a less liberal view of the West. And having a British spy pull the trigger, that was a stroke of genius. They always planned to kill you too, Mr Bond. Your body would have been discovered near the opera house and the whole thing would have been blamed on British intelligence. Nobody knew about your so-called defection or any of that. The Marxists need people to believe that the whole world hates them and that measures like the Berlin Wall are necessary to protect them. That was what they were planning. To turn up the temperature of the Cold War a notch or two. Or do I mean down? At any event, you rather spoiled it for them, killing their man. Shame about the girl. Who was she? She must have thought a lot of you, to try and help you like that.

'And now we have a problem. Like I say, the whole of Berlin is looking for you. You're safe here but not for long. Every moment you spend in the east, you'll be in greater danger. There are informants everywhere. The people in this room I would trust with my life and we are grateful to the good doctor for coming out at a moment's notice. But you can see Willie there, looking out of the window. Even having a light on at this time of the night might send a message to someone. He lives on his nerves. We all do.'

Otto said a few words in German to the younger man. There was a smile in the way he spoke but Willie answered briefly and unenthusiastically. Bond had a first-class command of the language and understood every word of the conversation. Willie had volunteered to help reunite German citizens with their friends and families in the West. He wasn't happy, getting involved with foreign spies. He thought Bond was a danger to them all.

Otto ignored him. He turned back to Bond. 'How do we get you across the border?' he asked. 'First of all, the sooner the better. Right now, you are invisible. Nobody knows you are even in the country. That's how it works here. The security forces are so paranoid that they never tell each other anything. That way, if anything goes wrong, there's less chance they'll get into trouble. They can blame each other without perhaps getting killed or sent off to the gulag themselves. In fact, I think it's best if you leave tonight. Nobody will be expecting you to walk through one of the checkpoints, not the same evening that you tried to kill the First Secretary.

'How are we going to do this? There aren't any tunnels in operation at the moment and the sewers have been closed off too. We can't approach any of the so-called "friendly" embassies. After what happened tonight, they'll be running scared. Normally, we'd set you up with a forged passport but last year the authorities added an entry permit which changes every day. You have to give it up at the frontier when you travel back into the West so that's put paid to that. We could consider the Scandinavian tour. Take you out by train from Ostbahnhof to one of the Baltic ports . . . Sanitz or Warnemünde and from there by ferry to Denmark. But once again, that'll take too long and anyway it's no longer safe these days. No. We've got to move quickly and we've got to be imaginative. Strike while the Iron Curtain is hot, so to speak.

'And as it happens, we've made certain arrangements which are still in place and which we can put into operation with immediate effect. We were already prepared with all the necessary paperwork and planning for a high-level defector. You can go in his place.' Otto paused as the doctor stretched out the needle with its length of bloody suture thread. 'I wonder if the name Karl Brenner means anything to you?'

Bond nodded. He had been told about Karl Brenner when he was in England, at The Park. Brenner was the ADC to Erik Mundt, a senior officer in the Stasi and a member of Stalnaya Ruka. He was the man who had first tipped off the British secret service to the conspiracy that had brought Bond to Russia – but he had been killed, hammered to death in the Hohenschönhausen prison before he could say what he knew.

The doctor sipped from a glass of water and began work on a third – or was it a fourth? – stitch. The needle prised its way back through the open lip of the wound and Bond winced.

'We agreed to help Brenner into the West in return for information,' Otto went on. 'We still have his passport and his identification papers, his Communist Party membership card and so on. We forged a letter from Hauptabteilung 2, the main counter-intelligence division of the Stasi, authorising him to cross into West Germany on a highly secretive matter of national importance. After what happened at the State Opera House tonight, such a letter will be all the more pertinent and it has been a fairly simple matter to amend the date. It's highly unlikely that any border guard will want to risk his own future preventing Mundt's personal ADC from pursuing the assassin who nearly killed his leader.'

'Brenner is dead,' Bond grunted.

'Yes. But let's just hope that nobody at the border

knows that,' Otto said. 'After all, he was murdered by his own people so I doubt that they'll have advertised it. More to the point, you're about the same age as him and you even look reasonably similar. We're fortunate here. Brenner was badly scarred in an accident on the autobahn some years ago. Fräulein Kruger here is a make-up artist with the Deutsche Film-Aktiengesellschaft or the DEFA. It's our state-owned film studio. Once the doctor has finished with you, she will get started.' Otto looked at his watch. 'It is ten thirty now. We don't have much time. There are no border crossings after midnight and I would like to get to Heinrich-Heine-Strasse at about five minutes before. Psychologically, that would be the right time, I think.'

'To slip through quietly?'

'No, Mr Bond. You don't understand the East German psychology. We will go through with as much noise as we can.'

The convoy arrived at the Heinrich-Heine-Strasse checkpoint at a quarter to twelve. There were two vehicles. The first was another Trabant, this one jet black. It was driven by a Stasi officer in uniform, with two more men in the back. It was followed by a very ugly, square van – a Barkas B1000. There was no reason for the van to be there but at the same time there was no vehicle on the roads of East Berlin that could terrify the general populace more. Even the border guards would be nervous when they saw it. The Barkas B1000 was used by the Stasi when people had to disappear. It looked like a delivery van but there were two small cells, cramped and windowless, built into the back. Victims would be snatched off the street. The doors would slam. They might never be seen again.

For the guards at Heinrich-Heine-Strasse, it was a reminder that it might be wise not to argue. The checkpoint had been chosen deliberately. By day, it was one of the busiest crossings, used for mail and other goods, close to the city centre with a wide stretch of road leading to Kreuzberg, in the American sector. But just before midnight it was almost empty. Heinrich-Heine-Strasse was less well known than Checkpoint Charlie just a few blocks away (which anyway would not allow East German nationals to pass through) and even less welcoming. It had the appearance of an assault course, hemmed in by drab apartment blocks and designed in such a way that even those equipped with the right papers might think twice before attempting to cross. A row of street lamps leaned inwards, casting a glow across the asphalt and revealing a twisting circuit of walls, high and low, humps and barriers, traffic cones and 'dragon's teeth', the road spikes that would shred the tyres of any car that attempted to break into the West. There were half a dozen guards in greatcoats patrolling the area, automatic rifles slung over their shoulders. Somewhere, a dog was barking ferociously, torturing itself and everyone else with the incessant noise.

At the same moment, three of the Trabant's doors opened. The driver and the two passengers got out.

Bond was dressed in a smart suit and tie, complete with a shining Order of Lenin badge pinned to his lapel. He was holding an official-looking attaché case in hands that were encased in black gloves. He would have been completely unrecognisable to anyone looking out for him. There was a livid scar running the full length of his cheek, the careful work of Fräulein Kruger of the Deutsche Film-Aktiengesellschaft. She had made the scar so vivid and pronounced that it obliterated the rest of his features. It was impossible to look anywhere else. Bond also had wire-frame glasses that added to his sense of authority. His hair had been given a coating of grease, pressing it close to his skull.

He was accompanied by the man he knew as Otto, now dressed in the full uniform of a senior Stasi officer, complete with silver shoulder braid, belt and medals. The driver, also in uniform, walked behind them with a self-important swagger. The three of them went into the nearest hut, an ugly square of grey concrete, for the first document check.

Otto did all the talking, presenting the passport, the exit permits and the official letter with the familiar heading of the East German ministry. All of these had been prepared for Karl Brenner with just a few of the dates carefully adjusted. The border guards, specially trained by the Stasi, examined everything carefully and snapped out a few questions to which Otto, acting as ADC to the very important Herr Brenner, replied. Meanwhile, Bond stood disdainfully to one side, allowing his indifference to speak for itself.

Loyalists and senior officers, acting for the regime, often came through Heinrich-Heine-Strasse on their way to the West and on a night such as this, with rumours still swirling about what had taken place at the Berlin State Opera, the urgency made complete sense. The two officials in the hut were tired, at the end of their shift. One of them asked a further question but this time he was barked down by the ADC. 'Do you have any idea what has happened tonight, Comrade? Do you really dare question my orders?' Once again, Bond understood every word. He stood where he was, maintaining a grim silence while Otto went on. 'You will do as you are told or, I can assure you, there is a van waiting outside to take you to rather less pleasant duties.'

It was all theatre but that was why it worked. This was no normal night and the sheer impudence of the performance – with not one but three actors and two official cars – did the trick. The papers were stamped. Copies were retained. The correct entry was made in the logbook. The two border guards saluted, just wanting to be away for the night.

Bond and his two escorts stepped back out into the street and exchanged formal salutes for the benefit of anyone watching them from the various guard huts. Bond turned smartly and, alone now, followed the road with its sandbags and glinting steel fences, heading for the first barrier. He heard a telephone ring, the Stasi men who had given him his clearance calling ahead. The barrier rose as he approached. He passed through and went into the second control hut for customs and currency checks. There were other people there, tourists and students on their way home before their day passes expired. Bond stood in front of another guard, who barked out a few questions at him. Otto had told him what to expect. He answered in terse monosyllables as if this was all beneath his dignity.

He knew he had arrived at the moment of truth. He was still a hundred yards from safety but even as he walked towards Kreuzberg and the West, the phone lines would be humming, his documents and his background being double-checked. His orders had been forged by experts. His passport and various IDs were authentic. But it would take just four words and it would all be over. 'Karl Brenner is dead.' If that first death had been recorded, Bond's own death would follow immediately.

He was allowed through the next barrier, along with the other late-night visitors. A single car drove slowly past, zigzagging between the concrete blocks that had been deliberately positioned to prevent it moving at more than a snail's pace. Bond resisted the urge to look at his watch. It must be two or three minutes to midnight. Soon the Heinrich-Heine-Strasse crossing would shut down. But the worst of it must be behind him. Freedom lay ahead.

What freedom?

Bond was exhausted. After his makeshift surgery, he could barely move without a bolt of pain, like a welder's torch, coursing through his stomach. He was sick from the kicking he had been given by General G. The cut on his arm was throbbing.

Worse than all this, he could still see Katya being ripped apart by bullets. He wondered how she had even found her way to Berlin. Presumably her father had allowed her to travel with him and had told her what he planned. It would have amused him to taunt her, to let her know that after everything she had done, it had always been his intention to ensure that the British agent was killed.

Bond was walking, his feet rapping out on the grey paving stones. The next border was getting closer. The dog was still barking, more distant now. It wasn't raining but the air felt damp.

It was over. He was finished. This time, he had made his decision. He should never have listened to Mathis all those years ago. Even then, he had known that there was no future in any of this. Here he was, pretending that everything was all right when there were probably victims of near-fatal car-crashes who were in better shape than him. Had he saved the world by saving the First Secretary? Had he achieved anything at all? Perhaps. But why did it always have to be him?

He had killed Katya as surely as if he had shot her himself. Bond was not an emotional man – at least, he never had been – but he couldn't get her out of his head. The look in her face. Those pathetic last words.

His fault.

As soon as he got home, he would resign from the secret service, and he wasn't going to allow anyone to dissuade him. There had to be another life; one that suited him and which didn't bring with it a mountain of pain and humiliation. He would sell the flat in Chelsea, move out of London. Why even stay in England? He had friends all over the world. There was René Mathis in France and Felix Leiter in America. Or what about Jamaica? He had always been happy there.

He had crossed the bridge. The East German control huts were behind him. Finally, the dog had tired of its own cacophony and stopped.

Bond knew that it wouldn't be easy. There was no way out for people like him. There were always the old enemies, waiting to catch up with him, the old habits he couldn't leave behind. He had lived with danger for too long and wondered if he would ever be fully alive without it. Instead of outrunning the days he would finally allow them to catch up with him. To hell with it. He had made his decision. He was going to write the letter this very night and this time he would send it.

The siren screamed out, shattering the silence of the checkpoint. The dog began barking again, joined this time by East German border guards shouting confused commands into the night sky. And then sodium lights exploded all around him, obliterating the darkness and replacing it with a brilliant white glare. Bond felt the light burning his eyes and put a hand up to protect his face. There were armed guards running into the compound. Ahead of him he could see security forces, American, suddenly alert, their own guns raised, wondering what was happening. There were about fifteen paces until the next barrier and entrance to the West.

The shouting continued. Bond didn't understand the words. He wasn't even sure if they were addressed to him. There had been other tourists making their way towards the West. It was perfectly possible that one of them had been identified as a criminal, a traitor, a dissident or whatever. The whole thing could be an exercise or a false alarm. Bond had not stopped. He heard the unmistakable sound of automatic rifles being loaded and knew that in just a few seconds shots might be fired. He could almost feel the bullets tearing into his back. He saw himself stretched out, face down on the asphalt.

It might not be him. It might be someone else.

Bond didn't care. He had made up his mind.

He kept walking.

Acknowledgements

This book completes my James Bond trilogy, which has covered his first assignment as 007 (*Forever and a Day*), his mid-career (*Trigger Mortis*), and now looks towards his final days . . . although Robert Markham and other authors have had their say about that. It has been a huge privilege to be allowed three encounters with a character who has made such a difference to my life and I will always be grateful to Ian Fleming Publications Ltd and the Ian Fleming Estate for giving me the opportunity.

Unlike my last two outings, I was unable to use original material for *With a Mind to Kill* but Bond aficionados will have noticed some help from the master. A few passages in my description of East Berlin in Chapter 20 have been lifted from Fleming's collection of travel journalism, *Thrilling Cities*, which I have drawn on before. Chapter 19 – 'The Inhuman Element' – carries the title that Fleming considered before he settled on *Moonraker*. Some readers may notice a few other 'Easter eggs' here and there.

Writing a James Bond novel demands months of research and although I visited Moscow and East Berlin in the early 1970s when the Iron Curtain was still very much in place, I needed help to create an authentic picture of this bleak and largely unhappy world.

I started with *Khrushchev's Cold War* by Aleksandr Fursenko and Timothy Naftali, which gave me a good understanding of Steel Claw's target and their need to be rid of him. It's interesting that in the spring of 1964, Leonid Brezhnev, the party leader Alexander Shelepin and Vladimir Semichastny (chairman of the KGB) actually did discuss the possibility of assassinating Khrushchev, perhaps in a plane crash. In the end, Khrushchev was dismissed by the Presidium on 14 October 1964 – about six months after this novel ends. He died in 1971.

Brainwash: The Secret History of Mind Control by Dominic Streatfeild told me everything I needed to know about brainwashing, the truth and the fiction. It also introduced me to the so-called 'magic room' where Bond is sent in Chapter 11. I drew on two other books: *The Rape of the Mind* by Joost A. M. Meerloo, which appears in the text, and *No Mercy, No Leniency* by Cyril Cunningham, a scientific adviser to the POW Intelligence Organisation during the Korean War and another C.C.

Several books gave me an idea of what it might have been like in 1960s Moscow. Among them were: *Destination Moscow* by George Mair, *A Russian Journal* by John Steinbeck, and *Moscow: A Short Guide* by A. Kovalyov, which was helpfully published in 1960. I must also confess to a quick reread of John le Carré's 1963 masterpiece, *The Spy Who Came In from the Cold*. There are a few nods to that book hidden inside mine. I would also like to thank Sir Brian Fall, who was our Russian ambassador in the early 1990s, for some very useful insights. Finally, Katya Leonova's doomed love story was inspired by a brilliant book, *The Whisperers* by Orlando Figes. There can be no more chilling account of what life was like for ordinary people living at the time of Stalin.

I am very grateful to Frederick Taylor, who has written a superb and comprehensive history, *The Berlin Wall* – and who also read the final chapters of my own novel, pointed out my errors, and helped me extract Bond from East Berlin. He gave me pretty much all the information I needed for the last section of the book, although I must also thank the author Giles Milton for directing me to the Berlin State Opera.

Sam King, the agent who guards Bond, is named after the teenaged son of Emma James, who kindly made a winning bid in an auction at the National Literacy Trust, a charity I am happy to support. My thanks to both of them and apologies for the long delay.

Finally, thanks to the team behind this book, starting with my agent, Jonathan Lloyd, and Jonny Geller, who represents Ian Fleming. The book was edited by David Milner, who has a quite terrifying knowledge of both 1960s history and all things Bond. Corinne Turner at IFPL read the manuscript at a very early stage and gave me a secret thumbs-up: her encouragement has been invaluable. Simon Ward – Publishing Manager at IFPL – provided great support just when it was needed. My assistant, Tess Cutler, organised my life and attempted to keep me calm throughout much of the writing. Thanks also to my publishers: Michal Shavit of Jonathan Cape in England and Jonathan Burnham at HarperCollins in the USA. Producing this book for them has been a joy.

It makes me sad to think that this is almost certainly the last paragraph which I will ever write in a James Bond novel, but I hope whoever comes next will have as much pleasure and personal satisfaction as I have had, and I wish them every success. When I was stuck in a foul boarding school back in the 1960s, James Bond was my one constant pleasure. The books (and films) were a lifeline and would later inspire, at least in part, my own hero – the fourteen-year-old spy Alex Rider. Bond is a unique creation. The books have had an extraordinary impact all over the world. It makes me proud to think that from now on I may be a foot-note in his history.

Ian Fleming

Ian Lancaster Fleming was born in London on 28 May 1908 and was educated at Eton College before spending a formative period studying languages in Europe. His first job was with Reuters news agency, followed by a brief spell as a stockbroker. On the outbreak of the Second World War he was appointed assistant to the director of Naval Intelligence, Admiral Godfrey, where he played a key part in British and Allied espionage operations.

After the war he joined Kemsley Newspapers as Foreign Manager of the *Sunday Times*, running a network of correspondents who were intimately involved in the Cold War. His first novel, *Casino Royale*, was published in 1953 and introduced James Bond, Special Agent 007, to the world. The first print run sold out within a month. Following this initial success, he published a Bond title every year until his death. His own travels, interests and wartime experience gave authority to everything he wrote. Raymond Chandler hailed him as 'the most forceful and driving writer of thrillers in England'. The fifth title, *From Russia, With Love*, was particularly well received and sales soared when President Kennedy named it as one of his favourite books. The Bond novels have sold more than 60 million copies and inspired a hugely successful film franchise which began in 1962 with the release of *Dr No*, starring Sean Connery as 007.

The Bond books were written in Jamaica, a country Fleming fell in love with during the war and where he built a house, 'Goldeneye'. He married Ann Rothermere in 1952. His story about a magical car, written in 1961 for their only child, Caspar, went on to become the much-loved novel and film *Chitty Chitty Bang Bang*. Fleming died of heart failure on 12 August 1964.

www.ianfleming.com

The James Bond Books

Casino Royale

Live and Let Die

Moonraker

Diamonds Are Forever

From Russia, With Love

Dr No

Goldfinger

For Your Eyes Only

Thunderball

The Spy Who Loved Me

On Her Majesty's Secret Service

You Only Live Twice

The Man with the Golden Gun

Octopussy and the Living Daylights

Non-fiction

The Diamond Smugglers

Thrilling Cities

Children's

Chitty Chitty Bang Bang

About the Author

ANTHONY HOROWITZ is one of the UK's most prolific and successful writers. He is the US bestselling author of *Magpie Murders*, which he adapted for TV and is soon to be seen on PBS. *With a Mind to Kill* ends his trilogy of James Bond novels that began with *Trigger Mortis* (2015) and *Forever and a Day* (2018). He has also written two books about Sherlock Holmes: *The House of Silk* has sold over forty-five thousand copies worldwide and had its tenth anniversary in 2021, and *Moriarty*, with its huge surprise ending, was an industry sensation. His bestselling Alex Rider series for young adults has sold more than nineteen million copies, and he created both *Midsomer Murders* and the BAFTA-winning *Foyle's War* for TV. In January 2022, Anthony was awarded a CBE for services to literature.